**When a deadly traitor
threatens to dishonor a top-secret agency,
A YEAR OF LOVING DANGEROUSLY
begins....**

Caleb Carpenter
Piercing eyes, menacing dark looks—
a powerfully seductive man!

*A man with more secrets than even his monstrous
reputation reveals, Caleb is determined to find a
bride to complete his empire—a woman who will
stand by his side as he conquers the Western world!*

Rachel Grunwald
Beautiful, blond, with a vulnerability no man
has ever touched...until now.

*This SPEAR operative has a personal stake
in bringing Caleb Carpenter—and his entire
compound—down. But going undercover as Caleb's
bride has unanticipated dangers once Caleb reveals
the true power of his passion....*

The Traitor
Known only as "Simon," he's due to make
an appearance at Caleb's compound....

*No one knows what's driving this deadly
villain, only that he seems determined to destroy
SPEAR's top man. It's up to Rachel to stop Simon—
before Caleb's seduction stops her!*

Dear Reader,

What is there to say besides, "The wait is over!" Yes, it's true. Chance Mackenzie's story is here at last. *A Game of Chance,* by inimitable *New York Times* bestselling author Linda Howard, is everything you've ever dreamed it could be: exciting, suspenseful, and so darn sexy you're going to need to turn the air-conditioning down a few more notches! In Sunny Miller, Chance meets his match—in every way. Don't miss a single fabulous page.

The twentieth-anniversary thrills don't end there, though. A YEAR OF LOVING DANGEROUSLY continues with *Undercover Bride,* by Kylie Brant. This book is proof that things aren't always what they seem, because Rachel's groom, Caleb Carpenter, has secrets…secrets that could break—or win— her heart. *Blade's Lady,* by Fiona Brand, features another of her to-die-for heroes, and a heroine who's known him—in her dreams—for years. Linda Howard calls this author "a keeper," and she's right. Barbara McCauley's SECRETS! miniseries has been incredibly popular in Silhouette Desire, and now it moves over to Intimate Moments with *Gabriel's Honor,* about a heroine on the run with her son and the irresistible man who becomes her protector. Pat Warren is back with *The Lawman and the Lady,* full of suspense and emotion in just the right proportions. Finally, Leann Harris returns with *Shotgun Bride,* about a pregnant heroine forced to seek safety—and marriage—with the father of her unborn child.

And as if all that isn't enough, come back next month for more excitement—including the next installment of A YEAR OF LOVING DANGEROUSLY and the in-line return of our wonderful continuity, 36 HOURS.

Leslie J. Wainger
Executive Senior Editor

Please address questions and book requests to:
Silhouette Reader Service
U.S.: 3010 Walden Ave., P.O. Box 1325, Buffalo, NY 14269
Canadian: P.O. Box 609, Fort Erie, Ont. L2A 5X3

Kylie Brant
UNDERCOVER BRIDE

Silhouette®

INTIMATE™MOMENTS®

Published by Silhouette Books

America's Publisher of Contemporary Romance

Special thanks and acknowledgment are given to
Kylie Brant for her contribution to
A Year of Loving Dangerously

For Aunt Marty, with love and fond memories

SILHOUETTE BOOKS

ISBN 0-373-27092-5

UNDERCOVER BRIDE

Visit Silhouette at www.eHarlequin.com

Printed in U.S.A.

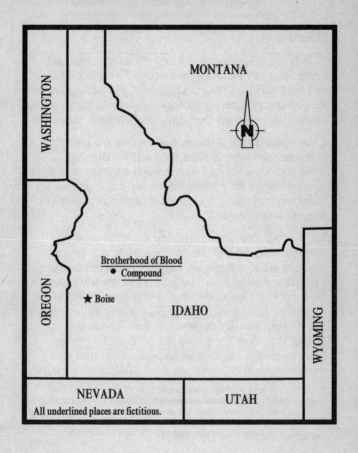

MONTANA

WASHINGTON

OREGON

Brotherhood of Blood
● Compound

★ Boise

IDAHO

NEVADA

UTAH

All underlined places are fictitious.

WYOMING

A note from gifted autor Kylie Brant,
author of over ten books for Silhouette:

Dear Reader,

This is my first opportunity to work with a continuity series, and I'm incredibly pleased to be included in A YEAR OF LOVING DANGEROUSLY. The plots are suspenseful, the heroes delicious and the heroines strong and courageous—all the ingredients for page-turners!

Undercover Bride is the second book in the series and poses the kind of dilemma I relish. After all, what could possibly go wrong when a female secret agent investigates a white supremacy group and its handsome, dynamic leader? As it turns out, plenty can happen—and does!

My writing shares time with my full-time teaching job, my husband and five children. Now that two of my kids are in college, we only juggle three athletic calendars each season. These days, the most time my husband and I spend together is sitting on a bleacher at a game of some kind! We're also veterans of emergency-room visits, usually the result of the aforementioned sports. But when the games are over, the housework done (sort of!), I can close the office door, turn on the computer and just dream away. And in between the frequent interruptions of phone, husband, children and dog, Rachel and Caleb's story unfolded.

I invite you to sit back, block out *your* distractions and immerse yourself in the results!

Sincerely,

Kylie Brant

Readers my contact me at: P.O. Box 231 Charles City, IA 50616.

Chapter 1

He didn't look like a man committed to spreading hatred, prejudice and destruction.

Rachel Grunwald tacked the color eight-by-ten glossy onto the padded wall before her where she could study it while she continued her workout. The photo of Caleb Carpenter managed to convey an aura of power; an invisible energy that all but crackled just below the surface. Based on physical appearance alone, she would have guessed the man as high-level military, or even as one of those exorbitantly priced motivational speakers that seemed to abound these days. As the leader of The Brotherhood of Blood, Carpenter was, in a manner of speaking, both.

She drew her arms up and slowly slid one foot behind her to rest on point. Eyes fixed dispassionately on the photo, she arched her back and raised her leg, the fluid movement as graceful as ballet.

Most would consider the man handsome. His piercing blue eyes contrasted sharply with his short, sleek black hair. Some might mistake the strength in his jaw as a mark of integrity; the squared-off chin as a sign of determination. Few, she imagined, would look at the man and guess him a racist who preached death or deportation for the non-Aryan and disabled.

She spun, her foot shooting out to land hard against the picture. If Carpenter had actually been standing before her, she would have just broken his nose. A slight frown marred her exquisite face. Her timing was off. She'd aimed for his nose. With an acquired patience, she ran through the move a dozen more times, until she was satisfied with it. In her eight years as an agent she'd found it most effective to neutralize an opponent completely, rather than to merely annoy.

She bent to the palm-size tape recorder on the floor and pressed Play. Moving to the long foam-packed punching bag, she swiped her face and bare midriff with a towel and waited for the quietly measured tones of a man she'd never met to describe her next mission.

"Angel. You're looking as gorgeous as ever."

Sending a rapid series of jabs and fake crosses to the center of the bag, she grunted at the recorded words. "Always the charmer, Jonah. If you only knew." She could feel the trickle of perspiration matting her blond hair, but disregarded it. A shower would revive the perfect looks she'd been born with, the looks that had given rise to the agency's nickname for her. The angelic face was as much a tool as the body she punished into well-honed condition. Both masked a will of finely forged steel.

"You've heard, I'm sure, about the events surrounding the kidnap and rescue of East Kirby's son. I'm sorry to say we failed to apprehend the kidnapper."

The mastermind of the plot, Rachel knew, was thought to be the same person attempting to destroy SPEAR, the top-secret agency she worked for, and the man at its helm, Jonah himself. All the agency had to go on at this point was a name Jeff had overheard one of his captors mention. She feinted right, then plowed her left fist into the bag, imagining for the moment it was the stomach of the traitor, a man known only as Simon.

"Jeff Kirby was found buried alive on The Brotherhood of Blood compound in Idaho, which is owned and operated by Caleb Carpenter. He was traumatized, but he'll be okay. A photo of Carpenter has been included. We need to discover the link between him and Simon. With your experience, of course, you're perfectly suited for the task."

The experience Jonah referred to was her specialty at anti-militia assignments. Her most recent task had been to infiltrate Comrades, a white-supremacist group hidden deep in the Appalachian Mountains of northeastern Pennsylvania. She'd moved her way up in the organization, from instructor of hand-to-hand combat tactics to junior advisor to the commander.

Panting, she moved away from the bag and grabbed one of the ropes that dangled from the overhead beams she'd left intact when she'd had the old barn renovated for her home. Scrambling up it, she kept her mind focused on the words coming from the machine, and off her straining muscles.

"Carpenter is said to be looking for a wife to complete his hold on the new union he's creating. He's considering candidates from all over the nation. I assume you'll have no difficulty arranging an introduction. And then in convincing him that you are a woman worthy of bearing his seed to propagate his empire."

Having reached the top of the rope, Rachel heaved herself to sit astride the beam, then rose to balance, arms outstretched. "Sure, Jonah," she murmured, as she tiptoed the length of the beam. Constructing a spin on pirouette, she crossed back to the rope and began her descent. "Pretend fiancée to a man handsome as sin who just happens to be Satan's counterpart? No problem."

"I knew I could rely on you." Was that a hint of amusement she heard in Jonah's voice? Not for the first time, she had the uneasy feeling that the man in charge of SPEAR was extremely familiar with the way she thought. An incredible feat for someone who was, for all intents, a stranger to her.

"We know it's Carpenter's stated intention to unite all the militia groups in the nation into one army capable of taking down the U.S. government." Jonah's voice hardened. "Obviously, he's positioning himself to become the new national leader. I need details, Angel. Who's he dealing with, and how does he hope to bring about the revolution? And finally, what tie does Simon have with The Brotherhood? His involvement, I'm certain, is critical."

She released the rope and dropped lightly to the floor. The tape was now silent, save for a faint whirring sound as its automatic destruction mechanism activated. Picking up the towel, she looped it around her neck, before reaching for the photo and recorder. She was accustomed to the abrupt end of Jonah's messages. Once he'd described the mission, the details were left to his agents. It made sense. She'd be the lone agent in the Idaho compound, and the danger of the assignment was such that she'd have to think on her feet. Any plans made were subject to split-second changes, depending on the circumstances.

The loft area held only her workout room, bedroom and bath. She walked through the bedroom now, tossing the equipment on the bed, and stripping on the way to the bathroom. She bypassed the oversize tub and stepped into the shower, setting the temperature just shy of frigid.

After the shower she rummaged through the kitchen for the makings of some sort of dinner. Her refrigerator held a pound of margarine and a bottle of wine. Since she'd been living in the Comrades' stronghold, she'd spent little time at home. She finally had to settle for a can of heated soup and a handful of stale crackers. After she finished, she poured herself a glass of wine. Now was the time to think about those details. Physically soothed, with the edge of adrenaline still humming, her mind would be sharper, her instinct more certain. First, though, she went to her office and shredded the picture of Carpenter. The slim celluloid tube the picture had been encased in, along with the recorder cartridge, went into the fire she'd started in the fireplace.

Her gaze fell on the flowers arranged in a vase and set on a table in front of the couch. A special courier had delivered them, with Jonah's message and the photo concealed inside. There was no use saving them. She'd be returning to the Comrades' stronghold in the morning. But she could enjoy their fragrant beauty for a few hours, at least. Picking up her glass of wine, she sank down on the black overstuffed sofa to think.

She let her mind drift, ideas half forming, to be analyzed, rejected, re-formed. Her gaze focused on the large sword prominently displayed above the fireplace. Its blade was still sharp, its point still keen. She'd carry the scar it had inflicted across her chest to her grave.

It served as a reminder. Training, intelligence and caution weren't always enough. Luck, or the lack of it, could be a powerful factor in any assignment. On that particular occasion luck had saved her life.

She tipped the wine to her lips and drank. The memory gave her no particular chill. Rachel had accepted the danger of her job soon after she'd been recruited by SPEAR on the college campus.

SPEAR. Stealth, Perseverance, Endeavor, Attack and Rescue, was an agency so guarded that most members of the government didn't even know it existed. Founded by Lincoln during the Civil War, the head of the agency answered only to the current president. SPEAR was called in when hope was lost, or the odds too great to be chanced by another agency. Death before dishonor was the inviolable code all SPEAR agents lived by. She was no longer amazed by the ferocity with which she embraced the doctrine.

Rachel rested the cool side of the goblet against her cheek. It had ceased to seem ironic that she'd become as much a zealot for her beliefs as had her father, although their views could not be more diametrically opposed. Had it not been for her miserable childhood, for her father, SPEAR would never have sought her out. She accepted that twist of fate, and poured everything she had into the agency which represented all she believed in. Truth. Justice. Loyalty.

It certainly wouldn't be fate she'd rely on as she considered her new mission. It wouldn't be luck. As darkness fell, she made no move to turn on a light. She'd operated in the shadows for long enough to be comfortable in them. And as the flames in the fireplace flickered to charred embers, she considered the best way to get close to Caleb Carpenter. Close enough to learn his secrets, to discover his strategy.

Close enough to destroy him.

At 0900 the next morning Rachel was in uniform seated at the conference table of Donald Parker, Commander of Comrades. Six other advisors were also in attendance. The meeting was a ritual, held twice weekly. Rachel wasn't certain how much input the more senior officials had into Parker's decisions, but from what she'd observed, the man preferred to keep most of the power for himself. That was the case with many of the militia groups she'd infiltrated. Paranoia was so rampant within the organizations that the leader did little delegating. It was a weakness that worked to the advantage of the government. Once the militia leader was removed, without another officer capable of salvaging the organization, its threat was eliminated. She supposed it was too much to hope that Carpenter had a similar leadership style. It would make the destruction of the Brotherhood all the more final.

"Take a look at this." The advisors were silent as they perused copies of a fax Parker handed out, the same fax message Rachel had arranged to be delivered to his machine that morning. "Any thoughts on it?"

Rachel was silent as she skimmed the information she'd

sent. The message was a copy of the mass mailings sent from The Brotherhood's Compound in Idaho. She never doubted that Carpenter's name would be recognized. The man had been making ripples in the white-supremacy movement for over two years, purportedly financing The Brotherhood's stronghold with his considerable personal wealth. The Brotherhood of Blood was one of the fastest growing militia operations in the nation, a source of grave concern to the U.S. Civil Rights Division.

"What's it to us if Carpenter wants a wife?" Lee Crandall, one of the senior advisors, said finally. "Seems to me with his money he could buy himself just about any woman he wanted."

"I heard he's got a real fancy compound out there," another man noted. "Using his own money to build it, too. Maybe we should start paying more attention. A guy with unlimited resources could be a threat."

"Or an ally." All heads turned in Rachel's direction. Here was the opening she'd planned for. "If The Brotherhood has that kind of financial backing it might not hurt to have someone there on the inside. Someone with ties to Comrades who gets close to Carpenter might be able to do us some good in the long run."

Parker leaned back in his chair and let his advisors debate the issue. Rachel said no more. She knew the commander was listening closely, despite the fact that his heavy eyelids were almost closed. With his crew-cut hair, square face and barrel-chested body, he still looked like the Marine drill sergeant he'd been over twenty years ago. He ran the organization like his own personal kingdom, and perhaps it was. A kingdom that bred on hatred for all people of color.

His beliefs were abhorrent and his tactics often shockingly violent. She'd wondered more than once if the man wasn't a psychopath. When he was spewing his organization's dogma his eyes would become a bit glazed and his face red as the hate-filled words seemed ripped from his throat. It was at those times that he reminded her of her father.

It was at those times she found herself despising him the most.

"Enough." Parker waved a hand and the discussion immediately ceased. "Let's move on. We need to discuss recruiting opportunities in the area. A structure is only as strong as its foundation. We've got to get new blood into the ranks. Ideas?"

The rest of the meeting passed without incident. The suggestions were frightening in their simplicity. Web pages, chat rooms, literature, student groups in high school and college…it occurred to her, not for the first time, that hatred had to be taught.

An hour later when the group was dismissed, Parker stopped Rachel before she could leave. "Grunwald. Sit."

She obeyed silently, waiting until the door had closed for the commander to speak. He studied her without a word for a few moments, his eyes giving nothing away.

"How was your visit home this weekend?"

Not even by a flicker of an eyelash did she reflect her surprise at the question.

"Fine, sir."

"And your mother? She's doing well?"

Rachel didn't have to feign her hesitation. The sudden knot in her chest was all too real. All too familiar. "She's about the same, sir." It didn't surprise her that Parker knew about her bi-monthly visits to her mother's nursing home in Philadelphia, but it did surprise her that he'd mention it. He'd never pretended to be a leader who cared about his members' personal lives.

The man took his time taking a cigar from the wooden box on the corner of his desk and lighting it. After puffing for a moment, he said, "I'd like to hear more about what you said earlier. About this Carpenter fax."

"I just wondered if an applicant from Comrades might be advantageous to us, sir."

His gaze shifted away from hers and he leaned back in his chair. "That's what I wondered, too. If we send someone who Carpenter doesn't choose, what the hell. It'd be a good-will gesture, the kind that might do us some good if The Brotherhood continues to grow. And if our applicant was selected as his wife—" he paused to exhale a stream of smoke "—well, that wouldn't do us any harm, either."

Voice carefully neutral, Rachel said, "Well, if you're considering applicants, I would suggest Western or Bailey, sir."

"I've already decided on the candidate, Grunwald. You."

"Me?"

The man nodded, and she knew the deal was made. Once he'd reached a decision he never strayed from it and he'd just been led, neatly, irrevocably, to the outcome she'd arranged. "We have to think of the future. I've never met Carpenter, but I've been keeping track of him. And I think he has one thing right. He believes that all the militia groups in the country will have to join forces to effect real change in this country. Revolution will come with strength in our ranks, and strength can only come through unity. When that time comes, I want to make sure Comrades remains among the leadership. An alliance between you and Carpenter could ensure that."

When she didn't answer, he continued, "I know this probably isn't the way you planned to serve, but change doesn't come without great sacrifice. You have to consider the good for the Aryan race, not just about yourself. Think about how this step could advance our cause. Think—" his voice dropped persuasively "—about how your father would feel about your work."

A faint smile crossed her lips, and her words were edged in irony. "Sir, I think about that every day."

* * *

Two days later Rachel was in a private limo, approaching the fortress that housed The Brotherhood of Blood. Parker had wasted no time proceeding with his plan. Rachel's candidacy, consisting of pictures and background, had been shared with The Brotherhood via faxes and phone calls. She'd been accepted for Carpenter's consideration.

What kind of man, she wondered, arranged for a wife in this manner? One who thought himself too busy, too important, to be bothered with the social rudiments of what society politely referred to as dating? Or one who had so little regard for women, for their importance, that appearance and background were the most important factors to be considered? The answer, she suspected, was both. The e-mail response from The Brotherhood had made it clear that Rachel would stay at the compound for a thirty-day trial period, and that she would have no say in Carpenter's final decision. She was content with the time frame. A month would give her plenty of time to determine the connection between Carpenter and Simon.

Glancing at her watch, she saw that it had been over three hours since they'd left the airport. They would be approaching the compound soon, but she didn't bother glancing out the windows. The glass was so deeply tinted that she could make out little more than filtered light and vague shapes. An effort by The Brotherhood to protect the secret of their site, she imagined. It wouldn't matter. Jonah knew exactly where the compound was located.

The limo slowed to a stop and the driver got out of the car. After a few minutes he returned to the vehicle, and began a slow approach. Security gate, Rachel guessed. She wondered just how protected the compound was. Certainly Carpenter believed in precautions. She was fairly sure that her bags had been searched at the airport, while she'd waited in the limo. However, she'd been undisturbed at the invasion of privacy. Though there were a few items among her personal belongings that should raise some questions, it would take an astute man, indeed, to find them, let alone identify them.

She reached into her purse and withdrew a compact mirror. With a critical eye, she smoothed her hair and renewed her lipstick. The beauty reflected in the mirror failed to register. It was a tool, nothing more. Looks could be as potent a weapon as any she'd ever wielded. She'd learned to use every weapon she had at her disposal most effectively.

The car pulled to a stop and she replaced the items she'd used in her purse. The back passenger door opened, and the driver extended a hand to her. Rachel accepted his help and stepped out of the car, blinking in the sunlight.

Hundreds of people were assembled at her side, facing a stage placed on a rolling green lawn. The troops were clad in black fatigues, and their voices swelled in unison as they shouted fervored agreement to the speaker's words. Above the stage on either side flew black flags emblazoned with a fisted hand clutching an American flag, dripping blood. The banners seemed to frame the man on the center of the platform, the man who had the troops transfixed.

Caleb Carpenter.

He, too, was clad in black, although rather than fatigues he was wearing dress pants and shirt. He paced back and forth across the stage, speaking into a microphone, and every sentence he uttered seemed to send the crowd into a frenzy.

Anticipation pricking her nerves, Rachel ran her palm down the front of her pink skirt to smooth wrinkles acquired by the long ride. Her eyes never left the man who stood front and center. He resembled a big jungle cat, dark and lethal, prowling the stage, roaring intentions of certain death for its prey.

"And I say to you—" the words boomed out over the audience "—we will topple this illegal government. We will tear apart its carcass and feast on the carnage. And upon the ashes of the corrupt, upon the ruins of the decadence, we will build a new union!'' He paused as the voices in the crowd swelled in agreement.

''There will be no mercy for those who have prolonged this moment—no compassion for our enemies. Those who defy us will be destroyed. The filth and unworthy will be deported or eliminated. Our new union will be untainted, and we will sustain it by strict adherence to the doctrine of The Brotherhood. We will set the standard for white purity in this nation.''

A howl of support came from the audience. Carpenter made no move to interrupt it. He stood with feet apart, fist raised, in a gesture of arrogant eminence. Despite the heat, Rachel felt a chill river over her skin. Carpenter was as vitriolic as any of the militia leaders she'd come into contact with, but he was clearly far more dangerous than most. He possessed a potent presence, one that reached out and gripped the minds of his followers. His words bared their deepest fears, fed the fires of their fanaticism. They were screaming and chanting his name now, and he remained still, head thrown back, his face a mask of triumph and determination.

The driver of the limo reached for Rachel's elbow, and she allowed him to lead her to the makeshift stage. Carpenter raised his hands to still the crowd, and when voices fell silent he began to speak again.

''Just as a revolution is a product of its loyal soldiers, so an empire is the sum of its leadership. Do I have your support?''

''Yes!'' the crowd roared.

''Do I have your loyalty?''

''Yes!''

Rachel was close enough to see the perspiration trickling down the side of Carpenter's face. He seemed impervious to the heat. His attention was focused on the people before him, and his own message.

"Our new white union must be guarded closely by a leader with the wisdom and courage to cull the misfits coddled by our society. I vow to be that leader for you, to remain committed to our goals and to build an undefiled empire from which shall spring sons to rule and daughters to serve. To that purpose," Carpenter stopped as the volume of the crowd increased. "To that purpose..." he repeated as the voices ebbed, "I continue to screen applicants for the position of my mate. It is imperative, as your leader, that I choose a woman of purity and integrity, one who will honor our commitment and dedicate herself to her role of begetting heirs to carry out our holy mission."

The crowd was completely silent now. There was an aura of expectancy in the air, and Rachel had an instinctive notion of what was about to happen next. The man at her side obeyed some unspoken command and motioned Rachel up the steps to the stage. As with every new case she worked, she could feel adrenaline spike through her veins. The game had begun. The boundaries were drawn, the stakes raised, and, although Carpenter didn't yet realize it, the outcome was determined.

The hush of the assembled troops seemed unnatural. She drew herself up to her full height and began mounting the steps, drawing closer to her quarry. She needed to call upon all her poise when she reached the top, when Carpenter turned the considerable force of his presence toward her and reached out a hand.

She walked toward him, her movements sure and deliberate. Their gazes locked. The brilliant blue light in his eyes gave nothing away, nothing except for a luminous, burning intensity. When she'd reached his side, he clasped her hand in both of his and, his gaze still fixed on hers, raised it to his lips.

Rachel forced a slight smile, despite the renewed shiver sliding down her spine. Under the beam of that charismatic gaze, encased in the warmth of his touch, there was no doubt in her mind that she was in the presence of true evil.

Chapter 2

Her pictures had failed to do her justice. Caleb openly studied the woman at his side as he led her from the dais and into the large home he'd built, which also served as headquarters for The Brotherhood. The photos had reflected Rachel's cool blond looks; the cheekbones that could etch glass, the lips fashioned for wild sin. But the pictures had failed to hint at the intelligence in that level blue gaze, the tensile strength in her grip.

Yes, he'd been prepared to be mildly aroused by her presence, but had never expected to be intrigued. And he'd been completely unprepared for his reaction upon touching her. A response had ricocheted through his system the moment their hands had met. It was involuntary, unfamiliar...fascinating.

What made this woman different from all the others? With her hair fixed in a discreet twist, and the light-pink suit she wore, she could have easily passed for one of the endless stream of available women his mother pushed at him whenever he visited San Francisco. He'd never felt more than a fleeting interest in any woman—until now. A man with his goals could ill afford to get sidetracked, and something told him any involvement with Rachel Grunwald would be a hell of a detour.

They passed through the huge opulent hallway silently, and he opened the door to his office, waited for her to enter. Because he was watching so closely, he saw her quick, all-encompassing glance.

"Please sit down. Can I get you a beverage?"

She went to one of the leather armchairs and sat, crossing one long, lovely leg over the other. Something clutched tightly in his belly, then released.

"Some ice water would be nice."

Her voice was low and smoky, layered with a hint of the northeast. He moved to the crystal decanters and ice bucket that were kept freshly stocked. "I owe you an apology. I shouldn't have kept you out in the hot sun after the long trip you've had." Smiling, he handed her the glass of water he'd poured. "I can almost hear my mother chastising me for my manners."

Rachel took the glass and sipped. "And does your mother live close enough to do her chastising in person?"

Shaking his head, he poured another glass for himself. "No, my family lives in San Francisco, but her lessons were ingrained at a tender age. I still live in fear of her lectures on deportment."

Rachel smiled back at him; it was impossible not to. The charisma his photo had hinted at was magnified tenfold in person. He sat next to her on the couch, maintaining enough distance between them to be considered proper, but still close enough to put all her senses on alert.

He drained his glass, watching her all the while over its rim, then set it on the table beside the couch. "So, tell me about Rachel Grunwald."

The composure that was so much a part of her had her settling back against the couch cushions, as she casually

straightened her skirt. "I assume Commander Parker sent
you a fax on my background. What would you like to
know?" She was, she thought, ready for anything. She'd
expected an inquisition; welcomed it. The sooner her credentials were accepted, the sooner she could start her investigation.

"What would I like to know?" He was as close as he
dared get; not as close as he wished to be. She smelled
female. Her perfume, something subtle and alluring, made
his palms itch. "Almost everything, I believe. Let's start
with your hair. What would you call that color?"

Those gorgeous blue eyes blinked. He enjoyed knowing
that he'd managed to surprise her. "I beg your pardon?"

"It first reminded me of polished brass." He reached out
a finger to smooth a strand that had worked free. "But I
don't believe the description quite does yours justice."

Why, he was *flirting* with her! It was so unexpected, yet
so jarringly familiar, that Rachel wanted to laugh. Amusement tinged her voice. "Blond. I call it blond."

"Functional, if unimaginative." He leaned back against
the couch, already craving a repeat of that light touch.
"Search of the perfect phrase will keep me awake nights."

Her brows skimmed upward. "Mr. Carpenter, I suspect
you've had a great deal of practice in the art of frivolous
conversation."

"Caleb." He noted her free hand, lying loosely on her
lap, free of any show of nerves. She wasn't intimidated;
wasn't even anxious. He liked that about her. He was liking
more and more about her by the second. "And I suspect that
you've been the recipient of a great deal of flattery in your
time."

"Ah, but none quite as accomplished as yours." She was
comfortable in the banter. Sexual attraction could often provide a convenient shield, blinding men to her true intentions.
She would be curiously disappointed if Carpenter proved to
be so uncomplicated. She was competitive enough to wish

for a worthy adversary. It remained to be seen just how worthy he would prove to be.

"You'll find that I'm curious about all sorts of things— whether your eyes are really an identical match for the deep waters off St. Thomas, how your mouth could so perfectly resemble my favorite shade of rose, and what would make a woman like you, one who's probably had a trail of poor fools in her wake since she could walk, agree to be a stranger's wife. At least," his eyes gleamed, "agree to be *considered* for the position."

His abrupt change of topic was designed to shake her. She mentally raised her estimation of him a couple of notches. His tactics may have worked on someone less prepared. "And I'm wondering," she brought the glass to her lips and sipped, "what would make a man like you, one who's obviously used to women swooning in his presence, consider complete strangers for the position."

He regarded her for a moment, then his lips curved very slightly in a smile that was somehow more genuine than the ones he'd graced her with previously. "So, there's a hint of temper beneath the tailoring. I'm…intrigued, Rachel."

He imbued the syllables of her name with a dark liquid essence that hinted at mysterious fires that remained contained. For the moment.

Her gaze was level. "Does it surprise you that a woman would be as committed to the future of the white race as you are?" She nodded her head toward the window. "I believe I saw women among your assembled troops outside earlier." He didn't answer for a moment, and she held her breath, wondering if she'd misjudged him. She had to rely on first impressions and instinct to guide her in the type of woman he would look for. Parker would never have stood for being addressed in such a manner, but she thought that Carpenter, *Caleb,* had more substance. Which, of course, made him more difficult to predict.

"Actually, it's been a very long time since I've been surprised by a woman." He watched her sip from her glass, and mentally applauded her poise. "But, I have a feeling that you're going to change that for me, Rachel."

Their gazes meshed. The brilliant intensity of his eyes was almost mesmerizing, she thought. Had she not seen them aglow with a fanatical gleam outside earlier, they may have affected her differently. But he was, she reminded herself, a zealot of the worst order. It shouldn't surprise her that he was charismatic. Recent history was full of fanatics who'd used a strong personal magnetism to draw followers to a cause—often with disastrous results.

A man entered the room, stopped short inside the doorway. "General Carpenter?"

"Come in, Kevin." Was there a shade of irritation in Carpenter's voice? Rachel observed closely, but could see no reflection of it on his face. "Rachel, meet Colonel Kevin Sutherland. He's my second in command."

"A situation has arisen that you should be apprised of." Sutherland wore the black fatigues she'd seen the troops outfitted in, and possessed the sunburned face of a man unaccustomed to spending time outdoors. In his midfifties, his fading red hair was still thick above a stern countenance. His name stirred in the deep recesses of her memory, but she was certain he hadn't been mentioned in Jonah's briefing. "A couple of the men on patrol told me those Hispanics were sneaking back onto the property. Probably coming through the pass in the southwest corner."

"The same ones who were run off a couple of weeks ago?"

The man shrugged. Clearly, to him, the people's identity were of little importance. "You want me to authorize the men to get rid of them for good this time?"

Rachel's blood iced. Surely the man hadn't just casually suggested murder. She'd been too long in the field to rush to conclusions. He could just as easily be talking about taking measures to make the property more secure. But the alternate possibility failed to completely satisfy.

"I believe you're right. Further action seems inevitable, but I'll handle it myself." Carpenter got up from the couch and walked over to one of two desks, opening a drawer and removing a gun. A Beretta, Rachel noted, her heart racing violently. And he was handling the weapon with an ease that spoke of familiarity.

Carpenter checked the cartridge, resecured the safety, then tucked the gun into the waistband at the small of his back. With grim purpose on his face, in his movements, he looked like a man readying for a mission. "I trust you'll excuse me while I handle some unpleasant business, Rachel. Colonel Sutherland will see you to your room."

He strode to the door and was gone. She considered her options, uneasily aware that she had none. She had no way of following the man; no way of observing, or preventing, what might happen next. Her heart was in a vise as she considered the possibility of civilian casualties occurring within an hour of her arrival at the compound. Rarely had she felt so helpless.

She rose, her next steps as yet unresolved, but Sutherland stopped her.

"Miss Grunwald, if you have a moment."

Rachel looked at the door then at the man. "Actually, I think I'd like to be shown to my room now, if that's possible."

"Certainly. I'll just keep you a few minutes." It was clear from his posture that the civility was merely perfunctory. Reluctantly, she sat in the seat he indicated.

Sutherland rounded the corner of the second desk in the room and sat down. He unlocked a drawer in it, took out a manila folder, and reached over the desk to hand it to her. "I think you'll find the information contained there to be sufficient for your complete understanding of your purpose here, but I'll summarize it for you. First, you must remember that you are a guest here, whose presence is solely reliant upon General Carpenter's wishes.''

Still preoccupied by her worry over Carpenter's intentions, she said distractedly, ''I understand that I'm here for a trial basis of thirty days, awaiting General Carpenter's decision.''

''That is not completely correct. You *may* be here for up to thirty days. The last candidate was sent away after less than three weeks.''

With a great deal of effort, Rachel shifted her attention from the situation that might be evolving between Carpenter and the trespassers. She forced herself to focus on the man before her. There was something in his tone, in his demeanor, that warned her. There was information to be had here. It was obvious that Sutherland was not completely happy about her presence at the compound. Again she tried, in vain, to remember why the man's name seemed so familiar.

She kept her words carefully neutral. ''I didn't realize there had been another candidate.''

His brows raised in what might have been derision. ''You thought you were the first? No, Miss Grunwald, actually there have been two others before you, both since deemed unsuitable. It is imperative that General Carpenter chooses the most superior mate. The future of The Brotherhood is dependent upon his heirs.''

From his choice of words, Rachel reflected, he could have been speaking of the finest stock of breeding mares. Perhaps, as far as he was concerned, that's all women were.

She indulged herself with a fleeting vision of a high back kick striking his arrogant square chin. Her voice was expressionless. ''I understand.''

He didn't appear to hear her. ''It will take a truly remarkable woman to prove worthy of Caleb Carpenter, worthy of the honor to be his wife. More than mere beauty will be necessary. Dedication to our cause, and loyalty to the death must be the standard by which each candidate is judged.''

"I believe my background speaks for itself."

Her quietly measured words seemed to bring him up short. For the first time he looked a bit disconcerted. "Yes." His fingers splayed over the desktop. "Hans Grunwald was a great man. You must be very proud of your father. He was truly a leader who lived his beliefs."

"And died for them."

"Your father was martyred for a just cause. None of us can ask for greater glory in our deaths than that." His eyes met hers again across the polished walnut desktop. "You have far to go, indeed, to live up to your father's legacy."

Farther still, Rachel thought, with an age-old weariness, to live it down.

"Of course, time will tell if you are worthy to continue your father's crusade." Sutherland pursed his lips and steepled his fingers. "And whether this is the avenue in which you will do so. At any rate—" he nodded toward the folder he had given her "—you'll find everything else you need to know in there. That information also outlines standards of conduct befitting someone in your situation."

Rachel slowly lifted her gaze from the folder in her hand. She knew she hadn't imagined the insolence that had crept into his tone. "Meaning?"

He made a dismissive gesture. "The last candidate was sent away for moral turpitude. The soldier found in her bedroom was dismissed as well."

"I see." One fingernail tapped slowly on the folder. "So I can safely assume that these lofty standards you refer to will provide protection for me, as well."

"Your protection is understood." Sutherland's face flushed at the intimation. "The Brotherhood respects a woman's sanctity outside of marriage. It is completely disrespectful of you to imply otherwise."

Voice even, Rachel replied, "No more disrespectful, Colonel Sutherland, than your earlier insinuation to me."

His jaw tight, Sutherland rose, indicating that she was dismissed. "The soldier outside the door will take you to your room."

As she exited the office, Rachel had the distinct impression that he wished he could dismiss her from the compound as easily.

The large richly furnished room she was shown to looked out over the front lawn. Her luggage was already there, stacked in a neat pile. She thanked the young soldier who'd accompanied her upstairs, and waited for the door to close behind him. The smile abruptly faded from her lips as she turned back toward her luggage. The first order of business was to check the security in her bedroom. It wouldn't be the first time a genial host had provided her with a room complete with hidden cameras or bugs.

She went to the largest of her suitcases and lifted it on her bed. Opening it, she removed a small CD player, set it on the bedside table, and turned it on. Unhooking the small remote attached, she tossed it, with seeming nonchalance, next to the suitcase. Then she went about unpacking, keeping a close eye on the small piece of equipment. The fake remote, in fact, housed delicate sensors that would detect any recording equipment in the nearby vicinity. By the time she'd finished her unpacking, there was no discreet telltale light winking from the remote. The room was free of security devices.

She quickly finished the unpacking. Checking her watch, she decided there was time to explore the upstairs before changing for dinner. She wanted to get a thorough map of the compound fixed in her head, and she'd begin with the house.

Palming the phony remote, she opened the bedroom door, then stopped short. The young soldier who'd escorted her upstairs was standing outside her room, leaning against the wall. He quickly straightened when he saw her.

Rachel smiled, a quick mask for her disappointment. "May I help you?"

Her words, or perhaps her sudden reappearance, seemed to have taken the young man by surprise. "No, ma'am." Standing at attention, he fixed his gaze squarely over her left shoulder. "Colonel Sutherland requested that I stay here in case you need anything."

She hid her dismay behind a regal nod. "How thoughtful of him. And of you. Perhaps you can tell me when dinner will be served."

"Dinner?" The soldier's face went blank. "The men eat at six in the mess hall."

"And does General Carpenter join you there?"

"No, ma'am. Not usually." Silence stretched, until comprehension dawned. "You'll be eating with the general, ma'am. In the dining room downstairs."

"And what time would that be?"

He finally looked straight at her, his expression confused. "I couldn't say, ma'am."

The smile she bestowed on him was dazzling. "Would you please find out for me? I don't think either one of us want to be responsible for keeping the general from his dinner this evening."

He looked torn for a moment, but her final sentence appeared to decide him. "I'll do that and be right back."

"Thank you." Rachel waited until the sounds of his retreat receded before opening the door wider and walking into the hall. She'd have to make her search quick.

She was not surprised to find that the door closest to her own was locked. She'd already discovered that her bathroom adjoined to what she could only surmise was another bedroom. The adjoining door had been locked, as well. It would be logical to assume that Carpenter had the suite next to hers. The knowledge had her nerves prickling. There was no doubt that their proximity would grant her easy access to search his quarters. It was the access the proximity granted *him* that lent to her unease.

Continuing down the hallway, she swiftly inspected the rest of the space upstairs. There appeared to be eight bedrooms in all, and none of the rest were occupied. Other than the locks in Carpenter's room, no other security devices were evident. Apparently the man was confident that the security at his front gate was sufficient to keep out unwanted guests.

She mentally took note of the number of windows and their distance to the ground. She would be most comfortable if she could plan at least three different escape routes from various regions in the house. But she'd need closer observation to measure exact drops and distances.

Returning to her room, Rachel entered the bathroom and picked up the hairbrush she'd set on the counter. Grasping it in both hands, she gave it a twist, and the brush separated at a barely visible seam. She reached inside the hollow handle and withdrew a slender wire. Without hesitation she went to the adjoining door and fell to her knees, wielding the flexible wire on the lock. Within seconds she had the door open and started on the one which would open to Carpenter's room. She gave a mental *tsk* of disapproval when it opened just as easily. A man in Carpenter's position should really be more careful.

She swung the door open and surveyed the rich furnishings, the desk strewn with paperwork. When her remote signaled the room was clean, she did a quick walk through. Another doorway in the room proved to be a large walk-in closet, and a third would lead to the hallway.

She strode to the middle of the room, turning slowly, her gaze sweeping the area. Something nagged at the edge of her consciousness. Her brow furrowed for a moment, then she mentally estimated the square footage of the area. It was a good size. But the next door down the hallway from this one had seemed farther away than this space would warrant.

Observing the room again, Rachel's gaze finally fixed on the paneled wall behind Carpenter's bed. Crossing the room to examine it more carefully, she found what she was looking for in the far corner—an almost invisible rectangular crack in the inlaid wood. Carpenter had built himself a secret room.

Again she was forced to revise her opinion of him. Clearly it would be a mistake to underestimate this man. Paranoia and a need for secrecy drove the leaders of these groups. Carpenter would be no different.

Rocking back on her heels a little, she eyed the paneled wall speculatively. There was no knob, no lock in sight. Most likely there was a spring mechanism hidden in the wood itself that would release the door. It would be complicated to break in, but not impossible. Rachel didn't believe in impossible.

Her interest was piqued, but further exploration would have to wait for another day. The sound of voices drifted over to her.

"Next time you disobey a direct order, I won't be so lenient." The words were faint, but unmistakable. "You were told to stay at your post."

Sutherland. Cursing mentally, Rachel hurried toward Carpenter's bathroom, closing and locking the door behind her. There was no longer any question in her mind that the colonel had set the young man outside her door to watch her.

She closed and locked her own bathroom door. With a quick adjustment of the shower, she had the water pounding down, drowning out the voices she'd heard. She slipped the remote into a pocket of the terrycloth robe she'd hung on the back of the door, kicked off her shoes and shed her pantyhose. She stepped under the spray fully clothed, then got out again. Wrapping the robe around her, she wrenched open the door and started into the bedroom, her hair dripping.

"Colonel Sutherland!" The shock in her voice wasn't totally feigned. She'd expected him to be pounding on her door, not standing halfway into her bedroom. The young man who had accompanied him was waiting outside the open door in the hallway, his eyes wide at the scene unfolding before him. Righteous indignation dripped from her every word. "What possible excuse could you have for barging into my private quarters?"

The colonel stared hard at her. "You didn't answer my knock."

"I was in the shower, sir!" The stage had lost a valuable actress in Rachel Grunwald. She literally shook with false fury. "Am I to understand that I can't bathe without fearing an intrusion?"

The soldier was taking in the scene with avid interest. Good. An audience only made the pretense more valuable. If Sutherland was going to align himself against her, she may need to discredit him in the future. The young man in the hallway could prove to be a witness if it came to that.

Sutherland had recovered. "I apologize. I mistakenly believed you were in need of assistance."

Ice edged her words. "In the future, please wait until your assistance is invited."

She thought for a moment she'd gone too far. Sutherland clenched his jaw and took a step toward her. Then he drew himself up, visibly reining in his temper. "Be careful here, Miss Grunwald. Be very careful." After delivering the warning, he spun on his heel and marched to the door. As he was pulling it closed behind him, the soldier called, "Oh, and ma'am? You'll dine with the general at six-thirty."

Surveying the panels of the closed door, Rachel took a deep silent breath. The magnitude of the scene began to register. Earlier Sutherland had made it clear he didn't ap-

prove of her presence here. Now it was obvious that in addition to Carpenter she had yet another powerful enemy to
contend with in The Brotherhood. It only remained to be
discovered why.

Chapter 3

She was exquisite in candlelight. As sounds of Chopin crashed around them, Caleb sipped from his glass, unmindful for the moment of the finely aged wine he tasted. Some would consider it sacrilegious not to savor every drop of the rare wine. It seemed even more sinful not to feast on the beauty before him.

"You're staring."

He inclined his head, unabashed to be caught in the act. Despite her accusation, she continued to eat the succulent pheasant. She was clearly used to male appreciation.

"You're very beautiful."

His words were a simple statement, and she accepted them with a shrug. "I've found that the true measure of a person lies beneath the surface."

He nodded slowly, setting his glass down. "Usually, although with some people what's on the surface is all there is. You're different, though. There's something about you, Rachel, that hints at layers, one wrapped tightly around the other, to conceal secrets you rarely reveal. It makes a man want to be the one to peel those layers back, one by one, and discover…everything.''

To disguise the slight tremor in her hand, she laid down her fork. There was no reason this man's words should affect her. His seductive words were just that, not an indicator that he suspected she wasn't what she seemed. But the shiver that skated over her skin wasn't completely due to a fear of his mistrust. She reminded herself that he was a master of words, one who used them as weapons, to cajole, threaten and condemn. Just as her father had. Thought of her father had the tremors abruptly dissipating.

''And what about you, Caleb Carpenter?'' Her tone was light, the reason behind the question wasn't. ''Is there a part of yourself that you seek to keep from the world?''

He chewed carefully, as if pondering her question. ''I suppose many would regard me as a very private person, yes. It suits my purposes to keep important matters to myself.''

''Is that what caused you to advertise for a wife, rather than seeking one out in a more traditional manner?'' Her words were almost a dare, although they were delivered innocently enough. The literature Sutherland had given her stated exactly what had caused Carpenter to search for a wife. He'd reiterated as much in his words to the troops shortly after her arrival today.

This time his answer was even slower in coming. He picked up a napkin and wiped at his mouth before answering. ''I confess I never thought overmuch about the qualities I would look for in a wife.'' His gaze warmed, and he reached over to enclose her fingers in his. ''And only recently have I begun to discover what those qualities are.''

The heat in his look was mirrored in his touch. She smiled, but after a moment, removed her hand under the guise of reaching for her wineglass. She preferred to avoid his touch. It had a way of clouding her thoughts, momentarily blurring her intent. The unfamiliar feelings were no doubt caused by a combination of fatigue and adrenaline.

However explained, they were annoying. Emotion had never been allowed to infiltrate an assignment. It never would be.

He was a man who would appear at home in a roomful of shimmering people, clad in a designer tux and cupping a cognac snifter in his hand. She didn't doubt that he was cultured, but knew the veneer could be an effective disguise. Most would never question his charming, civil mask. Most would never perceive the underlying element of quiet menace about him that he strove to conceal.

Conversation lagged, and neither made a move to end it. Caleb was content to study her in the resulting silence. She'd chosen a pale-yellow sleeveless sheath that was a perfect foil for her hair, which she'd again pulled up in a knot. Despite his earlier words, he knew the value in taking it slow with her. He'd been only eight when he'd spent time tagging along with the gardener on his parents' estates, admiring the roses. Anxious for the buds to unfurl into full bloom, he'd systematically peeled a full dozen of them, convinced that once he'd stripped the delicate petals aside, the rose would be fully visible. Instead, he'd been left with a path strewn with destroyed flowers, and a stern scolding. The man had learned much from the child; there would be far greater pleasure to be had if he peeled away the layers of Rachel Grunwald one filmy strip at a time. The patience it would take was no deterrent. Patience was a particular strength of his.

Her words interrupted his reverie. "You spoke of family earlier. Do any of them visit you here?"

His gaze dropped and he reached for his wine again. "No. I go to San Francisco to see them every month or so."

His answer was just short of brusque, but it didn't stop her from probing further. "Do they share our convictions for the future of the white race?"

The music changed, into something moody and melancholy. "My family is very traditional and extremely stubborn. We've agreed to disagree about what I've chosen to do with my life.'' Because the admission was accompanied by a twinge of regret, he pushed his chair back and rose. ''Are you finished? It's still early. I could show you the grounds.''

Rachel stood, a genuine smile curving her lips. ''I'd like that.''

The grounds, she soon learned, consisted of a lush, well-kept lawn surrounded by three hundred acres of land. The compound had been built on a plateau surrounded on two sides by the picturesque Sawtooth Mountains. As they rounded the house, Rachel saw again the buildings that dotted the vicinity, and asked about them.

''Some are living quarters for the troops. The few families here have their own homes. Kevin lives in one with his daughter. Careful.'' His hand lightly touched her elbow. ''The walk there is uneven.'' The shiver his touch evoked was due to the rapidly cooling temperature, she assured herself. The sun was already bleeding across the sky. ''The other buildings are for training purposes. The troops follow a daily regimen…weaponry instruction, hand-to-hand combat and so forth.''

He was describing a day much like any other she'd spent within various militias. ''I spent quite a bit of time in the Comrades compound teaching hand-to-hand tactics and martial arts. I'd be interested in seeing your facility, even in providing some instruction if there's a need for it.''

She caught him smiling, and arched her eyebrows. ''You find that amusing?''

He held up his hands placatingly. ''I'm not impugning your talent, believe me. But I don't like the thought of you wrestling with some of these gorillas here.''

''Gorillas don't frighten me.'' Still intent on scanning the area, she started a little when he slipped his gray suit jacket over her shoulders.

"You're shivering. The temperature drops quickly at night. Would you like to return to the house?"

She wasn't about to give up the opportunity to explore the compound further. "No, I'm fine." To her chagrin, he veered from the direction of the buildings, steering her to the gardens beside the house.

"You may enjoy taking a closer look at the garden tomorrow. Chad, the gardener, does a marvelous job." Even in the swiftly lengthening shadows, Rachel could see he spoke the truth. The plants were heavy with blooms, their fragrance stinging the air. It would be even more impressive during the day.

With seeming idleness she said, "He must be very talented. How did you convince him to take a job so far from civilization?"

Caleb halted, and together they watched the sun sink behind the mountains in a spectacular display. "I never saw a sunset like that in San Francisco. I've yet to grow tired of it." Belatedly, he answered her question. "Chad is one of our recruits. Those with particular talents often serve in a slightly different capacity."

Disappointment rose. She ruthlessly kept it from her voice. "How lucky for you that your recruits are so gifted. Dinner tonight was excellent."

With a touch on her elbow he guided her to a bench at the side of a path, and they sat. "Yes, Eliza is a jewel. She came to us from the Sons of Freedom. Have you heard of them?" Rachel had. "Their loss was my gain." His teeth flashed in the growing darkness. "I've put on five pounds since she's been here."

She smiled at the pun, but her mind was busy. She would have stood a better chance of extracting bits and pieces of information from hired help. From his words, she assumed that everyone on the compound was a part of The Brotherhood. Did that mean that Carpenter was paranoid or just very careful? Either way, her job had just gotten a little more challenging.

She pushed the thought aside and seized the opening he'd offered. "If I'm going to eat like that every night, it won't be long until I start tipping the scale myself. I'm used to being quite active."

Her words had the desired effect. "Of course you are. Feel free to use the training facilities any time you wish. They're stocked with state-of-the-art equipment."

"I'm not surprised." She turned to face him more fully. "From what I've seen there's been no expense spared in the complex. You must be quite proud of what you've accomplished here."

"Personal wealth makes a great many worries fade away. I feel strongly about what I'm doing. Your father was also a patriot for the cause, wasn't he? I remember reading about his death when I was in college. You must have been, what? Twelve?"

"Fourteen," she murmured, averting her gaze. She had to steel herself for the questions that would follow. She didn't want thoughts of her father crowding in at a time like this, not when she had the opportunity to build a tenuous bond with the man beside her. But the memory of Hans Grunwald would very likely prove valuable in forging that bond. He had, after all, died for the very convictions Carpenter so fervently believed in.

"I'm sorry." The gentleness in his voice was as much a shock as his words. "It must have been very difficult for you."

"He died a hero." The statement all but stuck in her throat, the words parroted from her mother. She'd never understood how her mother could regard as a hero a man who died carrying out an assassination attempt. Had never comprehended how a life of hatred and violence could earn a man a place as a martyr. Her failure to make that connection had led her straight to SPEAR.

Diligently, she shoved the jumbled pain and guilt back into the dark mental corner where she usually kept them. She had an assignment to do here. And memories of her father merely strengthened her resolve to destroy The Brotherhood.

Did Carpenter's family feel the same bewilderment and failure at the choices he made? Were they physically sickened when they saw the way prejudice had twisted their son, their brother, into something unrecognizable? She thought they must be. From what he'd mentioned, they didn't approve of his beliefs. She wondered if they'd experienced the same horrible epiphany she had, when she'd finally realized that beneath her father's face dwelled a monster.

"I've upset you." The pad of his finger caressed her jaw. It was difficult not to jerk away; the thoughts had left her strangely vulnerable.

She shook her head. "He inspired the same sort of loyalty from his followers that you do from yours, and he was a man who insisted on handling important matters by himself. Much as you did this afternoon after Colonel Sutherland interrupted us." She watched him carefully. "I was concerned when you insisted on confronting the intruders alone. Was there any trouble?"

He gazed into the distance, his profile etched in the darkness. "No, there was no trouble."

It was apparent that was all he intended to say on the subject. Rachel was far from content with his answer. "Good. I didn't hear any gunfire, but then, I didn't know how far away you were."

"Most problems offer an array of solutions. Force just happens to be the most final one."

And although her blood ran cold at his ambiguous answer, Rachel was really no closer to knowing what had transpired that afternoon with the Hispanics.

It came as no surprise to Rachel when she opened her door the next morning and saw the same young man, dressed again in black fatigues, leaning against the opposite wall in the hallway. She gave him a casual smile. "You must be an early riser. I hope you had time for breakfast this morning."

His countenance was stiff, and he focused on a point over her head. "Yes, ma'am."

She started down the hall, and he fell in after her. She wondered what he'd do if she stopped suddenly. Probably plow right into her. Clearly he had taken Sutherland's chastising to heart. She wouldn't dislodge him as easily today.

Rachel gave a mental shrug. The young man would be of no concern for a while. She was going to spend the next day or two familiarizing herself with the compound. After the conversation she had with Carpenter last night, she'd felt secure in doing so.

The omelet she had for breakfast was delicious, although she found it somewhat difficult to swallow with her guardian angel hovering nearby. Since the soldier didn't seem prone to initiating conversation, she tried to engage him. "If we're going to spend our days together, I think I should at least know your name."

He hesitated for a moment, before replying, "It's Private Sallem, ma'am."

"And I'm Rachel."

"Yes, ma'am."

She gave a mental sigh. "And what's your first name?"

He gave the question more consideration than it merited, before finally deciding it was harmless. "Raymond."

"Excellent." She smiled at him. He couldn't be more than nineteen or twenty. What could have led someone his age to the hate-filled world of The Brotherhood? Had he been raised in prejudice, as she had, or had he chosen it for himself? She found herself curious. "Do you have family in the compound, Raymond?"

"No, ma'am."

Her appetite satisfied, she rose from the table and walked from the dining room. "Where are you from?"

"Missouri, ma'am."

The hallway was lined with artwork she hadn't had an opportunity to study last night. She paused before each painting and sculpture. The selections could provide more details about Carpenter. Or they may only reveal a man used to surrounding himself with expensive beautiful things. The thought that he probably considered her presence here in the same light nearly made her cringe.

"Missouri is a long way from Idaho. How often do you make it back to visit your family?"

Although she wasn't looking at him, she could hear him shuffle his feet. "I don't have any family, ma'am. My mom died a couple of years ago. I've been on my own ever since."

Which might explain the attraction of the militia group, or others like it. If Raymond had sought out the group in search of a surrogate family, he couldn't have chosen less wisely.

Ironically, she felt the first stirrings of sympathy for the soldier. Surely in one so young it could not be impossible to show him the error in his thinking. As quickly as the thought occurred to her, she dismissed it. She'd faced down automatic weapons carried by far younger kids than Raymond. Disillusionment with the status quo seemed to be the lowest common human denominator. And she'd never been in the business of rehabilitation, at any rate.

She slipped on a pair of sunglasses she'd carried downstairs with her and led her young shadow outside and down the front steps. Her first destination was the garden she and Caleb had lingered in last evening. The place where he'd uttered that cryptic statement that had said everything, and nothing, about the trespassing Hispanics. Under the pretense of strolling through the grounds, she took her time studying the confines of the compound, at least what she could see of it from there.

The drive leading to the road in front of the house was at least a mile. Gates stretched across the entrance, connected to what she imagined was an electric fence line. Although she could see activity there, she was unable to make out the number of men patrolling from this distance. She made a mental note to investigate it later.

It wasn't necessary to feign fascination with the magnificent display of color before her. Although Rachel had no claim to a green thumb, she could appreciate the efforts of those who did. The garden was a fitting addition to the nearby mansion, and for the man who seemed used to the best of everything.

With seeming aimlessness, she exited the garden and began strolling toward the buildings, ignoring the young man at her side. But when they were within a hundred yards of the training facility, Raymond broke the silence. "Ma'am? You'll probably want to head back up toward the house. These buildings are used during the day for training operations."

"Perfect." She graced him with a bright smile. "I was telling General Carpenter last night how much I was missing my daily workouts, and he invited me to use the gymnasium facility. Is this it?"

"Yes, this is it, but I don't think the colonel would...that is..." His words trailed off when she whipped off her glasses to stare at him.

"The colonel?"

Raymond was clearly uncomfortable. "I—I mean the general. He probably wouldn't like it."

"But I've just told you that he okayed it, didn't I? So I don't foresee any problem."

Turning on her heel she strode to the entrance and pushed the door open. Carpenter hadn't been exaggerating, she discovered. The building was fully outfitted with top-of-the-line equipment. No expense had been spared training the men and women of The Brotherhood how to fight for the dogma they were dedicated to.

Despite the use for which it was intended, she had a grudging admiration for the equipment itself. She'd never worked out in such a well-maintained gymnasium outside of the agency's training facility.

She walked about the place, openly watching the drills going on in some of the rooms. And when she found a gymnasium empty, she lost no time entering. It was too much temptation to merely look at the various stations. Soon she was slipping out of her shoes and hoisting herself up on the balance beam to run lightly across it and back several times. Then spying an electronic sparring machine in the corner, she went to examine it. She was only peripherally aware of the moment when Raymond slipped away, probably to report to Sutherland.

"I see you're interested in our machine. Do you train?"

Rachel whirled around to see a red-haired woman about her age crossing the gym toward her. She was dressed in the customary black fatigues.

"I do, but I rarely have the opportunity to use equipment like this. You're very lucky. I'm Rachel, by the way."

"My name is Kathy." The woman surveyed her curiously. "I hope you fare better than the last two applicants. General Carpenter takes his responsibility to The Brotherhood very seriously, and his standards are quite high."

There didn't seem to be an appropriate answer for that statement, so Rachel didn't offer one. "The general invited me to use the facilities and I'm going to take him up on it. Is this gymnasium going to be free for the next hour or two?" As she spoke, she unbuttoned her shirt and shrugged out of it. Clad in a tank top and shorts, she sat to pull off her shoes. She always preferred to work out barefoot.

"There isn't a session scheduled for this hall until this afternoon. I'll be leading it myself."

Rachel bent her knee and lunged forward to loosen up. "Oh, so you're a trainer here." She switched legs. "I was an instructor myself in the organization I came from."

The woman looked pleased. "Really? Would you like a sparring partner? It's not often that I can find a worthy match here."

"Sure." She welcomed the opportunity. It was imperative to stay in shape during the assignment. It was impossible to tell when she would be called on to defend herself.

After a warming up for a few minutes, the women stepped into the middle of a ring drawn on the mat. For the first few minutes they circled each other, feinting a few times, gauging the strength and agility of their opponents. Watching Kathy's eyes, Rachel was able to estimate when her intent changed to something more serious, and easily dodged the first spin kick, dancing gracefully out of reach.

Kathy's face hardened. They circled again, and Rachel rushed in, landing a blow lightly in the woman's midsection. The other woman feinted left, and kicked out. Too late, Rachel moved away. The kick caught her in the shoulder with enough force to stagger her. If she hadn't moved at the last minute, it would have taken her down.

Her eyes narrowed. This was no ordinary sparring match, one to test speed, endurance and agility. Kathy wasn't checking her blows. From the look of determination on the other woman's face, she wouldn't be satisfied until Rachel was lying on the mat.

She had no intention of indulging her.

Rachel began to spar in earnest, determined to put an end to the competition. Again she watched Kathy's eyes. That's where the purpose would show, a split second before the hands or feet moved. She dodged a blow that would have rocked her chin back and waited for the next kick. When it came, she caught the heel of Kathy's foot and used her momentum to pull the woman off balance. She landed hard on the mat and Rachel followed her down, her knee to the woman's throat in a final demonstration of victory.

"Ah…an interesting exhibition." Rachel's head jerked at the sound of Carpenter's voice, and Kathy took advantage of her distraction to roll away and rise.

Rachel stood, her brows arched. "I wasn't aware we had an audience." Several men, including Sutherland and Raymond, were gawking from the doorway. Her attention, though, was focused on Carpenter, trying to gauge his reaction. He was, she decided a moment later, mildly amused.

Carpenter looked around him. "Dismissed, men." When it took a few moments for them to begin to disperse, he repeated himself, a thread of steel entering his voice. "I said, you're all dismissed. Back to your stations."

They exited quickly, and Kathy slipped out a side door, leaving Rachel and Caleb alone in the gym. Rachel went over to retrieve her shirt and shoes, and Caleb strolled after her. "Here." He tossed her a towel from shelf against the wall. "Not that you seemed to work up much of a sweat. Are you finished with your workout?"

"Actually…no. I had just started when Kathy offered me a match." She studied him carefully. "You told me I could use the facility."

His hands in the pockets of his trousers, he meandered over to her and leaned against the wall. "And I meant it. I just hadn't been prepared for the sight of my fiancée dumping the colonel's daughter on her behind." He shook his head, as if the memory of the sight still amused him.

Her attention fragmented. It was the first time the term *fiancée* had been used without a qualifier—like applicant or candidate. Another thought occurred. Stilling in the act of retying her shoes, she looked up. "Daughter. Kathy is…"

"Sutherland's youngest," he affirmed, eyes gleaming.

"One of our better instructors, too. You minimized your talents in this area."

The minimization, she was sure, had existed only in his presumption. She surprised them both by offering, "Maybe you'd like to get a closer look at my *talents*."

Her words seemed to have left him momentarily speechless. She must be a little shell-shocked herself, to have issued the impulsive invitation. Maybe it had been his amusement, as if the talents he'd spoken of had little more than entertainment value. Perhaps she was seeking to solidify their relationship as it was; that of adversaries.

At any rate, he was about to demur; she saw it in his eyes. With a pitying look, she promised, "I won't hurt you. I usually take it easy on a match opponent."

The verbal blow landed square on his ego. His gaze narrowed. "I don't."

She shrugged, smiled at him. "Then I won't either." She kicked her shoes off again and waited, as he moved more slowly to do the same. While he was getting prepared, she moved to the corner and worked off some of her nerves by pounding on the body bag suspended from a chain.

"Hopefully you're taking out your frustrations on that bag, and won't have much energy left for me."

She whirled and the bag swung back and bumped her hip. She didn't notice. He was barefoot, had divested himself of his shirt and had rolled up his pants. Her gaze followed the line of his leg to the hint of calf muscle showing below the hastily rolled cuffs. Her eyes traveled upward to linger over his flat belly before fixing fascinatedly on his bare chest.

She swallowed. His tall body was rangy rather than broad, sinewy rather than bulky. A perfect V of black chest hair covered lightly padded muscle. It was impossible not to appreciate the picture he made. Objectively speaking, of course.

Her objectivity fled when her gaze landed on his face.

The slightly amused smirk on his lips might be considered cute by some. She longed for nothing more than to knock it off.

He made a come-and-get-me gesture with his hands. "I'm ready if you are."

She strolled over to the ring, and waited for him to follow. "Oh, I'm ready, all right."

She eyed him as they circled in the ring, as each tried to detect the first hint of weakness in the other. In hand-to-hand warfare she had to use her weaknesses, as well as her strengths. If the opponent outsized her, she would have the advantage of speed. Against superior strength, she would still have agility. The only rule of combat was to never, ever fight battles she couldn't win.

She was determined to win this one.

He moved in with a right jab aimed for her stomach. She ducked under his arm and spun, delivering a kick to his kidneys. She didn't temper the force and knew it stung, even without the reproachful look he fixed her with as he rubbed the spot. "That hurt."

This time it was she who smirked. "It was meant to."

There wasn't a smile on his lips, but his eyes gleamed. "Something tells me that you think you're pretty hot stuff on the mat."

"Something tells *me* that you've spent your share of time stretched out on top of it."

He shook his head, a flicker of humor crossing his face. "Baby, I'm going to make you pay for that one."

With a mask of renewed resolve on his face he kept moving, blocking her feint and right cross, jabbing out, catching her firmly in the shoulder. "Ready to stop yet? I'd hate to really hurt you."

She bared her teeth. They continued to circle each other warily, waiting for an opening, searching for a vulnerability. She landed one more kick to his belly, and was almost downed when his foot shot out behind hers and he gave her a push that should have toppled her. She held on to his arm to regain her balance, then wrested it behind him. It was a trap. She knew it as soon as she moved; she didn't need his husky laugh to tell her so. She should never have gotten that close to him. Nearness dissipated her advantage. Her mobility was threatened. She released him, clasped both hands, and drove her elbows into his rib cage.

Although his breath released with a satisfying whoosh, he had the presence of mind to grab her before she could spin away, and used his greater strength to wrestle her to the mat. Where he landed smack on top of her.

She used her elbows to wedge some breathing room for herself and forced herself to meet his laughing gaze.

"I didn't dare tell you this while you were intent on knocking my block off, but I have a confession to make. I have to admit to experiencing a certain, ah…fascination at the sight of two scantily clad women fighting."

"Sparring."

"Whatever." His teeth flashed and there wasn't a hint of contrition in his smile. "I guess that makes me a pervert."

"Well, it makes you male. Of course, the two terms aren't mutually exclusive."

His chuckle seemed to roll up from the pit of his belly. She imagined that she could feel every roll and pitch of it as it worked through his body. Every inch of his long length was pressed close to hers. Angles against curves, heat to heat. The pounding of her pulse no longer had anything to do with her exertion, and everything to do with their position. It was time to fight dirty.

She let her eyelashes flutter, and parted her lips. Her body softened against his. She didn't have to feign her breathy gasps for air. She saw the instant the laughter faded from his eyes, to be replaced with primitive masculine intent. His knee pressed between hers, and his mouth descended slowly, his gaze fixed on hers.

And a moment later he stilled, his lips a fraction away, male discomfort evident on his face. "Ah...you know that your knee is in a very tender spot...you *do* know."

She smiled sweetly.

"My mother is expecting grandchildren."

"Then I'd advise you to get up. Slowly."

With exaggerated care he rose, moving back cautiously while she stood, as well. He watched the self-satisfied look settle upon her face and it brought an answering smile. Damn, if she wasn't something. Unexpected, alluring, intriguing. And sexy enough to melt a glacier.

He stepped forward, stuck out a hand. "Truce?"

She eyed it suspiciously, before putting her hand in his. The moment their fingers clasped he yanked her against him, and wrapped his arms securely around her waist to keep her there. "Remember," he whispered, his lips close to hers, "never trust an opponent. Especially one promising peace."

His mouth closed over hers for a quick, teasing sampling, but lingered when reaction rocketed, smashing expectations. There was more here than he'd anticipated, far more to be shared than a casual kiss between acquaintances. He paused, his lips motionless on hers for a heartbeat. He'd faced danger often enough to recognize it, often enough to avoid it when possible. A visceral instinct was warning him now, screaming at him. It wasn't like him to ignore it. It wasn't like him to rush in regardless, to mindlessly dive into sensation.

He deepened the kiss for a heated, hungry taste. Her tongue glided along his in a velvet dance and need slammed into him. Inner warnings went ignored. The battle changed, became passion warring against passion, strength pitted against strength.

He hauled her closer. Her arms welcomed him, twined

around his neck and enfolded him in a greedy embrace.
Their mouths mated, tongues battling and bodies straining
against each other. One of her hands raked into his hair, the
other gripped his shoulder. The evidence of her desire
stripped his mind clean.

She was a medley of wild flavors and silken textures. Her
mouth was pure sin and was rapidly driving him beyond
reason. The arousing scent of her lingered in the curves and
hollows of her neck, and behind her ear. He swept his palm
down her spine, cupped her bottom, damning the fragile bar-
rier of clothes between them. He wanted to explore her. He
wanted to find all the secret places that made her gasp and
moan and beg. He wanted to drink the cries from her lips
and wring them from her again and again, until he'd marked
her for his own.

And the depth of that wanting shocked him. It fired an
alarm through his system that wouldn't be stilled, that
couldn't be ignored. He lifted his head, although need still
pounded through his veins like a locomotive. The cessation
of pleasure was keen, and it took effort not to reach for her
again. Because it took such effort, he took a step away from
her. And then another.

"I'd better get back to the office."

He barely recognized his voice, edgy and ragged. He
watched her eyes, still dazed and slightly drugged-looking
and it was all he could do to keep from dragging her to him
again, pulling the damn holder from her hair and tangling
his fingers in the thick blond strands. Deliberately, he turned
his back and walked over to where he left his clothes.

After a moment, she did the same. Buttoning her shirt
was a task that required concentration. Donning her socks
and shoes gave her an excuse not to look his way. But not
looking at him couldn't stem the tide of emotions flooding
through her. She needed time; time to get things back in
perspective, time to reset her course.

Her fingers faltered over knotting her shoe, and she gave a mental curse. She ordered her flagging composure back by sheer force of will. It wasn't as if this was the first time she'd been kissed by a thoroughly reprehensible man, one being investigated for his involvement in heinous activities. Fingers stilling in their tasks, she drew a deep breath and released it.

But God help her, it was the first time she'd enjoyed it.

Chapter 4

By the time Rachel had been at the compound a week, she'd developed a detailed mental map of the house. While boring Raymond by her seemingly endless fascination with the ornamental woodwork, the fine wallpaperings and furnishings, she observed exits, determined possible escape routes and household schedules. Admiring the bounty of the flower gardens from different windows of the house, she mapped distances, drops and roof pitches. She was finally satisfied that the only potential places of interest in the home itself were the locked areas in Caleb's bedroom and the office he shared with Sutherland.

It wasn't difficult to evaluate the risk factor of searching both. Getting in and out of Caleb's room would be relatively easy to accomplish, especially when she had a firmer grasp on his daily schedule. The office would require more thought. She hadn't yet observed a time when it was unoccupied. It would clearly be an opportunity that would lend itself better to nighttime reconnoitering.

She'd also learned a great deal about Caleb Carpenter. In

the course of their dinner conversations it had emerged that they shared a similar taste in books and movies, with both of them preferring mysteries and thrillers. They liked dogs above cats, and enjoyed basketball over baseball. They differed over their favorite museums, he preferring the Louvre and she professing an enjoyment in exploring the Smithsonians. But both preferred classical music, and enjoyed physical activities that pitted them against the elements.

She thought she'd learned a lot about the man with what he didn't say, as well. She knew he was tough; he'd have to be. He was obviously smart, well-educated, cultured. His smiles came more frequently than his frowns, and his voice could be serious one moment, filled with amusement the next. Always though, his blue eyes gave nothing away, at times appearing shuttered, deliberately secretive.

And she knew, with an intuition independent of logic, that he was dangerous.

Rachel was about to take a measure of that danger. A man who distrusted her posed a far greater threat than one who did not. It was time to find out, once and for all, whose orders ultimately kept Raymond so closely attached. She eyed the bored-looking young soldier at her side speculatively. She was ready to begin the next stage of her operation, and having one of The Brotherhood's soldiers tagging along was an obstacle that would have to be eliminated, one way or another.

Turning abruptly away from the window she was standing before, she nearly collided with Raymond. She strode past him down the hallway. She was hoping that the idea for a guard didn't spring from Carpenter. If he didn't trust her, at least a little, he'd be doubly wary. It suited her purposes to keep her primary adversary relaxed.

Caleb hadn't seemed very relaxed, however, for the past several days. Although they still had dinner together every night, he excused himself soon afterward, leaving her to her own devices. She'd welcomed the space his absence created.

It gave her time to collect her own composure, to come to terms with her reaction to his kiss. Rachel's strengths had always been her cool steady calm and her clearheaded logic. She should know better than most that separating the good from the evil in a person was impossible. Rather than two different sides, the qualities were irreversibly entwined. Her father's good traits hadn't been enough to save him from the demonic hatred that had eventually destroyed him.

It was deeply troubling to discover desire could even momentarily overcome her loathing for everything Carpenter represented. But after a few days she'd been able to dismiss the emotion as an aberration fueled by long-dormant hormones. There was no denying, however, that the emotional distance Caleb had been displaying made the task easier.

"Miss Grunwald!"

Rachel threw a quizzical look over her shoulder. Raymond's expression was panicked. "You can't go in there. The general and the colonel shouldn't be interrupted."

She gave a careless smile, her hand on the knob of the office door. "I won't keep Caleb long." She knocked once, deliberately pushing the door open almost immediately.

"...no better way to accomplish nationwide recognition and respect than with some carefully planned bombings and assassinations. We've certainly got the arsenal for it, thanks to Sim—" Sutherland's words broke off abruptly as Rachel entered the room.

"Oh." With a self-conscious air, Rachel stopped in her tracks. She sent an apologetic shrug to Caleb. "I'm interrupting you. Please excuse me." She began to back out of the room, bumping up against Raymond, who was hovering behind her.

Caleb watched her, his face impassive. "Careful. You're causing a human pileup there."

"You *are* interrupting us, Miss Grunwald." Sutherland said. "Perhaps your business can wait until this evening."

''Of course.'' She gave an easy smile and began to turn away.

''That won't be necessary.'' There was a hint of command in Caleb's voice which had her pausing. ''I'm not so busy that I can't spare a few minutes.'' His gaze went to Raymond, and his brows rose. ''Is there something I can help you with, soldier?''

The young man went a deep dull red. ''No, sir, General.''

''Oh, he's with me.'' Rachel waved a dismissive hand. ''At least, he's the soldier who's been assigned to me. And he warned me about interrupting you, so the fault is mine.''

Caleb's expression went thoughtful and he continued to stare at Raymond, who began to fidget nervously. ''Assigned to you?''

Rachel had her answer. Carpenter knew nothing about the constant posted guard on her, so Sutherland was to blame, as she'd suspected. She was given no time to ponder the reason. Caleb turned his piercing stare on Sutherland. ''Colonel, please take the soldier with you and give us five minutes.''

He didn't wait for them to obey before switching his attention back to Rachel. ''You left your hair down.''

His simple observation was oddly disconcerting. So was the flame of heat in his eyes. After his polite reserve of the past several days, she was dismayed at the return of that familiar intensity. It seared her, bathing her with warmth and making her all too aware of the last time he'd looked at her that way. And the way she'd responded.

She reached up to push her hair over her shoulder, the genuine embarrassment in the gesture foreign to her. ''It's usually simpler to just pull it back....''

''I like it.''

The distance between them closed as he stepped toward her and the other, more intangible distance that had existed between them for the last several days, suddenly evaporated. He reached out and combed his fingers through the loose strands curving beneath her jaw and Rachel went completely still.

"It looks good on you." It softened her face, made her perfect features seem less remote. More touchable. And because he wanted to touch, badly, he clasped both hands behind his back.

Turning abruptly and crossing to the service cart tucked into a corner of the room, he asked, "Can I get you something to drink?" He glanced over his shoulder and saw Rachel shake her head. "I have some of that iced lemonade you like so well."

Relenting, she accepted the glass he poured for her, wondering how he'd known that she stopped in the kitchen each afternoon for some of this delicious drink. She wondered uneasily what else he might have observed, as well.

She met his blue gaze with her own, and raised her glass. After taking a sip, she said, "I apologize again for barging in on you. I just wanted to ask if it was all right to borrow from your library. You have quite an extensive collection, and I haven't had the time to read for a while."

He gave a careless wave of his hand. "You don't need to ask permission. You're to make yourself completely at home here. And don't worry about the interruption. I can always spare a few minutes for a beautiful woman. Especially one that I've been neglecting lately." The reasons for that had never seemed less rational. Certainly limiting his time with her hadn't erased her from his mind. Not when she still lingered at the edges of his thoughts, a teasing distraction to the very serious matters at hand.

It was exactly the seriousness of those matters that had had him carefully avoiding her for the past several days. He couldn't afford to lose sight of the goal that was so close to achievement he could almost touch it. A goal that would be the fruition of years of single-minded dedication.

His fingers clenched as he watched Rachel lower her glass. Her lips were moist. He knew exactly how they would taste, with the sweet, tangy drops clinging to them and the succulent sweetness that was all her own. And he recognized just how thoroughly he'd been deluding himself for the past week. He may have kept his physical distance from her, but she'd continued to represent just as much a diversion.

Consideringly, he raised his glass and drank. Women didn't distract him—ever. They were pleasant companions, and he enjoyed their company, but when it was time to part, they were forgotten. Never had one caused his thoughts to stray and his sleep to fragment. A faint frown crossed his face. It still surprised him that Rachel was managing to accomplish what all the others could not.

"You're staring again. I'm surprised your mother didn't extinguish that particular trait of yours."

He smiled, slow and wide, and never took his gaze from her. "It's not the only character flaw she failed at erasing from my tender psyche, just perhaps the most annoying one."

Rachel strolled to a leather sofa and sat, observing the room curiously. She hadn't been in it since the day of her arrival. Computers sat beside each of the two desks. She wondered briefly how long it would take her to break the security codes on them.

"Are you thinking about trying your hand at it?"

Her hesitation was only slight, before she completed the act of crossing one leg over the other. "Trying my hand...?"

"At correcting those character flaws my mother failed at." His teeth flashed in a wicked grin. "I'm modest enough to admit to a few, and patient enough to submit to your tutelage."

"Oh, don't worry. I'm not planning on being one of those wives intent on improving their husbands."

"No?" He seemed almost disappointed. "What will you be intent on?"

She shifted away from the sensitive subject. "It's a little

premature to be making any plans. I have three more weeks left in my trial period here.''

His smile faded, and his expression turned reflective. ''Yes, you do.'' Draining his glass, he set it on a nearby end table. ''Maybe we should be making better use of that time. We could begin after dinner tonight. We'll take a ride, so you can see more of the compound.''

Interest piqued, she agreed readily. ''We should plan on dining earlier than usual. Daylight fades more quickly here than it does back east.''

He gave a slight nod. ''Please tell Eliza to plan dinner for five-thirty.'' He walked by her side to the door of the office. He waited until she was ready to walk through the door before adding, ''Oh, and Rachel.'' She looked back quizzically.

''Leave you hair down for me.''

Leaning against the doorjamb, he watched her walk away with a gait that was all the more provocative because it was natural. If Rachel Grunwald was going to prove to be a distraction regardless of how much time they spent together, he reasoned, why should he limit that time? He'd never been a man to deny himself the pleasures of life, although admittedly, it would be the first time he'd consciously chosen to allow them to mix with business.

He shifted his gaze to Sutherland and Raymond, who was barely old enough to vote, but ready to sacrifice his life for The Brotherhood and their beliefs. ''Soldier.'' The young man snapped to attention. ''You've been reassigned. You may go back to the detail you held prior to Miss Grunwald's arrival.''

The soldier swallowed nervously, flicked a glance at Sutherland, and then nodded. ''Yes, sir, General.'' From the pace he set as he strode toward the door, his eagerness to vanish was clear.

Caleb turned and went back to the office, returning to his chair. After a moment, Kevin followed, closing the door behind him. When the other man remained standing, Caleb raised a quizzical brow. "Something on your mind, Kevin?"

Sutherland's mouth was pressed in a thin flat line. "No, sir."

It didn't take much perception to realize the man was livid. "I think there is. Why don't you spit it out so we can get on with our earlier discussion?"

"All right." The colonel paced toward the desk, emotion carving deep furrows into his brow. "You countermanded my orders to that soldier, and undermined my position. I can't command the men's respect if you're going to proceed that way."

"I disagree that I undermined your position, Kevin." Caleb's desk chair squeaked as he leaned back in it. "Your place is my second in command, so the men shouldn't think it strange that my orders take precedence. That's what we train them for, isn't it? To follow orders?" When the man remained silent, Caleb's gaze narrowed. Sotto voce he inquired, "Or maybe it's you who has forgotten who's in command here."

The colonel held his gaze for a long tension-filled moment, before finally looking away. "I haven't forgotten, sir."

"Good, because I don't tolerate disrespect in my ranks. This is not a democracy. I'm in charge and I make the decisions." A long pause followed, during which neither man spoke. "But, as always, I value your opinions. So I'm going to listen while you explain to me why you assigned a guard to Rachel Grunwald."

Sutherland faced him squarely, not backing down an inch. "I would think that would be obvious, sir."

"Indulge me."

"Very well." The man took a deep breath. "Because of the problems we had with the first two candidates I thought more proactive measures would be useful this time. We don't want a reoccurrence of the trouble we experienced with them.''

Mention of the first two prospective candidates was jarring. Caleb hadn't spared either of them a thought after they'd been dismissed. Somehow he knew that even if Rachel left the compound, memories of her wouldn't be so easily banished. ''Well, I hardly think it likely that we'd be so unlucky as to have attracted another candidate with sticky fingers or wandering eyes.''

Grimly Sutherland surveyed him. ''I don't think you take this situation seriously enough, sir. It's imperative that you select the perfect mate. She must be worthy of you, and of her position in The Brotherhood. Surveillance of the candidates isn't out of line.''

Caleb linked his fingers atop his desk, a picture of steady composure. ''We caught the other two young women in their peccadilloes easily enough, didn't we? I'm sufficiently confident of our security here without assigning young soldiers to fool errands. I have more important plans for our troops, and it's imperative that each soldier learns these particular lessons well.''

Sutherland looked at him, interest clearly battling with ire. In another moment, interest won. Grasping the back of the chair Caleb gestured to, he pulled it closer to Caleb's desk and sat. ''It sounds like you've been making some plans. I hope you'll consider my earlier proposal. Some carefully chosen hits should gain us valuable attention.''

As the other man talked about his suggested targets in the state and surrounding area, Caleb rose and strolled to the one of the front windows. The lawn sprawled in a vivid-green carpet rolling toward the gate securing the front of the property, a mile in the distance. Boundaried on the other sides by mountains and canyon, The Brotherhood had etched out its own little kingdom, in the midst of nature's majesty. And he'd scratched and fought to build that kingdom; every inch a testament to his dedication and commitment to the only cause that had ever mattered to him.

Sutherland droned on about his ideas for attaching The Brotherhood's name to violence and destruction. The man was partially right; both would be in The Brotherhood's future. But it would be Caleb at the helm, directing it every inch of the way.

Turning from the window he spoke, his voice low, but laden with such authority that the other man immediately fell silent. "You have the right idea, Kevin, but you're thinking too small. What I'm planning is on a far grander scale. Think international organizations. Embassies. Specialized agencies."

The colonel stared at him, a small vicious smile curling his mouth. "Big ideas, General. Are they possible?"

Caleb slipped his hands into the pockets of his Italian linen trousers. "All visions are possible, Kevin, with the proper planning and financing. Do you doubt that I can provide both?"

Sutherland shook his head. "I'm amazed at what you've accomplished so far. But what about our unification efforts? Details for those hits will take months to finalize. Then again, the postponement may be worth it," he said, interrupting himself. "They would certainly gain us the respect of all the other organizations in the country."

"There will be no postponement. We'll continue to meet with the heads of the western militias as scheduled. Regional unification is the first necessary step toward becoming one national entity. And once the west comes together, the first move we'll make to flex our power will be the cooperative hits in New York City and D.C."

The man's head jerked up, and he stared hard at Caleb. "New York City and D.C…the northeast and south?" Even before the sentence was fully formed, comprehension flooded his expression. "You chose those areas for a reason."

"I think the militias in those regions will be suitably impressed with our show of strength, yes. Proving what we're capable of once the western militias join together will make a most persuasive argument for what we can accomplish as one national union."

It was clear from the other man's face that he was still trying to assimilate the finer points of the scheme Caleb had just outlined. Kevin was better suited as a detail person, often losing focus of the big picture. Caleb had had his eye on the big picture for so long he imagined it was engraved on his mind. To simplify, he said, "This strategy achieves three things simultaneously—it unites the western militias, demonstrates to the militias in the rest of the country the power of joining together, and destroys powerful organizations which support the filth. The last, of course, is a bonus."

Caleb walked over and poured himself another glass of the lemonade Rachel favored. Thoughts of her lingered at the outer edges of his mind like drifts of fog hazing the air. He no longer fought it. He'd given up believing there would ever be anyone he would be willing to share his life with, in every sense of the word. But Rachel seemed different from any other woman he'd met. Therein lay her danger.

"So who gets the credit?"

At the question, Caleb's attention snapped back to Sutherland. "That's the beauty of it, Kevin." He raised the glass to his lips and drained half of it. "We don't claim credit. Why would we call federal attention to ourselves when we're beginning our unity effort?"

The colonel frowned. Clearly they'd come to a part of Caleb's plan that disappointed him. "We have to be ready for the reality that one or two of the largest groups will fail to see the importance of unity, the necessity for it. One might even get the idea of blocking our growth. If so, there will be evidence found at the site of the hits that casts suspicion on that particular group." He finished the lemonade and set the glass on the finely polished wood table. "All the credit, and the subsequent law enforcement interest, will be directed toward them. I'll see to it personally."

A long moment passed before Sutherland threw his head back and laughed out loud. "General, you could out-devious Machiavelli himself."

Caleb inclined his head. "Thank you, Kevin. I consider that a compliment. Our success in this endeavor should go a long way toward national unity, and ultimately, revolution."

Sutherland went to his desk. After carefully unlocking a drawer, he drew out a legal pad. "Let's get started on the logistics now. We have a lot of details to map out before we progress with the meetings."

A faint, hard smile curled Caleb's lips. "Nothing in writing. No paper trail. No damning evidence."

The look Kevin threw him was startled. "Surely we can plan to get rid of the evidence later, sir. Something of this size is going to take careful deliberation. Reams of paperwork."

"Something of this size takes the utmost discretion." On that Caleb was immovable. "I've been in this business long enough to know that a little paranoia can keep us alive. Trust me. The plans are fully formed, and operational. Now all that remains is to put them in place."

Long after the colonel had left the room Caleb stared moodily out into the bright sunshine spilling over the front lawn. He'd given Sutherland just a piece of his strategy, enough to intrigue him, to whet his appetite. A good leader kept classified information to himself for as long as possible. It wasn't an issue of trust. Caleb knew exactly how deep Sutherland's loyalty ran. But even the best-laid plans were subject to change. And as he contemplated the spread of his compound, he mentally shifted those plans to include Rachel Grunwald.

Chapter 5

After delivering Caleb's message to the cook, Rachel took her time selecting a book from the library. She knew, from close observation of the housekeeping schedule, that she couldn't conduct an uninterrupted search upstairs for the next twenty minutes or so. The time period should still allow her almost two hours for her search, one and a half, if she wanted to play it safe.

She needed the minutes alone to think about the snippet of conversation she'd overheard. Sutherland had been about to identify Simon as the supplier of The Brotherhood's weapons, she was certain of it. And it was much too coincidental to believe there could be anyone else of a similar name involved with The Brotherhood on such a level.

Her gaze narrowed as she considered the possibilities. It fit too well. Supplying illegal weaponry was a lucrative activity. The profits would certainly help Simon finance his plot to betray SPEAR. If she was able to discover where The Brotherhood's weapons were kept, she might also find a clue to help verify her theory of Simon as the arms supplier.

Deliberately, she tamped down her eagerness to proceed to Caleb's quarters immediately. Cool rational logic was a quality she prided herself on. Strategy based on the heat of emotion could only put the investigation at risk. She forced herself to linger in the library, and found herself marveling at the scope of Carpenter's literary collection. There were rare first editions of Poe, Byron, Twain and Joyce. Her fingers stroked richly bound leather sets of Shakespeare, Hemmingway and Plato. And then her hand faltered. Couched between the fluid magic of the bard and the tomes of great thinkers were housed several shelves of the most vitriolic hate teachings published. Another shelf held books preaching ethnic cleansing and white supremacy. And settled among these was a four-inch wide screed detailing the doctrine of The Brotherhood.

Rachel's hand slowly moved to the volume and removed it. Bound in leather as rich and detailed as was the bard's prose, the 512-page doctrine could have been yet another rare collection of literary art. But what Rachel found between the pages was anything but.

There is no place in our new society for the mental incompetents, the old and infirm. Those not strong enough to help in our endeavors are ultimately worthless. Their elimination from our society, through death or deportation, shall free up billions of dollars in revenue, which shall be detoured to valid expenditures which further the goals of The Brotherhood.

Swallowing hard, Rachel flipped to another chapter.

The only bonds that will matter in our new government is loyalty forged through blood. Not the bonds of birth, nor those of marriage. And so brother shall be set against brother, son against father and the victor shall be he who puts his faith in The Brotherhood.

Could Carpenter truly believe that? Rachel wondered.

There should be no doubt that a man who led such an organization, a man who had authored such a treatise was capable of horrendous deeds. But what was she to make of a man who wrote such and then spoke of his family with such indulgent devotion? He'd made it clear that his family disagreed with his views. Were they, then, among those nonbelievers he would destroy? Or would their bond to him ultimately save them? Was he a complete monster or a hypocritical one?

Her stomach gave a single savage twist. She turned to yet another chapter.

For the mud races, all non-Aryans and those of sullied mixed blood, there can only be mass deaths without mercy. They shall be treated with less compassion than that with which a hunter would gut a deer, for their usefulness is far less. Their humanness is nonexistent. The strongest of the filth may be saved only for the most severe constraints of slavery, to serve their true masters, the image of the Creator, the white man.

Rachel closed the book, shuddering. Her fingertips tingled, as if the hate spewed across the pages had singed them. The words seemed to leap from the page and fire memories best kept distant, locked away. Echoes of similar phrases still huddled in the corners of her mind, words spoken in her father's voice, its thundering command reduced to a whisper that had never fallen completely silent. She'd given up believing it ever would.

The writings shouldn't be a surprise, after all. But it wasn't only the words that had her stomach clenching and releasing in nauseating repetition. It was the fact that they'd been authored by Caleb Carpenter. If she'd ever harbored the slightest suspicion that there was more to the man than his beliefs, it had just splintered.

Glancing at her watch, she took a deep breath and shoved the book back on the shelf. Grabbing the selection she'd ostensibly come to get, she headed out of the library toward

Carpenter's quarters. And toward answers she was in an increasing hurry to find.

Fifteen minutes later she carefully replaced the final pick instrument in the small leather case holding her tools. The lock on the desk in Carpenter's room had taken her less than thirty seconds to pick. Not for the first time, she sent a silent thanks to Del Rogers, another SPEAR agent. While she'd excelled at most of the skills taught at the agency's training facility, locks had initially given her some problems. Del had offered to give her a few lessons. He'd proved so adept at it that she'd accused him of an industrious and misspent youth. As she replaced her tools in their packet, she could mentally picture the light in Del's amber eyes as he'd laughed at her accusation.

It's all in the wrist, Angel.

Using both gloved hands, she eased the top drawer out. The first thing that caught her attention was a large black ledger. In it she found documentation itemizing the expenses for setting up and maintaining the compound. Her fingertip skimmed down the page. The detailed accounts of expenditures were staggering. Carpenter's pockets must be deep indeed to incur this kind of continued expense. She rifled through the pages until she found a section labeled Artillery. This time the magnitude of the expenses made her brows raise. Handguns, machine guns, shotguns, grenades, dynamite. The Brotherhood of Blood had armed themselves for revolution. And quite possibly had made Simon rich in the process.

Going through the rest of the desk's contents quickly, Rachel found nothing more of interest. She was struck by the fact that the entire room lacked any personal touches. There were no pictures, no phone numbers or addresses for family…nothing. For a man who claimed great affection for his relatives, Caleb kept no mementos of them nearby. She had a picture of her parents sitting on her dresser; one of her father on the table beside her bed. They served her well as props, reminding others of the commitment her father had been known for. Caleb's room, however, was void of any such keepsakes, odd for a man who remained close to his family. It caused her to wonder which of them was putting on a bigger pretense.

She quickly checked to make sure she'd left items in the desk as she'd found them before relocking the drawers. Checking her watch again caused her to pause. More time had passed than she'd thought. Regardless, she crossed the carpet silently and dropped to her knees before the secret door. She'd always been a firm believer in exploiting every opportunity to the fullest.

There would be a trick to the opening, there always was. The right amount of pressure, against exactly the right area, was most likely the way to coax it open. Finding that spot, however, was not going to be easy. First she ran her fingertips over the area surrounding the barely visible seam. No luck. Next she spent precious minutes examining each whorl in the wood grain. Again, failure.

She squatted on her heels, eying the door balefully. It was quickly becoming a personal challenge for her. She resigned herself to the fact that it might take many trips such as this one before she found the mechanism. Nevertheless, she went back to work. She never backed down from an obstacle.

The opening itself wouldn't be regular sized; closer to four-by-six feet. It made her wonder what was kept in there. An entrance that wide was needed for storing something of size. She estimated about where Carpenter's arm would extend if raised before him, and went over every inch of that area. Still nothing.

Not to be deterred, Rachel took a moment to think. She was focusing on the obvious. What if Carpenter had been more devious? Dropping to her knees, she ran her fingers lightly over the lowest panel. And then switched to the one on the left. And there she found success.

Cleverly concealed in the edge of the panel was a mechanism that had the door sliding open. A broad smile crossed Rachel's face. But her smugness faded when she saw what filled the opening.

A second door. And the lock on it wouldn't be child's play. With a sigh, she reached for her tools again and went to work. It was a full twenty minutes before she'd unlocked the door. Exhilaration filled her as she turned the knob and pushed inward. The space was dark, and shadowy shapes towered over her. Rachel reached for the slim penlight flashlight she carried with her and played the narrow beam over the room.

Crates were stacked to the ceiling on all sides. She drew closer, and shone her light over the writing on a box. And then over another one. She continued flicking the beam over row after row of endless stacks, mentally tallying the numbers stored there. The final amount was staggering.

She'd just found The Brotherhood's ammo room.

"I'm glad you agreed to come with me this evening," Caleb said, over the sound of the SUV's engine. "Farther away from the compound there are some really beautiful areas of the property. Surrounded as we are by mountains and canyon, there are actually places nearby that look untouched by humans."

And somewhere on this same property, Rachel reminded herself silently, there was a place primitive enough to hide a kidnap victim; to keep him buried alive. What did Carpenter know about Jeff Kirby? And what was the connection between the kidnapping and The Brotherhood of Blood?

Unable to put those questions into words, she asked another. "How do trespassers get on the property with the way it's surrounded? I've noted the security at the front gate."

They hit a rock on the path, and the vehicle bounced wildly. There wasn't anything as civilized as a road where he was taking her. What they were following looked like little more than a path.

"They come through a trail that winds between the mountains. There's a pass in the southwest corner." Her gaze followed the direction his finger was pointing. "Up there. A group of Hispanics squat in the foothills on the other side waiting for the potato season. Local farmers hire extra help during the harvest. The temperatures stay relatively cool, and they figure no one will bother them."

With seeming idleness she observed, "I'm surprised any intruder that far away from the compound would be discovered. Surely you don't post patrols over the entire property."

"Security is something we take very seriously here on the compound. We had some…unpleasantness at one of the corners of the property a couple of weeks ago, the result of a major breach. We've upgraded our patrols to make certain it doesn't reoccur."

Rachel's heart beat wildly. His remark could have been echoing the direction of her earlier thoughts. Could he be referring to the rescue of East Kirby's son? The timing would be right. But she'd yet to figure out why The Brotherhood would have been involved in it.

As they jolted along even more rugged land, he spoke again. "You may have noticed Colonel Sutherland is a stickler for security. Hence your assignment of a guard." His tone was wry. "I hope you weren't offended."

Surprised, she chose her words carefully. "I understood, of course. A man in your position can't be too careful."

"Kevin sometimes overly concerns himself about my position. At any rate, the young man has been reassigned." Sighting some landmark that wasn't obvious to Rachel, he turned the vehicle to the right. "The guard was completely unnecessary, and I told Kevin so. If someone is to be assigned to watch you closely—" he reached over and skated a finger over her knuckles "—then I'd prefer it to be me."

His finger trailed warmth over her skin. She wished she could believe the only message in his words was flirtatious.

She wished she could convince herself that there wasn't a more sinister underlying meaning.

"Is the air conditioner too high?"

She jerked at the question, taking the opportunity to move her hand. "Yes, a little."

He reached out to adjust the control. "Bad habit of mine. My internal thermostat seems to be set higher than most people's."

She'd noticed. There was something about his heated touch that drew an unusual reaction from her. One she was loath to admit to.

They passed two soldiers in a jeep, and Carpenter raised a hand in acknowledgment. She wondered if they were returning from serving on the patrol he'd mentioned. It was impossible to tell just where the men had been stationed. The pastureland seemed to stretch before them on all sides.

Caleb steered the vehicle on a trail toward the mountains to the south. They traveled in silence for a time, until Rachel noticed a building in the distance. "What's over there?"

He glanced at her, then at the direction she was indicating. "That's where the troops practice their shooting."

"It's a shooting range." Her discovery came upon the heels of his words. She pressed the button to lower her window and leaned out to get a better look. "Let's stop."

He hesitated, then made the mistake of looking at her again.

There was such a hopeful light in her eyes when she turned back toward him that he could feel his reluctance swiftly melting. "You know, most women reserve that kind of enthusiasm for a shopping mall. Roses. Dancing."

Rachel lifted one narrow shoulder in a shrug. "I'm not most women."

That, he decided, was one of the understatements of the century. "Do you shoot?"

Again the shrug, this time accompanied by an impatient toss of that bright blond hair. "I do all right. And you?"

He allowed the vehicle to slow, then turned it in a wide loop. He echoed her words with a sense of irony. "I do all right."

Realizing he was acceding to her request, she flashed him a quick, delighted smile. The force of it struck him square in the chest. His fingers clenched around the steering wheel. God, the woman was potent. He realized at that moment, that it was the first truly genuine smile he'd seen from her; one unguarded, without the polite distance she usually maintained. In her spontaneity, she was literally heartstopping. If they could package her charm, they'd have a far more powerful weapon than any he'd managed to acquire for The Brotherhood. "Your dates must find your interests somewhat…eccentric."

Caution reared, and with it, logic. She chose her words carefully. "I was raised differently from most girls, I expect. My father started teaching me to shoot when I was eight." His death had given her the opportunity to quit practicing; she hadn't touched a gun again until she'd been recruited for SPEAR. But the old talent hadn't withered from disuse. She was one of the best marksmen in the agency. In truth, she had a dual purpose for wanting to see the shooting range. She was almost as eager to utilize the facility as she was to get her first glimpse at some of the weapons that Simon may well have supplied.

"Well, let's see what you're made of, champ." He slowed before a large L-shaped building. Rachel was out of the vehicle as soon as Caleb put it in park. She looked toward the north, from the direction they'd traveled. The house wasn't visible from here. She'd need to have wheels to examine every corner of the compound, if it came to that.

She followed Caleb inside the building. While he spoke to the soldier standing behind a counter, she ran her gaze over the selection of firearms in the glass cases lining the walls.

"How's it going, Tommy?"

"No complaints."

Rachel glanced at the man Caleb was addressing. He was short and burly, with a shaven head and onyx eyes that gave nothing away. He had the appearance of a street fighter, with his battered nose and watchful expression. He returned Rachel's scrutiny unblinkingly.

"Tommy Mahoney, Rachel Grunwald." Caleb made the introduction offhandedly. "Tommy and I have worked together in the past. When I started the Brotherhood, I hand-picked many of my recruits, and he was one of the first. He's a top-notch soldier and what he doesn't know about weapons isn't worth knowing." To Tommy he said, "Rachel insisted on stopping by to show off. I was going to take her to some of the more picturesque places on the compound, but apparently she finds the scent of cordite more exotic than that of wildflowers."

She ignored the second sentence and took offense at the first. "Show off?"

"Excuse me." The laughing light in his eyes belied the contrition in his tone. "Perhaps I was too blunt. Exhibit your prowess? Display your talent? Strut your stuff?"

She ignored the other man, who was watching their verbal sparring closely, and arched a brow. "Don't tell me your ability with guns is as pathetic as your hand-to-hand tactics. Maybe you need to spend more time training with the troops." She stalked by the men and ran a quick, judicious eye over the weapons in the cases. Although there was an admirable range of firearms, there weren't more than a half dozen of each, perhaps less than a hundred guns in all. She knew better than to believe that this was the sum total of The Brotherhood's weaponry stockpile. The cost that Caleb had documented, as well as the crates of ammunition she'd discovered in his secret room led her to believe otherwise.

Strolling before the cases, she examined the samples until she found one that interested her. She reached for a 9mm Glock, one that reminded her of her favorite piece she'd been forced to leave at home. All she'd been able to effectively conceal in her luggage had been a small, yet deadly, plastic derringer, one made specifically for SPEAR. She had but a moment to enjoy feeling the weight of the pistol in her hand, before it was snatched away from her. Surprised, she met Tommy's glower.

"I handle all the firearms in here. You point to the one you want, I load it and give it to you. Sign that book by the door while I get the ammo."

Backing away, she went to do as he'd directed. Glancing sideways at Caleb, she saw amusement on his face. "Tommy's in charge of the weapons on base."

"He's very diligent." Moving to the register he'd indicated, she ran a casual eye over the signatures scrawled on the pages. Apparently anyone who trained daily was required to check a gun out, and back in, with Tommy first. The page she was looking at was dated that day. With a studiedly careless movement, she knocked the book to the floor, earning her another scowl from Mahoney. Mumbling an apology, she picked it up and flipped through the pages slowly, until she came to the one she was to sign. It was apparent from the dates on the pages that this process had been followed since The Brotherhood had been created. She hadn't had time to register many names, although she observed Caleb's and Sutherland's had been signed several times.

She felt, rather than saw, Caleb come up behind her and stepped aside, allowing him to sign in.

After he'd done so, he crossed to the door and led Rachel down a hallway and into the shooting range. Like everything else on the compound, she discovered, it was first-class. There were a dozen shooting stations, complete with automatic returns on the targets, for the shooter to check accuracy. One lone man was practicing at the far right, but otherwise they were alone.

"What do you think?"

"Top quality all the way," she responded lightly. "Do you find time to use it yourself?"

"He gets out here often enough to set an example for the men." It was Tommy who spoke behind her. "A well-armed militia is nothing if they're not well-trained, right, General?" Caleb merely nodded as he took the firearm Tommy held out to him. Expertly, he flipped the safety and rechecked the gun. Rachel's gaze fixed on the weapon in his hand. It was another Beretta, a match for the one he'd taken from his desk the day she'd arrived.

Tommy handed them both a set of earguards, and went back to the shed. Rachel strode to one of the empty stations and flipped a switch, sending a fresh human outline target two hundred yards away. Caleb positioned himself in the lane next to her. They both slipped on their earguards and she took her stance, the Glock feeling smooth and natural in her hand. She sited and fired, drilling a hole through the center of the outline's face. Then, spurred by an unmistakable sense of competition, she emptied her chambers.

Turning, she flipped the switch to bring the target forward again. She lowered her earguards and said nonchalantly, "The balance is off. It pulls a bit to the left."

A slow tuneless whistle escaped him, and the corners of his lips twitched. Bullet holes riddled the face of her target outline, completing it with eyes, nose and a wide smiling mouth. "Hotshot, huh? I doubt the gun is the problem. You drop your wrist a fraction of an inch in between firings."

Nothing he could have said would have offended her more. "I've never dropped my wrist in my life!"

Unperturbed, he put his earguards back on and took up his stance. "Maybe not, but you're doing it now."

Seething, she watched as he sent the target back, a good fifty yards farther than hers had been. Then with deadly accuracy, he began firing. Moments later, he had the target returning. Anticipation turned to an absurd sense of disappointment when she saw only a few holes in the paper. "You only hit it three times."

"Did I?"

The target fluttered to a stop before them, and she immediately saw her mistake. She'd been partially correct; there were only three holes positioned where a person's forehead would be. But one hole was larger than it should have been. Several of his bullets had passed through exactly the same area.

It was her turn to whistle. "You're a heckuva marksman. I'm impressed."

He gave a lopsided smile, carelessly handing over his empty semiautomatic to a waiting Tommy. "This isn't my usual method of impressing women, but with you, I'll take any opportunity I can get."

They walked back toward the vehicle with Tommy gazing after them. Rachel didn't respond to Caleb's remark, but all her senses were humming. He'd made quite an impression all right. He impressed her as a thoroughly dangerous man.

Chapter 6

She dreamed of her father that night. She was fourteen again, back in the nation's capital, squinting in the blinding sunlight. She could feel the warm caress of the sun on her shoulders; felt again the anticipation layered with boredom. It was the first real vacation her family had ever taken, and she was anxious to visit the sights she'd been reading about. But instead she was stuck with her mother and a crowd of strangers, all milling about for a glimpse of the two visiting dignitaries who were making international news with their countries' unprecedented peace accord.

The scene unfolded before her, memory supplying her unconscious with an eerily accurate depiction....

There were the long black limos pulling to a stop, a show of security before the doors opened; the shouted questions from the media as the smiling leaders waved at the crowd; the press of bodies, as the mass of people surged forward for a closer look.

And then her other senses took over, just as they had that day, fourteen years ago. The sharp cracks of rifle fire; the

*screams of the crowd; the panicked expressions all around
her; and most vivid, the sibilant, triumphant hiss from her
mother; the tightening grasp of her fingers on Rachel's
shoulders when one of the dignitaries crumpled to the
ground.*

Rachel frowned in her sleep, unwilling to relive the nightmare; yet as helpless in the dream as she'd been so long
ago.

*People stampeding in the opposite direction; Secret Ser-
vice with guns drawn, raised skyward; more shots. And then
a body falling, down, down, each second of its descent an
eternity. The body twisted in the air, in a strangely graceful
arc. The pavement rushing up to meet it, the impact as the
lifeless form met unforgiving cement...*

She jolted up in bed, her breathing loud and ragged. Shak-
ily, she reached up a hand to push her damp hair back from
her face. Funny how the nightmare was always the same,
like the unchangeable details on a movie reel. And always
she awakened at the identical time—the moment of impact.

Swinging her legs out of bed, she moved to the window.
She could see little in the darkness, but the sight was preferable to the one that still lingered in her mind. She hadn't
been privy to the real plans that had brought them to Washington that day; she hadn't even paid much attention to the
reason for the parade they'd attended. But the instant she'd
seen that figure toppling from the sky, a comprehension far
developed for her years had claimed it. Identified it. She'd
watched the man falling to his death, knowing, with an in-
nate, inexplicable understanding, that it was her father.

She hugged her arms around her waist, struggling to regain control. Reaction always followed the dream. The shudders that racked her body were as involuntary now as they
had been that day so long ago, and just as debilitating. The
shamed horror; the mingled grief and relief a tangible entity.
He'd never hurt anyone else. Not ever again.

A long racking breath escaped her, and she tilted her head,

focusing her gaze intently on the sliver of moon that hung low in the star-kissed sky. Perhaps those brief moments of memory wouldn't have survived with such clarity if they hadn't been captured by the media, and rerun endlessly on news programs the days following the assassination. But she thought otherwise. Tragedy had a way of carving out its own spot in the consciousness, and rarely relinquished its grip. The memory served a purpose, at any rate. It helped underscore the validity of her goals, the strength of her determination.

But it never failed to shred her heart, and tear at her emotions.

Driven to move, Rachel strode to the bathroom and slipped into her robe. At home she would go to the loft upon awakening from the dream, and punish her body into exhaustion with grueling physical activity. Here she had fewer options. But getting out of this room, away from that bed was imperative.

Silently, she made her way downstairs to the kitchen. She rummaged through the cupboards for a glass, then filled it with ice. Pouring it full of lemonade took longer than it should have. It was a task to focus on, and she desperately needed something, anything, to distract herself from the remnants of the scene that still prowled the edges of her mind.

Unable to sit, she strode about the large well-equipped kitchen, both hands clasped tightly around the glass. Her nerves would be too edgy for sleep anytime soon. She may as well read, plot strategy, or go over the details she'd discovered about The Brotherhood so far. But instead she continued pacing, as if by her movements she could escape the memories that swarmed from her past.

How long would she continue to feel this blanketing regret, for having despised what her father had been? It wasn't as if there weren't sweeter scenes to remember from her younger years; sitting on his lap, riding on his shoulders, being tucked into bed at night. But somehow those memories had been suffocated by time, and a growing realization of what her father had been. What he'd believed in.

Rachel gave herself a mental shake. It had ceased to matter long ago. Once she'd been old enough to reason, she'd begun to question the teachings he forced on her, the ones her mother had supported. Retribution for daring to disagree with him had been swift and painful. Witnessing the rages he was capable of, whether while watching a newscast or when talking to the crowd which always seemed to fill their living room, she'd become afraid. And in the long hours of questioning by an endless stream of men in suits, knowing her father had been responsible for the assassination, she'd felt anger, shame, exhaustion. But never, not once, had she felt surprise. Somehow the lack of that emotion had seemed the saddest of all.

Awash in old regrets, she felt, rather than heard, a presence behind her. Whirling, she saw the shadow of a man in the doorway. She identified him by shape alone, and something else, an awareness of him that she'd never been able to completely suppress. A sliver of panic sliced through her. She didn't want to face Carpenter now. Not when her emotions were raw and her senses heightened. But he reached out, turning on the overhead light. And while she blinked to refocus, she drew her defenses closer and commanded her frayed emotions to order. Vulnerability was something she avoided, and it would be a dangerous indulgence around this man.

"I hope I didn't wake you."

He watched her with eyes that saw too much, said too little. "I was working late and heard someone in the kitchen." He nodded toward her glass. "Is there any more of that?"

Fetching the lemonade gave her an excuse to turn her back on him, another few seconds to calm her fractured nerves. She took her time with the task, and when she turned to him again, she felt slightly more centered.

"Do you work late often?" She handed him the glass, and picked up her own.

"Do you have nightmares often?"

She froze in the act of raising the glass to her lips. It took tangible effort to complete the action. "What makes you think I had a nightmare?"

He made an impatient gesture with his hand. "Let's just say, I recognize the signs."

More nights than he cared to remember he'd awakened, sweating and shaking. More memories than he cared to retain picked the midnight hours to haunt. For the life of him, he couldn't imagine what would have brought Rachel out of sleep, drenched and trembling. But before he left this room, he was determined that she would tell him.

He circled the area, keeping her before him when she would have turned away. He'd vowed to peel the layers from her, one at a time, but he'd never expected, had never wanted to see Rachel like this—emotions so raw, so brittle they were almost painful to watch. He observed them flit across her face too quickly to be identified. And then he watched her visibly smooth razored nerves and adopt a bland polite mask that was so obviously a disguise that it was almost an affront.

Stopping before her, he crooked a finger under her chin, felt the effort it took for her not to flinch away. "Tell me."

She retreated from him; not physically, but the distance was there all the same. He dropped his hand, never taking his eyes from hers.

"It was nothing. I have dreams sometimes."

Her voice wasn't completely normal, but it was an admirable attempt. It was also clear that she meant to say nothing more.

"Disturbing dreams, apparently."

Apparently. She gave a ghost of a smile and sank into a chair. He did the same. "Of the day my father died." Her voice trailed off, and when she spoke again, it was almost as if she'd forgotten him entirely. "It was so hot…beastly, the way D.C. gets in July. I could see heat waves shimmering in the air. If I hadn't heard the shots, I would have thought I was watching a mirage fashioned by sun dogs."

He stilled suddenly, completely. "Shots. You were there?"

The question seemed to yank her attention back to him. Again he had the impression she'd been speaking more to herself. "Yes, I was there with my mother."

He now understood a measure of the horror that had been revisited on her tonight. For a young girl to witness her father's death had to have been traumatic, terrifying even. It was no wonder she had nightmares. The memories must inflict tremendous emotional scars.

Looking at her with new eyes, he mentally reevaluated her. He'd been struck by her strength when they'd first met, yet he wondered now if he'd underestimated her. What kind of woman had grown from the girl? What kind of tenacity would have been fortified from the specters of her childhood?

The answers wouldn't be forthcoming tonight, of that he was certain. He could already read her reaction to her candor. Without moving a muscle she was drawing in her defenses, folding into herself. Perhaps if he wasn't such an expert at the same trick himself, he wouldn't have noticed. But he was, and he had. And although he understood the need she had to reestablish control, he rose and closed the distance between them, both physically and emotionally. He pulled her into his arms, driven to offer comfort in the only way he knew.

She was stiff in his embrace, fighting the contact, fighting the need. He kept his touch soothing, innocent, and he felt the exact moment when the fight streamed out of her, the ebb of control faltered and for an instant, just for the length of a sigh, she sank against him.

"There are some ghosts," his lips brushed against her

hair, "that will haunt us a lifetime. The way we learn to live with them says more about us than if we'd managed to forget them completely."

She lifted her head and looked at him then, questions in her eyes, on her lips. But when she would have asked them, his head lowered and he sank his lips against hers.

This wasn't the rush of sensation he'd felt the first time he'd kissed her. Instead of crashing over him, threatening him with the undertow, the waves of desire were secondary to the very real need to provide comfort. He desperately wanted to believe that it was her beauty that drew him; her distress that held him. But he understood passion and he understood pity. This was more. Whatever it was scared the hell out of him, even as it lured him back for another taste.

His lips brushed over hers, again and again, before he changed the angle of the kiss and pressed deeper. She swayed against him, helpless under the contact. She was used to greed and she was used to urgency. But this depth of tenderness was so unfamiliar that it literally rocked her system. She clung to him, afraid the new sensation would destroy her, wondering if it already had. Surely it wasn't normal to respond to his gentleness with a tripping pulse and a heart doing a slow spin in her chest. She waited for the kiss to heat, to change. It was all the more devastating when it just grew sweeter.

When he drew her closer she complied, feeling boneless and strangely pliant. His skin was warm to the touch where it was bared; at his throat, on the arms exposed by his rolled-up sleeves. There was a sinewy power beneath the skin that beckoned roving fingers, that spoke of a stolid strength under the cultured exterior. Her neck arched as his mouth dropped a string of gentle kisses across her collarbone. And in the floating haze that encompassed them, she thought how very strange it was that the first person in her life to offer her tenderness was the very man she'd come to destroy.

The thought had logic returning, in a cold icy rush that

froze her from the inside out. She broke away on a gasp, avoiding his eyes. She wasn't capable of speech; not when her emotions were a senseless tangle inside her. So she turned and walked away, wishing she could leave all the tumult behind, knowing she carried it with her.

He let her go, when every instinct he had urged him to reach for her again. It was better she had time to tame wayward emotions; far better that he did the same. Her vulnerability had fostered his own, and he didn't recognize it; couldn't allow it.

The early hours of the morning were always a bastard for regrets and self-doubts. Knowing this didn't stop them from coming, from lingering. All his life he'd been blessed with a gift for timing. Being in the right place; meeting the right people; asking the right questions. But now his miraculous timing had failed him. If there was anything on earth that he could undo, he wished that Rachel Grunwald hadn't come to him at this time, in this way. He wished he was a decent enough man to put her needs above his own goals and send her away.

But most of all, he wished he didn't know that he couldn't change a thing. His course had been set long ago. Lives were in the balance. The future direction of the country depended upon his success.

And if using Rachel could provide him with a way to realize his ambitions, he really had no other choice.

Rachel rarely wasted time second-guessing herself, but the events of the night delayed any chance of sleep. The minutes crawled into hours, allowing plenty of time for her to stare morosely out into the darkness. Self-delusion would hardly be helpful in the midst of a dangerous assignment, and was impossible, at any rate. There was no denying the flash of feelings that Carpenter's tenderness had evoked. While she'd always prided herself on her control, he was able to draw emotions from her with a touch. She could no longer blame her awareness of him on long-dormant hormones. It wasn't any man who could slip beneath her guard and spark feelings much better buried—it was *this* man. She could curse the situation, but she couldn't change it. And she'd compounded the issue by allowing Carpenter to see a vulnerability, something a good agent never did. Where one was vulnerable, one was weak.

Even as she castigated herself for lowering her defenses, she grew intent on damage control. Most situations could be used to advantage if one knew how to shift the tides away from herself. She was nothing if not resourceful.

And so through the long hours of the night, when it would have been comfortable to flee emotionally from the memory of his touch, she dwelled instead on how to turn it against him. The chemical reaction that sparked between them, the more elusive feelings that had been triggered last night, would have to be honed and utilized.

She only hoped that in destroying Caleb she didn't end up destroying a part of herself, as well.

Rachel was surprised to see Caleb the next morning. Although they always dined together in the evening, he'd never joined her for another meal. Eyeing him carefully as he seated himself at the table across from her, she wondered at his purpose. The long hours she'd spent awake last night had had her sleeping later this morning, and it was long past the time when he would have normally been breakfasting.

''Good morning.'' Caleb sat back and allowed Eliza to pour him a cup of black coffee. He picked up the cup, and despite the steam rising from the brew, sipped cautiously. He looked like he needed the caffeine, Rachel thought shrewdly. Although as impeccably groomed as always, she detected a weariness in his eyes that would be a match for her own this morning. All in all, he looked as if he'd spent as endless a night as she had.

There was a gentle clink of china against china as he set

his cup back on the saucer. His gaze was as assessing as hers had been a moment ago. "Did you get any sleep at all?"

She tried for a smile, was aware that it would appear forced. "And here I thought I'd covered up the damage."

"You look lovely, as always. But I know better than most that sleep can't always be summoned. Perhaps you can catch a nap this afternoon."

"Don't worry about me." Her voice was amazingly normal as she lifted a bite of fresh fruit to her mouth, chewed and swallowed. "I've been taking care of myself for a long time now."

"Yes, I suspect you have. Which makes me all the more concerned about you. Everybody needs somebody at times, Rachel. Even you."

If she'd thought she was prepared for a reference to last night, she'd been wrong. Her only consolation was that any discomfort she showed at the topic would be expected. Still, it went against everything in her to soften her words, to smile directly at him. "You were very kind last night, and you're right. I'm not used to leaning on anyone else. I should thank you."

"I imagine last night was a first of sorts for both of us." Her interest sharpened at his comment, but he went on. "I wanted to tell you myself that I'll be leaving for a while. I'm not sure how long I'll be gone, but at least three days."

"I see." Instincts began to hum and it was an effort to sound nonchalant. "Where are you going? To visit your family?"

He reached for his coffee again. "No, this will be a business trip. I have several stops to make across the western states. But I'll be back as soon as I'm able. You're to make yourself completely at home while I'm gone."

"Are you traveling alone?" She made no attempt to keep her interest a secret. He would expect it, and information he would share freely decreased the amount she'd have to discover on her own.

"Colonel Sutherland will accompany me. We leave within the hour. I'm going to be addressing the troops in a few minutes, and I thought it best if you made an appearance, as well."

"Of course," she said immediately, her mind racing. She had no doubt that she would be able to put his absence to good use. With both he and Sutherland out of the house, it would be a perfect time to step up the pace of the investigation. After last night, she was in a sudden hurry to get this assignment wrapped up quickly. Before she made a fool of herself again. Before she tricked herself into seeing something in Carpenter that just wasn't there.

Then his hand reached across the table to clasp her own, his thumb skimming the top of her knuckles. "Rachel...I need to ask. Do you have any doubts at all about your reasons for coming here?"

She looked at his hand touching hers and her answer was automatic. "No, of course not."

His gaze was searching, but whatever he was looking for, Rachel was determined he wouldn't find it. He removed his hand from hers, and picked up the suit jacket he'd hung on the back of the chair beside him.

He rose and Rachel followed, wondering why his answer hadn't erased the concern from his eyes. "What time will you speak to the troops?"

He glanced at his watch. "In about ten minutes."

"I'll go change and meet you out front in five."

A ghost of a smile flickered across his mouth. "If you can change in five minutes, you're a rare woman indeed."

Her brows skimmed upward. "Did you doubt it?" She felt his gaze on her as she started down the hallway and toward the stairs. She halted only when she heard his voice again.

"I've decided when I get back and things settle down again, that you and I will go on a trip."

She turned back to him, his words forming a cold hard knot in the pit of her belly. "What kind of a trip?"

He crossed his arms on the newel post and leaned against it. "To Philadelphia. You visit your mother twice a month, don't you? I don't want you to have to forgo that because of the time you're spending here. I'll charter a jet."

He had no idea, she thought frantically, just how much a problem it was. Her mother blamed her for the emotional distance that had always existed between them. In the years before Rachel went to college, the two of them had been like strangers, cohabiting in the same house. Seeing her mother remind Rachel of all the lies that lay between them, lies that were a necessary part of her cover for SPEAR. Gloria Grunwald thought her daughter worked for a fictitious antiquities dealer, one Rachel frequently had to accompany abroad. Her visits invariably left her feeling drained, helpless and guilty. She had no desire to have someone else witness the emotional distress the visits caused her, especially not Caleb Carpenter. A savvy strategist never willingly displayed a weakness to the enemy. "That's kind of you, but it really isn't necessary. I explained to my mother before I left that I wouldn't be able to make my next visit."

He gave an impatient shrug. "But you are able. Let me do this for you, Rachel." His gaze was strangely intent, and she knew, with instinct that owed nothing to logic, that he was thinking of last night. Of her reaction to the dream; of the grief and regrets that he'd helped soothe.

She gave a jerky nod and turned away, feeling his eyes on her as she walked up the stairs. It wasn't the first time that Carpenter had surprised her with the depth of his research on her. And it certainly wasn't the first time she'd surprised *herself* with her reaction to *him*.

She shut off the troublesome thoughts while she hurried to slip into a dress and sandals, then drag a hairbrush through her hair. Reaching for the pins to put it up, her hand hesitated midair. Old habits died hard. Her reflection in the mirror regarded her soberly. And because she didn't want to examine that reflection too closely, she turned away and went outside to join Caleb.

He was already on the dais that had been hastily erected for the occasion, talking to two men who were adjusting the microphone system. He stopped speaking when he saw Rachel, one side of his mouth curling upward. Making a show of consulting his watch, he informed the two men, "Make a note of the time and date. A woman was early. Next I expect the grounds to open up and seas to part."

"On behalf of women everywhere, I'm offended." She climbed the steps to his side.

"On behalf of women everywhere, you should be worshiped as a goddess. My mother and sisters' idea of *on time* is a fashionable forty-five minutes late."

"Well," she turned away, watching the troops file into rows before the stage, "I'm not one of your sisters."

"I had noticed." A quick glance discerned that the hint of irony in his voice was matched by the gleam in his eye.

They were interrupted by Colonel Sutherland, who climbed the dais and captured Caleb's attention. Rachel experienced a sense of déjà vu as she watched the audience. Hundreds of men, far fewer women, joined the crowd, their uniforms forming a sea of black. Unlike the first day she'd arrived, she noted a few familiar faces in the throng. There was Kathy, easy to pick out of the crowd with her dark-red hair, and Raymond, standing on the edges, with a look of excitement on his face. Scanning the mass of people, Rachel was jolted by yet another face she recognized, an unsmiling one. Tommy Mahoney.

There was a man she'd rather not meet up with in the middle of the night. She didn't know whether Mahoney's hairstyle reflected his beliefs or personal taste, but she was perceptive enough to realize that the air of latent menace surrounding him was very real. Unfortunately, her search for the Brotherhood's store of weapons would most likely fall under the cover of darkness. It was imperative that she report to Jonah on how well-armed this militia was. The agency had to be prepared for whatever it would face if an assault on the compound became necessary. From the amount of ammunition she'd uncovered, she expected to find The Brotherhood well-armed, indeed. Tommy Mahoney struck her as a man who took his job very seriously. She hoped his diligence didn't extend to the midnight hours.

As if feeling her eyes on him, the man's gaze met her own and held. And when Caleb turned to slip his arm around her waist and bent to whisper something in her ear, Mahoney's expression grew speculative.

Distracted, she looked at Caleb. "I'm sorry, I didn't hear you."

"I said I had a chair brought up to the stage so you wouldn't have to stand." She crossed to the seat he motioned to and sat gracefully. A sense of irony surfaced. Seated at Caleb's right hand, she had displaced Sutherland, who now stood to the left of Caleb. If the man felt any slight from the change, it didn't show. He stood rigidly erect beside his leader, his bearing every bit as regal as a monarch surveying his loyal subjects. His was the first voice to boom out through the microphone, settling the crowd instantly.

"Welcome to my Brothers of Blood. It is exciting news that has brought us before you today, news that will prove our deep commitment to our cause. The general and I are about to commence on a journey that will be the fruition of all we've been toiling for. General Carpenter has asked to speak of this himself, to explain to you all just how close we are to attaining our dreams." He stepped back, and gestured to Caleb. "General."

Stepping forward to the microphone, Carpenter made no move to speak. It would have been pointless, at any rate. The applause and cheers which greeted him were deafening.

He raised his arms out to the crowd, and the noise increased in intensity. Rachel swallowed as she watched the display of hero worship. It wasn't a question of what these troops would do for the man; it was a question of what they *wouldn't* do.

At a single gesture from Carpenter, the crowd fell still once more. "My fellow soldiers...you have worked cease-lessly for the rights of the superior white race, and your efforts will not go unrewarded. All the hours spent in train-ing, in drills and formations is about to pay off. We are on the brink of a new alliance. One that will multiply our size by ten, and spread the holy word of The Brotherhood across the western states. One that will terrify the filth and unwor-thy, and give the politicians in Washington reason to lock their doors in fear."

There was something about the timbre of his voice, mag-nifying the considerable presence of the man. Rachel was almost as transfixed as the crowd, but for far different rea-sons. His was a persuasive tone, whether inciting a racial war or whispering soothing words of comfort. She wondered bleakly how many personalities the man had, or if each dif-ference he showed was merely a facet of the whole. She, better than anyone, knew that a man couldn't be measured by pieces, but from his total. And she didn't trust this con-fusion she was beginning to feel about him, the blurring of edges that should have remained sharply delineated.

"Colonel Sutherland and I embark today on a mission to unify the major western militias. Our success will mark the beginning of The Brotherhood's goal for one national or-ganization dedicated to the destruction of this Zionist gov-ernment. This move represents a giant step toward ridding our country of all those who pollute it with their repugnant bloodlines and life-styles. When we return, and do not doubt that we will return successful, we can start counting the minutes until we will begin the ethnic and cultural cleansing of the mud races, the gay abomination and the elitist liberals who condone their presence in our midst.''

There was a burst of cheers from the crowd, and Rachel scanned the faces arrayed before her. She'd seen this kind of fanaticism before, in the various militias she'd infiltrated. And even earlier, on the faces of the people who'd filled their house while her father was alive. She'd learned to look beyond the veneer to find the person beneath, but now she wondered if she hadn't been ignoring the obvious when it came to Carpenter. Why should she feel this horrified dismay watching hatred twist his face, to hear his speech full of violence and bigotry? He was, after all, only underscoring her reason for being here. But that didn't explain the sick distaste she felt hearing his words, seeing their effect, and the insidious memory of another man, another agenda, with frighteningly similar notions about the supremacy of the white race.

Sunlight slanted over the stage, a natural spotlight for the orator addressing the crowds. The black flags with The Brotherhood's insignia waved lazily in the breeze. Heat waves shimmered in the air, and a feeling of vertigo clutched at Rachel's stomach. Carpenter's words were lost to her as that hot July day fourteen years ago melded for a moment with the present. The microphone system let out a screech of static and Rachel jerked in her seat, unable to prevent an involuntary glance skyward.

An instant later reason reasserted itself. She wasn't in D.C. and this wasn't her father's followers gathered. Disconcerted by the flashback, she turned her attention instead on Carpenter's message.

"Upon our return be prepared to work harder, longer and with increased diligence. The troops of The Brotherhood must be known as the best trained, the most able, and the most knowledgeable. It is my own men who I will depend on to bring about the downfall of the filth and unworthy. It is to my own officers I will look for input on toppling the national government. Mark this day as the beginning, soldiers and officers alike. A beginning of our dreams, a beginning of death tidings to our enemies... a beginning of the end.'' Caleb raised both arms in the air, fists clenched. ''Let the holy war commence!''

This time he made no move to still the crowd, but basked in its approval. And only long minutes after the people had quieted, and begun to file away, did he turn and look at Rachel. His expression arrested he said, ''What is it? You look upset.''

The smile on her lips seemed stiff, and she had to swallow around a knot in her throat. ''Nothing. For a moment or two you reminded me of my father, that's all.''

''That's good, isn't it?''

''Yes.'' She met his gaze dispassionately. ''That's very good.''

Chapter 7

Carpenter's absence was an advantage that Rachel was determined to maximize to the fullest. After careful thought, she settled on the study as her first nocturnal target. With no one else in the house at night, she'd be able to take her time breaking through whatever security was protecting the office and the computers inside it. It was a luxury she hadn't counted on.

Until then, it was important she maintain her normal schedule. And so she went up to change before heading to one of the gyms, spending her time working off unwanted emotions with grueling physical activity. After a shower and lunch she finagled a jeep from the soldier in charge of the fleet of vehicles, and headed to the shooting range. It was busy, with lines of soldiers waiting their turn, so Rachel returned to the jeep and explored the area for a couple of hours. It was the canyon that drew her. The sheer ragged drop from plateau to the river snaking a mile below was a sight of raw breathtaking beauty. It occurred to her that Jonah hadn't mentioned exactly where on the compound East

Kirby's son had been buried alive, but it almost certainly had to have been in the foothills of the mountains surrounding two sides. The plateau itself was too flat, and vegetation too undergrown to have kept the spot a secret for long.

She returned her attention to the canyon, going so far as to drop to her belly and hang head and shoulders over the edge. It would be a challenging climb, she thought, itching already to try it. There appeared to be few ledges and jutting rocks. A climber would have to rely on cracks between the stones for footholds. She wondered if she could convince Carpenter to let her try, or to make the climb with her.

Thought of Caleb had her rising, and striding back to the jeep. It was a delicate balance she was going to have to strike upon his return; to draw him closer with the chemistry that flared between them so easily, yet somehow manage to keep herself emotionally aloof on any real level. She needed for him to relax his guard, something he would only do if he trusted her completely, or if she could distract him to a point of making him careless. A month ago…a week ago she would have had no doubts that she could do so and skate away unsinged. But she'd felt the fire of his touch on two occasions now, and was less than certain that she was going to walk away from The Brotherhood without getting badly burned.

She drove the jeep back to the shooting range, and found that the numbers waiting had dwindled. Rachel was surprised when she entered the building to find an unfamiliar soldier behind the counter.

"Where's Tommy?" she asked, looking around. He'd been so adamant about handling the firearms himself, that she couldn't believe he'd leave the building attended by someone else.

The man behind the counter shrugged. "He was needed elsewhere on the compound. Do you want to talk to him? I don't know when he'll be back here."

Rachel shook her head and made her usual selection of a

Glock, watching while the man performed the same operations Tommy did each time she came. Signing in at the register, she flipped the pages with seeming nonchalance. Not surprisingly, the pages she scanned didn't list anyone by the name of Simon.

She spent longer than usual in the alley, engrossed in the process of aiming, firing, and reloading. Finally, aware of the time, she handed her gun to the man behind the counter and strode back to the jeep. The time she'd spent exploring the canyon's edge had her running later than usual, and she drove back as fast as she dared. Every rut and rock in the path had the jeep bumping and jolting. Steering should have commanded all her attention, but troublesome thoughts drifted across her mind, and refused to be banished. She doubted she'd be free of them until she'd come up with some kind of workable plan for dealing with Carpenter.

Intent on a quick shower before dinner, Rachel strode to her bedroom, opened the door and entered. But just inside her doorway she came to an abrupt stop. She swept the space with her gaze, the inexplicable instinct that had frozen her in place turning to certainty.

Someone had been in her room.

She reached a hand behind her and pushed the door closed. Only then did she move slowly across the area. Most people wouldn't have noticed, she mused. Most people weren't trained to note the most minute of details. But although she didn't doubt that care had been taken to prevent it, clues had been left behind in the wake of the search. The picture of her and her father on her nightstand was facing the door, rather than the bed, as she usually kept it. She might be forgiven for believing the housekeeper had been careless today, if that was the only oddity she noted.

She crossed the expanse of carpet and dropped to her knees before the bureau. The drawers had obviously all been removed, and then replaced. A crack appeared below the bottom drawer that hadn't been there before. Rachel drew it open, surveyed its contents. The drawers had been replaced in the wrong order, causing an incorrect fit. She removed each of the drawers again, and peered at the inside of the dresser. It was as empty as it had been when she arrived on the compound. She replaced the drawers, switching the order of the bottom two so they glided shut smoothly.

Sitting back on her heels, she thought for a moment. She didn't have time to go over the entire room right now, but she'd return after dinner. There wasn't a doubt in her mind that the room had been tossed, and a pretty decent job done of it, too. The questions remaining were who had done it, and why.

Dinner was a rushed, solitary affair, and Rachel was glad to escape the dining room. Not even to herself would she admit that she'd missed talking with Caleb, and the way their conversations would wander from subjects as diverse as world politics and their favorite cartoon strips.

Upon returning to her room, she examined the space inch by inch, taking the precaution of scanning it with the phony remote. Although she found a few more hints that her things had been searched, there was no evidence of hidden security devices. So the objective of the intruder hadn't been to bug her room.

She frowned, one foot beating a rapid tattoo on the carpet. Had the trespasser meant only to search her things? She would be unconcerned if the culprit had managed to find her gun; she felt sure she could think of an excuse that Carpenter would find plausible. A careful check had convinced her that the items she'd brought along to help with the investigation hadn't been discovered. At least their real use hadn't. So there had been no real harm done.

But the questions continued to burn a pathway through her mind. If she hadn't known Sutherland was away with Caleb, she would have immediately assumed that he was the culprit. But other than him, she could think of no other suspects. It was possible, of course, that he'd left orders for someone else to conduct the search in his absence, but that possibility only added to the puzzle.

While night fell over The Brotherhood of Blood's compound, Rachel continued to turn the questions over and over in her mind. She failed to come up with a single answer.

The beam from the security light mounted outside the front door spilled into the front window of the office. Rachel dodged the obstacle by moving to the far end of the room before crossing to the desks. Like the previous two nights, she'd set her alarm to awaken her shortly after midnight, long after all the household help would have left for the evening. She'd found the door to the office to bear a very decent lock, one that took her all of fifteen minutes to pick the first night. She managed it in five this time, and slipped into the room.

She'd ascertained the night Caleb had left that there was no other security system in the room, and now made a bee-line for Carpenter's computer. She'd already searched his desk, unsurprised to find nothing there of interest. He was not a man given to leaving important information lying around. She was damning his caution now. She'd spent the past two nights trying, without success, to break the security code on his computer.

Slipping behind his desk, she turned the computer on and stared intently at the screen. Tonight she was determined she'd unlock the computer's secrets. She'd had no luck trying to guess his password the first night, and had then decided her only hope was to bypass the security system on his computer altogether. She had no doubt that when she did so she'd be able to get into Sutherland's as well.

Stifling frequent yawns, she worked ceaselessly at her task. But it wasn't until 3:00 a.m. that she succeeded in thwarting the system.

She gave a grin of delight as Caleb's named files appeared before her. She opened one after another, skimming the material contained, quickly becoming absorbed. One file listed names and phone numbers for the leaders of every major militia in the country. Rachel scanned the list quickly, recognizing many of the names. She lingered over the ones that had *x*s by them. She guessed he'd marked those situated in the western part of the country. The ones that even now he was urging to join him.

She sat back in the chair a moment, thinking. It was obvious, both by Jonah's briefing, and the speech Caleb had given days ago, that he had embarked on the first stage of his master plan. He was clearly attempting to unify one section of the country at a time, working up to his goal of one unified militia in the United States. But she knew too well the pitfalls he would face. Over and over again when she'd infiltrated a militia she'd been struck by the paranoia among the leadership. They closely guarded their secrets, and most often didn't communicate with other organizations. Whatever success he met in convincing the other leaders to join him would be silent testimony to how much credibility the Brotherhood had already managed to build.

She continued to open files, her mind racing. The details of Carpenter's strategy must be impressive indeed, for him to believe that the most powerful western militia leaders would follow his guidance. Finding out what that plan was just might provide the information Jonah had sent her to gather. And lead SPEAR right to Simon.

She spent a great deal of time perusing a database listing The Brotherhood's members. No one by the name of Simon was listed among the names. The discovery only strengthened her belief that she'd been correct to conclude that Simon was The Brotherhood's arms supplier. But her conclusion still lacked verification. It was incredibly frustrating to not be sure whether Simon was the traitor's real name or just one of an assortment of aliases.

When Rachel finished with Caleb's computer she moved to Sutherland's. Disabling the security system, she proceeded to scan his files. There was one of particular interest. Labeled simply Candidates, the database was filled with more than one hundred names of applicants for the position as Carpenter's wife. Next to each was a date, presumably indicating when the application had been received. Notations had been made in another column. Most simply said Rejected with a short accompanying note of reason. Two of the candidates' names drew her eye. They were obviously the two who had come before her. Notations were made of the length of time each had spent at the compound. One listed reason for dismissal as stealing, and the other as moral turpitude.

Rachel made a face. Sutherland had a flair for the dramatic. She doubted that phrase existed outside of employment contracts. A moment later she quickly sobered. She'd found her own name, with only the date of her arrival noted. The rest of the columns were blank. So far. She had little doubt that Sutherland would love to see her make a mistake as the other two women had done.

The fact that both previous candidates had been caught in a misdeed seemed odd in itself. Why would any woman who was interested in becoming Mrs. Caleb Carpenter, despite the circumstances, take such chances with her position? As Caleb's wife a woman stood to gain money, power and a certain prestige. Yet according to the data before her, both of the other two women who'd been accepted for candidacy had been caught in some sort of wrongdoing. That was more than odd, it was coincidental. Rachel had never trusted coincidences.

She closed out of that file and opened another, titled with Sutherland's initials. And from the first page of the document Rachel knew she finally had one of her many questions answered.

The file consisted mostly of newspaper stories downloaded from the Internet. All of them were dated more than five years ago, with the oldest more than a decade old. And all of them featured Kevin Sutherland.

Rachel leaned closer to the screen, instantly engrossed. She'd had that nagging sense of familiarity with the man's name since her arrival, yet she'd never placed the reason for her sense of recognition. But here it was, laid out in black and white. And the moment she began to skim the first article, she was filled with chagrin that she'd needed this reminder.

Sutherland had been a vocal militia leader in the late eighties. Based in North Dakota, his organization, The Aryan Army, had been credited with several bombings of African American churches and Jewish synagogues, in addition to being suspected in the disappearance of two Native American men in Minot. Rachel clicked from article to article. Sutherland's entire arrest and trial process was outlined. The government had failed to gather proof of his personal culpability in the crimes, beyond conspiracy charges. He'd been sentenced to ten years in a federal prison, during which time his militia organization, in disarray from the arrests of several of its members, had dissolved.

With a quick mental calculation, Rachel figured the man had served less than six years of his sentence. Carpenter must have recruited him shortly after his release.

The oldest articles didn't mention Sutherland or his militia at all. They detailed bombings in the Midwest, unsolved murders and assaults on people of color, a biracial couple and a gay man. Rachel clicked out of the file with nausea twisting in her stomach. Some people kept scrapbooks of their accomplishments; in this age of technology, she supposed, it was far easier for Sutherland to keep his on a computer file. She wondered in the next moment if the man had used the file as a personal résumé of sorts for Caleb, or if none had been needed. Surely Caleb had been well-aware of Sutherland's past. Undoubtedly he'd been recruited because of it.

Shaken, she opened each remaining file, only to find nothing more of interest. She looked out the window and saw that the sky was turning pale gray, signaling dawn's approach. She needed a few hours' sleep before she stumbled down to the breakfast table.

But as she secured the computers and relocked the office door, she knew sleep wasn't going to be so easily accomplished. It was obvious that Caleb had handpicked Sutherland for The Brotherhood. He'd chosen a man with a past shrouded in violence and death as his most senior officer. Carpenter and Sutherland were actually more similar than different. They shared the same goals, the same beliefs, and both harbored the potential for violence.

If she needed any further evidence of what kind of person Caleb was, his alliance with Sutherland provided it.

"You present a compelling case, Caleb." Patrick Dixon stared at him across the restaurant table with glittering green eyes. "As they say, however, the devil is in the details. And it's the details of your unification efforts that I'll want to hear more about."

Caleb hooked his ankle on the opposite knee and returned the man's regard confidently. He and Sutherland had deliberately left Dixon until last, wanting to spend as much time with the head of Freedom Reigns as was necessary. Of the thirteen militia leaders they'd visited within the last few days, Dixon was by far the most powerful.

Assassinations, bank robbery, jail break…the man had a most impressive background. Caleb's plans could go forward without Dixon, but it seemed a shame to have to do so. The feds had put the man on their Most Wanted list last year. Rumor had it that when Dixon had found out he'd thrown a party. And then he'd disappeared. The fact that he'd agreed to meet with Caleb in a discreet public place proved that he recognized the growing influence of The Brotherhood.

"Uniting the western militias is only the first step toward my goal of one national alliance. Once we're joined, our power will be infinite."

The trio fell silent as the waitress returned to fill their coffee mugs. Once she'd departed, Dixon asked, "Why do it by increments? Why not work on national unification at once?"

Caleb sipped cautiously from his steaming mug. The restaurant had the dubious distinction of serving some of the worst coffee he'd ever tasted. With a slight grimace, he put the coffee aside. "It's tempting to rush in, but there's far greater value to be realized with smaller steps. We'll be unable to draw other militias if their leaders aren't assured a voice in our new organization. It's imperative that our leadership remain solid throughout the rapid growth we'll experience in the unification process. Those who join us originally, of course, will stand the best chance of holding the most powerful places in the new leadership."

Dixon leaned forward slightly. Clearly Caleb had his attention now. "And how would we decide on the leaders and their positions?"

"Their roles will be determined by the value of what they can offer the new organization." It was Sutherland speaking now. "All can promise followers, but obviously those bringing finances, arms and experience will be worthy of the most powerful positions."

Dixon brushed a miniscule bit of lint from his Armani suit jacket. "From what I hear of your finances, Carpenter, you'd count yourself at the top of that particular pile."

Negotiations had just turned delicate. Caleb chose his words carefully. "Ego has to take a back seat to the good of the new alliance. Our strength cannot rest on one man. Too often groups fail when the one at the helm dies or is imprisoned. The way to avoid that is to have the power in the hands of two or three, with active voices of a dozen others."

Several moments went by as Dixon digested this information, but Caleb wasn't fooled. There was definite interest there. A virtual promise of a leadership position in the highest placement would go far in enticing him.

"As I said, you present a compelling argument. How many others have you targeted for this discussion?"

"We've been in contact with twelve others militias in the western part of the states. All have expressed interest."

Noncommittally, Dixon said, "Well, count me as cautiously interested, as well. I'd expect certain concessions based on the value of what I'd bring to the union." He picked up his coffee mug. "And a leadership role, of course."

Caleb eyed him steadily. "If your war chest is as great as you lead us to believe, I don't think granting those concessions will be too burdensome."

A hard smile played across the other man's lips. "Perhaps we can do business, Carpenter. I'll contact you when I've had more time to consider it."

Satisfaction surged through Caleb. He made certain it didn't show. He waved the waitress over and asked for the check. While she prepared it, Dixon observed idly, "Didn't I hear that you had some upcoming nuptials to celebrate?"

"That hasn't been determined yet." Both Dixon and Caleb looked at Sutherland, who flushed, but continued. "General Carpenter is currently considering a candidate for that position. No final decision has been made."

"You may have heard of her father," Caleb said to Dixon. "Hans Grunwald." He stopped when an arrested look passed over the other man's face.

"Are you saying your fiancée is Rachel Grunwald?"

"She's a candidate only."

The other two men ignored Sutherland's correction. "That's right," Caleb said coolly. "Do you know of her?"

"I spent a brief time in the Michigan Coalition about five years ago. Rachel was a member. Well, well, well."

Caleb wasn't sure what it was he heard in the man's voice, but he was certain he didn't like it. There was a little flare of something directly under his heart, then just as quickly it was banked. He'd never experienced jealousy, would have denied it if it occurred to him. So the tension filling his limbs must have sprung from protectiveness.

"You're a twice-blessed man, Caleb. Rachel is one of a kind. Face like an angel and nerves of steel." Dixon's eyes met Caleb's then, and widened slightly at what he read there. "Not that she had the time of day for me back then, of course. But a man's allowed his fantasies, isn't he?"

Caleb's fingers slowly clenched into a fist. Lucky for Dixon that fantasies didn't transform into reality, or he'd be nursing a shattered jaw. "I'll give Rachel your regards."

"You do that," the other man said musingly as Caleb and Sutherland prepared to leave. "If you and I are able to do business together, I'll look forward to seeing Rachel again."

Sutherland said, "We look forward to hearing from you." Caleb contented himself with a short nod before heading out of the restaurant. For the first time Caleb was having grave doubts about the wisdom of getting further involved with Dixon. And those doubts had nothing to do with the future of The Brotherhood and everything to do with Rachel.

After her round of shooting practice, Rachel drove a hundred yards directly east to the canyon's edge. She was drawn to it more and more frequently. She'd spent part of each afternoon contemplating the breadth and depth of the area. There was something calming in the majesty, in observing the eagle's flight and watching the river below carving its way across the land. It was the one place that she seemed able to think clearly in recent days.

But there was a difference today; clarity was difficult to achieve. And she knew that had less to do with her lack of sleep in recent nights and everything to do with Caleb's eminent arrival.

She was eager to discover what he'd achieved on his trip. She knew that his intent had been to garner support for the unification efforts, beginning in the west. Greater strength meant The Brotherhood would have more money, more weapons, more power. And soon she'd have to face the man who meant to control all of it.

Her considerable acting prowess was going to be sorely tested before her mission was accomplished. She needed to pump Caleb for additional information, acting as though she admired his goals, his ambition, his commitment.

The only thing that was truly admirable about the man was his ability to seem two like different people at once.

She shook off the morose thought impatiently. This job might turn out to be the challenge of her career, but there was far more at stake. She had more than her assignment to consider. There was her judgment hanging in the balance, as well.

Never before had she allowed self-doubt to infiltrate her decisions, and she damned herself for permitting it now. Self-doubt clouded perceptions, made decisions murkier and skewed her focus. She'd need to be doubly diligent to achieve her goal here, and to try to protect herself in the process. Because there was no longer any denying that Carpenter could get to her in a way no other man ever had.

There was a slight sound behind her and when she turned her head he was there, as if summoned by her dark thoughts. She watched him approach on foot. He must have left his vehicle in front of the shooting range, along with his suit jacket and tie. She'd only seen him so informally dressed on one other occasion; the night he'd surprised her in the kitchen.

A flush heated her skin. Avoiding that memory was definitely in her best interests. But he seemed determined to make that impossible. Already he was rolling up the cuffs of his shirt and loosening another button at his neck, in concession to the heat.

"Tommy said I'd find you out here."

She swallowed hard around a rapidly forming ball in her throat. "Yes. I've gotten in the habit of exploring here in the afternoons. Sometimes I travel farther south, but the canyon never fails to fascinate me."

He obviously didn't share her affinity for the view. He stopped several feet away from her. "I've never found anything particularly fascinating about it, myself." He kept his gaze firmly fixed on her face, and a small secret smile curved her lips.

"Don't tell me you're afraid of heights."

He shoved his hands in his pockets and rocked back on his heels. "*Afraid* has such a negative connotation. Actually I'm ambivalent about heights."

She remained unconvinced. "Really? Then it won't bother you if I do this?" She stretched out, as she was accustomed to doing, with her head and shoulders well over the edge.

"For God's sake, Rachel, get away from there!" The concern in his voice almost disguised the thin thread of panic. "If you fell there'd be nothing left of you to rescue."

"I wasn't considering falling." She switched positions so that she was lying along the edge, one arm dangling over the side. "I have, however, been considering asking you to join me rock climbing."

"I'd rather stick needles in my eye."

She laughed; she couldn't help it. The grim fervor in his voice was silent testament to his real dread. And it was curiously uplifting to hear him admit to a very human fear.

"However did you manage traveling across the Golden Gate Bridge?"

"By choosing inside lanes and not looking at the view. I mean it, Rachel, come away from there."

She stood slowly, and bent to dust off her jeans. Catching his eye on her again, she waved her arms, as if losing her balance. "Ooh, look, Caleb, I'm going to slip. Save me, save me."

A reluctant smile tugged at his mouth. "You're really an impudent brat, you know that?"

"It's been said." Her amusement vanished as quickly as it had appeared. "Did you have a successful trip?"

"I think so."

"How many militia leaders do you think you convinced to join you."

"It's hard to say yet, and I refuse to have a discussion with you until you come away from the edge."

"All right. If you're really sure you won't join me." She moved away from the edge, although she kept a wary distance between the two of them. Experience had taught her that the fewer times she allowed Carpenter to touch her, the safer she'd be.

"Actually I met an old friend of yours." Caleb's gaze was unwavering on her as she raised a quizzical brow. "Patrick Dixon."

She made a noise of disinterest, hiding her intense dislike for the man behind a bland mask. For the first time she considered that this assignment could have been even more impossible; she could have been chosen to investigate Dixon. A sleazier human being she'd never encountered, and that was aside from his repugnant bigoted views. "*Friend* would require a stretch of semantics. We belonged to the same militia several years ago."

When she said no more, a slow burn flickered to life in his belly. "He remembers you fondly. Sent his regards, in fact."

"If you're going to team up with Dixon, watch your back, Caleb." The advice was offered before she could temper it. "A less trustworthy man would be hard to find."

His face was unreadable. "You sound like the voice of experience."

"Experienced enough to know that he'll take whatever he

can get his hands on, and that he's not all that particular about where he *puts* his hands.''

Not for the first time, Caleb was reconsidering his forbearance with the man earlier that day. ''Is that personal experience talking?''

''I broke two of his ribs before he learned to keep his hands to himself.'' The memory still had the power to satisfy. ''I would have preferred his nose but his first instinct was to protect that pretty-boy face of his. It left him exposed.''

He regarded her with sheer astonishment for an instant before laughing out loud with pure delight. ''Rachel, I do believe I missed you.''

His words had the same effect as a dash of cold water. Instantly she regretted having shared so freely. ''You can take care of yourself, of course. There's no reason to believe you couldn't control Dixon or others of his ilk.''

''No reason at all.'' There was a still amusement evident in his voice. ''But right now those men are the last thing I want to think about. Why don't you come over here and welcome me home properly?''

Her system froze for a moment, before she forced a smile to her lips and moved forward. The numbness was fleeting, to be replaced with a mingled dread and anticipation of his touch—and her reaction to it. As Caleb drew her into his arms, she saw Tommy in the distance, watching them with his familiar enigmatic expression. And then that sight, as well as all thought, was obliterated as Caleb's mouth claimed hers again.

She'd been determined to remain unmoved in his embrace, determined to contain the storm of response his touch elicited. But it was difficult when her system pitched and churned as his sure, knowing lips moved against hers. Her body recognized his touch now, and responded of its own accord. The dark, dangerous taste of him swirled through her, arrowing deep in her belly, tendrils of fire curling in its wake. His hard, hungry mouth devoured hers, demanding a response. Involuntarily, her fingers speared into the thick dark hair at his nape, and her lips opened under his. Her tenuous grasp on logic faded as need battered at her senses. Even with one hand clutching his shoulder, anchoring herself, she had the sensation of free-falling, as if she'd finally gotten too close to the precipice he'd warned her about.

She never considered the moment of impact.

Chapter 8

The figure in black clung to the shadows, avoiding the slivers of moonlight slanting between the buildings. The soldier on patrol walked by, not two feet from the place of concealment. The figure went still, not breathing, until the soldier moved on, his footsteps fading in the darkness.

Rachel cupped her hand around the face of her watch, shielding its glow when she checked the time. The soldier had been a minute and a half early. From the observations she'd made during her nocturnal forays the last few nights, there were usually twenty minutes between rounds.

She backed away, in the opposite direction of the soldier. It was time to make her way back to the house. Dawn would arrive in another hour. And she needed to get at least a few hours sleep. Caleb had questioned her more than once the last few evenings when he'd caught her yawning. So far she'd managed to convince him that her unaccustomed idleness was to blame for her tiredness. But for her own sake, she needed to get some decent rest. These late-night explorations were taking their toll, and she had to keep her senses sharp.

An open expanse stretched between her and the house. There were no buildings, trees or shrubs for cover. Rachel crouched down and scurried across the area as quickly as she could. Had anyone seen a movement, they'd have been forgiven for believing it a night creature hunting for prey.

She dodged into the shadows of the house and followed them around the corner to where she'd left her rappeling line dangling from the window of her bedroom. With swift, sure movements, she fastened the safety harness, and grasped the line with both hands. Using the line for support, she walked up the side of the house as nimbly as a spider returning to its web.

Ducking into the open window in her room, she silently removed the hooks and stays from the sill and divested herself of the equipment. She replaced the screen, then loosened the hood and stripped off the thin black jacket she wore. Before hanging it up, she took the night scope from the zippered pouch pocket, and returned it to its case. One of the handiest items made for SPEAR, it resembled a 35mm camera.

She kicked off her black leather slippers and struggled out of the black leggings. After she'd put the clothing away and slipped into a nightgown, she turned her attention to the rappeling equipment. The slender coated hooks she screwed back into place, until they resembled clothes hangers again. The line was clicked back onto handles, and returned to an ordinary length of jump rope. The harness passed nicely as a back brace; an old sparring injury that sometimes kicked up, if she was asked.

It would have been far less trouble if she could have risked slipping out the kitchen door at night. The security lights posted at both entrances would be easily disengaged, but doing so would alert the guards. And there was the additional reason of not wanting to chance running into Caleb if he worked late in his office again.

Her investigation of the last few nights had eliminated one possibility: the weapon cache wasn't concealed in an underground room or tunnel in the vicinity. Her search had failed to turn up anything out of the ordinary.

The sky was lightening, heralding dawn's approach as she slipped into bed. And when she closed her eyes sleep descended swiftly, the undertows dragging her toward unconsciousness. Despite her exhaustion, her slumber was restless, filled with dreams of hidden arsenals and an enigmatic man with secrets in his eyes.

"You slept late."

Damning her luck, Rachel looked up as Caleb strolled into the dining room. Most days she was able to avoid him until dinnertime. The lie slid easily from her lips. "Yes, I did, a bit. I had trouble sleeping last night."

He stopped in the act of swiping her coffee cup and narrowed his gaze at her. "Nightmares again?"

She shook her head, wishing she'd come up with a different excuse. "No. Just old-fashioned insomnia."

He sipped from her cup and handed it back to her, the gesture curiously intimate. "My grandmother always said that comes from having a guilty conscience." He frowned, struck by a thought. "Or maybe that's just something she said to me."

"No doubt."

He smiled at her dry tone. "I'll have you know that I was pathetically misunderstood as a child. My grandmother and my father disagreed over the best way to curb my...ah...youthful high spirits. Thankfully my father won out and I narrowly avoided being sent to a prep school. He thought an all-male local private academy would be punishment enough."

"And was it?"

"Among other things I learned to roll my own cigarettes and make a very passable fake ID." At his raised eyebrows, he shrugged. "I had to meet girls *somewhere*."

"It sounds to me like that prep school might not have been a bad idea," she observed blandly. "And totally deserved."

He crossed his arms to lean on the back of the chair beside her, and assumed an injured expression. "I'd expected a little more sympathy, Rachel."

"Did I sound unsympathetic? I didn't mean to. I have nothing but sympathy for the members of your family who had to put up with you during your formative years."

He winced. "That's harsh. Something tells me you didn't hold teenage boys in high regard."

"Most male youths should be locked up at twelve and not released until they become twenty-two or human beings, whichever comes first."

"You *are* harsh. My grandmother's going to love you."

Caught up in the vein of lighthearted banter it was all too easy to visualize a scene where she met his grandmother. She could almost see the woman in her mind already, a grande dame who typified class, with strong opinions and a tart tongue. And then reality crashed through that image, smashing it beyond repair. She would never meet Caleb's family and they wouldn't welcome her if she did. She was, after all, the woman set to betray him. While she was investigating The Brotherhood's link to Simon, she would try to earn Caleb's trust, gain his confidence. And when her time here was over, she would turn over every shred of evidence involving Caleb that came her way to any agency seeking to build a case against him.

She doubted very much that the Carpenter family would hold any high regard for the woman who brought down their son, regardless of their feelings about how he was choosing to live his life.

She'd suddenly lost her appetite. Patting her lips with her napkin, she asked, "Are you playing hooky today?"

"I wish. I'm waiting for Kevin to arrange a secured conference call for several of the leaders we met with last week."

Pushing her chair back, she rose. "How's that going? Are you getting many positive responses?"

"We've exceeded our expectations, actually." The satisfaction in his voice was reflected on his face. "Most are already expressing interest. Only Dixon is playing coy, not committing himself, but I know it's only a matter of time. He couldn't let a deal like this happen without assuring himself that he'll be a major player."

She nodded. "That's my take on him, too. What's your plan once you have the western states joined?" She held her breath, wondering if he trusted her enough to share some details with her, willing him to do so.

"The future plans I'm most concerned about at the moment involve you. That's why I came in here to catch you this morning. I wanted to tell you that I haven't forgotten my promise to take you to Philadelphia for a visit. I should be able to get free in the next day or so."

Dread filled her, stealing her voice. She'd already learned the danger of exposing vulnerability to this man, and it was an experience she was loath to repeat. "No," she said flatly. "I told you before that won't be necessary."

"I think it is." The tone of his voice brooked no resistance. "You need to get away." His tone changed, its sensual timbre stroking her nerves. "And I'll admit to being anxious to spend some time alone with you."

She must have disappointed him with her silence, but Rachel was incapable of forming an answer. She didn't know which thought terrified her more: Caleb at her side while she visited her mother, or the prospect of spending time alone with him.

* * *

As had become her custom, Rachel worked out in the morning. Following that, she trailed through the buildings in a seemingly aimless fashion. Her intent was anything but. One of the structures might well store the arsenal, and she was increasingly desperate to find out how extensive it was. First, however, she needed to *find* it. So she poked about, checking doors and closets, mentally measuring space. And while doing so, incurred the wrath of at least one instructor.

"You're interrupting our session." The soldier left the group he was leading in defensive tactics to approach Rachel, who stood just inside the door. "If you're looking for a free gymnasium, try gym three."

Rachel smiled politely and murmured an apology, backing out of the room. She could have told the man she'd tried gym three; as a matter of fact, she'd searched every nook and cranny of the entire building, save this gym. She was no closer than before to finding where the weapons were concealed.

She'd have to return later in the afternoon to finish, but she didn't hold out much hope that the buildings held any clues.

Her lunch was solitary, which suited her just fine. It had been much more comfortable when she'd only had to face Carpenter at dinner. The charade she was playing with him was far more draining than any other she'd experienced. Far more risky. She'd sensed a subtle change in his attitude toward her since he'd returned from his trip. He seemed to find reason to touch her more often, a casual stroke of a fingertip on her arm, a hand that lingered at her back, his body brushing hers as they walked in the garden. But he hadn't kissed her since the day of his return. If she didn't know better she would guess that she was being seduced; gentled to his touch, much as a horse shaman would tame a wild mare. The analogy brought her no humor. If that was Carpenter's goal, it was backfiring. Each seemingly innocent touch put all her senses on alert.

It would be too easy to be lulled by the face Caleb usually wore with her: the cultured, articulate, witty scion of one of San Francisco's oldest families. It would be too effortless to allow herself to believe that someone with his qualities couldn't possibly be capable of the kind of evil Jonah suspected him of.

She couldn't allow herself to lose sight of the fact that all the evidence suggested that Jonah was right. She'd heard Caleb speak of his plans, she'd heard him incite his troops for a racial war. She'd seen the numbers for the stock of weapons he'd acquired, and discovered enough ammo to arm a good-size battalion. It really shouldn't be so difficult to withstand the kinder gentler side he presented to her. All she had to do was look at him and imagine him wearing her father's face.

Strangely restless after lunch, she headed toward the vehicle barn. She almost thought better of ordering a jeep to drive to the shooting range. A long walk might be just what she needed to cure this odd mood that lingered, but Idaho was having unnaturally warm weather. She didn't relish a hot walk in the sun.

At the shooting range, she waited for a silent Tommy to load her gun for her. She no longer needed to verbalize her selection. When she walked in the door he took a Glock down without a word and motioned her to the register book. She spent a long time in the shooting gallery, going back to have him reload the weapon several times. The whole setup struck her as a somewhat laborious process; she hadn't encountered one like it in any of the militias she'd been involved with. She wondered if the extra precaution was Caleb's idea or whether it was due to Tommy's overdiligence.

Later, she sat in the jeep, torn between two equally strong desires to return to the house for a nap and go to the canyon's edge. Her energy level was flagging due to her late nights. But the canyon beckoned her. It was the one place on the compound that she felt truly alone. And nature's beauty never failed to have a calming effect on adrenaline-spiked nerves.

She braked twenty feet from the edge, but the jeep continued to move. Next she tried slamming the brake to the floor. The jeep kept rolling. Her gaze dropped to the brake, as if to convince herself that she was indeed using the right pedal. On the slight slope nearing the cliff, the jeep picked up speed. Stomping on the emergency brake didn't slow the vehicle's approach.

Reflexes had Rachel turning the vehicle in a sharp right, her maneuver throwing up a cloud of dust. The edge of the canyon loomed, impossibly close. She opened the door and jumped from the jeep, hitting the ground in a dizzying roll. She had one last glimpses of the vehicle, back wheels spinning for traction, before it began to teeter on the cliff. And then she came to a sudden painful stop, stars burst behind her eyes, and everything went black.

She never saw the jeep slip over the edge of the cliff and begin a silent dive to the deep canyon below.

Images blurred, shifting in and out of focus, and when she tried to concentrate on them her head put up such a furious protest that she closed her eyes again.

"Don't try to move."

She gave no thought to obeying that harsh voice. Rather, it was the vicious surge of nausea threatening that kept her still for the moment. She took several deep breaths, then became aware of hands running over her body. Weakly, she pushed them away, but they returned. She opened her eyes, willed them to focus. "Get away from me."

"Shut up." She could hear other voices now, other sounds, but it took all her effort to concentrate on making sense of the scene before her. And when she finally recognized the man who was handling her so familiarly, she scowled.

"Well, now I know I'm not in heaven."

Tommy ignored her, talking to another soldier nearby. "Did you call the general?"

"Yes, sir, I did that right away. He should be here shortly."

Those words gave her the strength to sit. It was bad enough that Mahoney had seen her weak, unconscious. She wouldn't allow Caleb the same view.

"Didn't I tell you not to move?" he barked, as she fought for a sitting position.

"Didn't I tell you to shut up?" she mumbled, successfully batting his hands away.

"No ma'am, that's what he told you," a helpful voice reminded her.

"Oh. Well, ditto." And then she couldn't waste any breath talking. It took all her strength to keep from slumping backward. Explosions of pain were going off in her head. Gingerly, she put her hand up to investigate the source. Her fingers came back bloody.

With brisk, impersonal movements, Tommy lifted her eyelids and peered into her eyes. Squatting back on his heels, he announced, "You may have a concussion. How many fingers am I holding up?"

Her stomach pitched and rolled. "On which hand?" She'd had medical instruction as part of her training period with the agency, but it was experience, rather than knowledge that invalidated his diagnosis. She'd been concussed after a particularly nasty fight in a filthy alley in Barcelona. She recognized the signs, and she was fairly certain that she didn't have a concussion. Just the grandfather of all headaches.

"Get out of the way. What happened to her?"

She winced as the loud tones seemed to echo endlessly in her head. Caleb crouched down next to her, in the spot vacated by Tommy. "Rachel, all you all right?" He turned to glare at Tommy. "What the hell happened here?"

"I'm fine." His attention snapped back to her. She tried for a weak smile. "Next time I'll ask for a stunt double."

His voice went to simmer, but was all the more dangerous for the control barely leashed. "I want some answers, fast."

"She must have lost control of the jeep, General." Tommy's words were expressionless. "You can see the marks there," he pointed, "where it happened. She was lucky she was able to bail out before it went over."

Caleb's face went still. "Are you telling me that her vehicle went over the cliff?"

"Yes, sir."

For a moment Rachel forgot the pain, the churning sickness in her stomach and watched in utter fascination while emotion worked on Caleb's face. And when he turned his gaze on her again, the weakness that coursed through her had nothing to do with the effects of the accident.

"How badly are you hurt?" The rough edge of strain in his voice was a marked contrast to the gentleness in his hands as he seemed determined to check for himself.

"Nothing appears to be broken." It was Tommy who spoke, and his words served to yank Rachel from a reverie of the senses. She caught Caleb's hands in hers, in an effort to halt his touch. His fingers had trailed heat in their wake, the kind of heat that was growing all too familiar. All too risky.

"I'm fine. Just a bump on the head…" She broke off and flinched as he found the wound for himself and probed tenderly.

"You're not fine," he bit the words off savagely. "You're *bleeding.*"

"Nothing that looks like it needs to be stitched, though," Tommy said.

"Head wounds always bleed profusely." For some strange reason, Rachel found herself trying to reassure him. "A cold wash cloth and a shampoo and I'll be fine."

"She can be moved?" he asked Tommy. At the man's

assent, Caleb rose. "Bring the jeep over here," he commanded one of the soldiers.

Slowly, carefully, Rachel struggled to her feet. And then swayed, as she fought to remain upright. Caleb turned back to her and cursed.

"What the hell do you think you're doing?" His arms went around her. She was ashamed to admit she was glad for the support. While sitting, her head and her stomach had been her primary concerns. Standing allowed her to take stock of the rest of her body, and various parts were joining with a loud chorus of complaints.

"I'm standing. Although I'm rapidly rethinking it," Rachel said in a thin voice. The ground shifted under her feet, and she found herself in Caleb's arms. His face moved in out and out of focus, and there was a roaring in her ears.

"I can walk." Her words were pathetically weak.

"I know you can, baby."

"I'm not gonna faint," she mumbled. Sheer force of will had to count for something, didn't it? "I never faint."

His voice barely registered through the rush of black unconsciousness. "Just close your eyes. I've got you."

"You have to eat something."

"I really don't think that would be such a good idea right now." It was Rachel's stomach that was convincing her. The waves of nausea had subsided, but she was left with an overall queasiness that threatened at the mere mention of a meal.

Caleb frowned, and put the cover back on the scrambled eggs. "The doctor said—"

"The hell with the doctor," she snapped. "I'm saying no, at least until I can be assured the food will stay down."

Eyebrows lifting, he settled back in the chair he'd pulled close to her bed. "You're cranky."

His mild observation had her screwing her eyes shut and wishing he'd disappear. "Sorry." Her voice sounded so pitiful that she would have shaken herself if the action wouldn't have worsened the throbbing in her head. "I don't have a lot of practice being a patient."

"That's okay. It's really kind of nice to find something you're not good at."

She opened one eye and sent him a jaundiced look. "Your sympathy is overwhelming."

"Not at all. I'm thrilled to have found someone who's more obnoxious in their sick bed than I am. My mother will be amazed."

Slumping back against the pillows, she tried ignoring him. Maybe he'd take a hint and go away.

"You got a great deal of sleep. That has to be a good sign."

Not bothering to open her eyes, she retorted, "That has to be a miracle, considering that you were waking me up every fifteen minutes."

"Every hour," he corrected her imperturbably. "Doctor's orders."

"I very much doubt it. They don't recommend that anymore, even if they do suspect a concussion. Which I don't have."

"You could have had one."

"But I didn't."

"You could have been killed."

His quiet words had her eyes flickering open, and she exchanged a long sober look with him. "I wasn't."

"No." He gave her an faint smile, but there was a look in his eyes, a dangerous burn. "But not from lack of trying on your part."

Now she was the one frowning, wondering what he was getting at. "Look, I tried to turn at the last minute, but it was too late. I'm sorry about the jeep."

"I don't give a damn about the jeep!"

She stared at him, instantly wary. It occurred to her then that she'd never heard him raise his voice before. She'd also never seen this look on his face, as if he was barely restraining an urge to do something violent.

He recovered almost immediately. His voice was even when he repeated, "I don't care about the jeep. I care about you, Rachel. How the hell could you have taken such a foolhardy risk? And for what? The thrill of it?" He stopped, his throat working, and then he got up, jammed his fists in his pockets and began to pace. "If I have to, I'll assign another soldier to you, if only to keep you from dreaming up any more of these harebrained schemes—"

Her voice incredulous, she demanded, "You think I deliberately tried to drive that jeep over the cliff? Are you crazy?"

"No, I think you took one too many chances, got too close to the edge and weren't able to stop in time. It was sheer luck that you could bail out of the jeep before it went over. But luck is unreliable."

"It was the brakes that were unreliable, Caleb." His gaze flew to hers, held. "I might have been going a little faster than I needed to, but I braked in plenty of time, at least twenty feet away from the edge."

His face went still. "Are you saying the brakes failed?"

"I had the pedal all the way to the floor and it didn't slow at all."

"Did you try the emergency brake?"

She frowned, trying to remember. The throbbing in her head intensified. "I think so. It all happened so fast. The cliff was coming up so quickly...I tried to turn, but the jeep skidded around...." She shook her head, which was a mistake. Closing her eyes, she swallowed until the pain subsided. "I figured my best chance was to jump, so I did. I never even saw it go over."

He didn't remind her of the reason for that. The rock she'd hit had been covered with blood. *Her* blood. His stomach clenched. When he spoke, his words were chosen carefully. "I didn't mean to put you on the defensive. I just want you to be more cautious with your safety. There are plenty of natural ways we can meet our end in this world without courting new ones."

She took a deep breath, feeling ridiculously weary already. She'd needed sleep, but this bone deep exhaustion went far beyond a few missed hours in the last few nights. "Caleb, look at me. Do I seem stupid to you? Because only a stark raving lunatic would try to pull a stunt like the one you're describing."

His look sharpened. "You mean the brakes...really failed?"

The fight streamed out of her, leaving her weak and aching. "They seemed all right on the way to the shooting range. I didn't notice anything wrong until I was on my way to the canyon."

She didn't open her eyes to double check, but she could hear the grim purpose in Caleb's voice. "Sounds like I need to have a serious discussion with the soldier in charge of our fleet." Too tired to care, Rachel welcomed the sleep that was threatening to pull her under again. She heard Caleb leave the room, but she could drum up no sympathy for the man who would soon be on the receiving end of his temper. Through his carelessness, the idiot had almost gotten her killed.

"Gin."

"You're cheating again."

"I am not cheating. There's no need. You suck at cards. Pay up."

Caleb reluctantly thrust his hand in his pocket and pulled out another dollar, which Rachel snatched and added to the mound of money before her. Pursing her lips primly, she picked up the cards and shuffled. "You are an exceedingly poor loser. Luckily, you're rich. No one would play with you otherwise."

His fingertips tapped restlessly on the small table he'd

moved into her room. "Cards aren't my thing. I prefer to be more active."

"So do I," she said meaningfully. "Just say the word and you could go back to your office and I'll just amuse myself."

"Nice try." He fanned out the cards she'd dealt him and frowned. If he hadn't been watching so closely he'd have sworn she'd pulled a fast one. How could he continually get such lousy hands? "The last time I left you to amuse yourself I came back to find you practicing your martial arts moves."

"Every muscle I have is stiff." She drew a card and discarded another. Her voice was just shy of sulky. "I've been in this bed an eternity."

"You've been in bed for two days," he corrected dryly. He picked up her discard and reconsidered his hand.

"I'm getting up tomorrow, if I have to go out the window."

"Maybe at dinnertime."

"Breakfast."

"Lunch. And that's my best offer. You'll still need to take it easy and rest frequently. The doctor said that bed rest would be good for you."

"Then that doctor's a quack. Where'd you find him, anyway?"

"He's a follower. I had him flown in from Boise."

That had her pausing, and raising her eyes to his. "You flew him here?"

"I was concerned, Rachel." With a gesture he reminded her it was her turn to play. "I thought perhaps Wonder Woman had met her untimely demise. You're not invincible, you know."

"I know." The words were shaded with irony. If she were invincible the past forty-eight hours wouldn't have affected her so strongly. She wouldn't be so moved by his show of concern, his efforts to feed her, to entertain her. She wouldn't find it touching that he was neglecting attending to business, and playing card games he despised, just to ensure she got the rest he insisted she needed.

Invincible. She only wished she were. Because surely a woman would have to be invincible to remain unaffected by Caleb Carpenter.

Chapter 9

"This trip you're planning seems ill timed, General."

Caleb finished jotting a phone number down on a piece of paper, then looked up after he slipped the number in his wallet. Tucking the wallet back in his pocket, he asked, "In what way, Kevin?" His usual unflappable colonel was looking more than a little disturbed.

"Things are rapidly coming together. Ten western militia leaders have already pledged their support, and in my opinion Dixon is only holding out to up the ante a little. And word of our unification proposal is already spreading. We've had…what? Four calls from across the country?"

"Five." Caleb checked the knot in his tie and picked up his suit jacket, folding it over one arm. "We've got momentum going for us, Kevin. The Big Mo, the politicians call it. And we're going to ride the crest right into forming our own national government."

"That's what I mean, sir." Sutherland was making no effort to keep the disapproval from his tone. "We've never had more on our plate. As well as taking calls, we have plans to make. There's strategy to define, starting with our time line. We have to begin giving specifics. Our new partners are full of questions and we have to be ready to provide answers soon, or we risk sabotaging—''

"Kevin." Caleb's voice was quiet, but effectively stemmed the rest of his words. "I'll only be in Philadelphia overnight. You field the calls for me today and take care of things around here. I'll be back tomorrow afternoon and we'll get to business then."

"Philadelphia?" The man's interest sharpened. "You're going on business then?"

"Not business, no."

Sutherland's mouth went flat. "Not business. You've been somewhat distracted the last couple of days, sir. I'm concerned about when your attention is going to return to the problems at hand."

"Your concern is beginning to sound very much like something else, here, Kevin." The words were uttered pleasantly enough, but there was no denying the steel underlying them. "Are you questioning my judgment? My commitment?"

"Of course not!"

The vehemence in Sutherland's denial may have been genuine. Caleb chose to believe that it was. "Rachel's on the mend now, so when we return you can be assured that my energy will be focused on business once more."

But his reassurance went unheard. Sutherland's face went still. "Miss Grunwald is accompanying you to Philadelphia?"

Caleb checked his watch. He had four minutes before Rachel was due to join him. The car that would take them to the jet was kept was already waiting out front. "That's right. She needs to visit her mother. I said I'd take her. I trust you to handle things in my absence. Now if you're satisfied, I have to meet Rachel." Without waiting for the man's assent, he began striding toward the door.

But the expression on Sutherland's face as he watched him go was anything but satisfied.

Rachel put the car in park, fingers clenched on the steering wheel, her only outward sign of the emotions that were circling and colliding violently inside her.

"Is this it?" Caleb lowered the newspaper he'd been reading, to survey the rolling property of the Good Shepherd Care Center. He glanced at the woman beside him. "You're right. I would never have found it. How far out of the city is it?"

"Only about four miles out of city limits, but this turnoff can be tricky to find." She unfastened her seat belt, but made no move to exit the car. Instead she dropped the keys to the rental car into her purse and then sat clutching it on her lap.

Caleb watched her curiously. "Are we getting out?"

"No." She tried to temper the blunt answer with a smile. "I mean, there's really no reason for you to come in with me. Mother's strokes have left her unable to speak. If you want to wait in the car, I can just dash in long enough to say hello, and—"

"Nonsense." To her dismay, Caleb opened the door and got out. "She's all the family you have and I'm anxious to meet her." Rachel took a deep breath and accepted defeat. Slowly, she joined him in the parking lot and led him to the front door of the center.

As they walked to the front desk, Caleb looked around curiously. "I've never been in a nursing home before. My maternal grandfather died when I was young, and my other grandparents are still fairly healthy and living in their own homes."

"I'm sure everyone would like to live out their years in their own homes," Rachel answered, her voice tight. "It's just not always an option." Upon reaching the front desk, she gave her name, acutely aware of the keen look Caleb gave the pretty Asian receptionist. "Nice to see you again, Rachel," the woman said. "Company is just what Gloria needs." An RN jotting notes on a chart nearby looked up and smiled, nodding.

Caleb was silent as they walked down a hallway. His attention was directed at Rachel. He'd never seen her this tense, her nerves so exposed, not even on the night he'd comforted her in the kitchen. He was curious about the cause. More, he was intrigued, eager to explore another side of her life, even one she was obviously reluctant to share with him.

They paused outside a door and he could see resolve stiffen her spine, the angle of her chin lifting. And when she pushed the door open, her greeting was cheerful, with no hint of the tension that had been building steadily since they'd boarded the jet that morning.

"Hello, Mother. Dr. Paulus, it's good to see you again." Rachel bent to kiss her mother's cheek. She could feel Caleb's presence behind her, although she refused to look at him. "I've brought a friend with me today. This is Caleb Carpenter."

Caleb stepped forward and picked up the woman's limp hand in both of his. "Rachel has spoken of you, Mrs. Grunwald. I'm happy to have the chance to meet you."

Rachel stepped aside to have a brief conversation with the doctor, while Caleb kept up a pleasant one-sided chat about their flight, the weather, and the Eagles chance of a winning season. By the time Rachel turned back to them, she could tell he was running out of topics.

"You've had your hair done. It looks lovely. Would you like me to read to you today?"

Gloria Grunwald blinked once, signaling no. Rachel wasn't surprised. Her mother would never willingly allow her to do a thing for her. She rarely would do anything for herself, either.

Her voice firm Rachel said, "The doctor says you aren't

cooperating in rehab, Mother. You know if you won't try, your muscles will atrophy. Then you'll lose all hope of ever regaining any movement back.''

Her only answer was a long look from blue eyes too much like her own. A look filled with resentment. Bitterness. A look guaranteed to flood Rachel with an inevitable, overwhelming tide of guilt.

She'd encountered that look too often over the years, ever since it had become clear to her mother that Rachel wasn't going to take up her father's cause, that she had no sympathy for her parents' beliefs. Gloria would go to her death believing Rachel had failed her. It would be at least that long before Rachel stopped wondering the same thing. Not for her refusal to embrace dogma that was abhorrent to her, but for her inability to find something, anything, to spark an emotional connection with the woman who bore her.

Although she and Caleb stayed just over an hour, the time seemed interminable. No efforts Rachel made were met with any response, other than that accusing, unblinking stare. And when the afternoon nurse came in to cheerfully check Gloria's vitals, a broad smile on her ebony face, the resentment in Gloria's eyes was clear. She glared at the nurse, then aimed her gaze at Rachel. Her message was unmistakable.

Traitor.

Certainly nothing could feel as bitter to a woman of Gloria's beliefs than to end her days helpless, being tended by some of the people she'd spent her life unreasonably despising. And in some deep part of herself, Rachel acknowledged that she had indeed betrayed her mother, although in a much different way. Because Rachel should feel more than duty, a sense of obligation to this woman.

She swallowed hard around an all too familiar knot in her throat. Surely she should be able to find something in her mother to love.

Caleb studied Rachel over the globe of his wineglass. She seemed subdued, but her color was better than it had been earlier in the afternoon. The dress he'd ordered sent up to her room sheathed her form lovingly, the black fabric an elegant contrast to her blond hair and creamy skin. Even the accessories he'd chosen fit. He'd expected his actions to elicit at least an arch comment regarding his familiarity with women's clothing. But she'd said very little since they'd entered the lounge, other than to utter a polite thank you.

He thought he understood the cause of her somber mood, but he wasn't going to let her use it to shut him out. He bided his time while she sipped her wine. It was no hardship. Watching Rachel, whether she was quiet or animated, was peculiarly rewarding.

"Did you get any rest this afternoon?"

"A little." She looked up, caught his gaze, and her mouth turned down ruefully. "All right, not much."

"You're still upset."

The quiet observation didn't surprise her. She knew she'd need to prepare for his questions, for his curiosity. It was that knowledge that had kept her awake, staring at the ceiling from the four-poster hotel bed. Formulating answers. Answers that didn't stray too far from the truth, yet would satisfy. But in this case the truth was so painful that she wished desperately for a convincing lie to hand him. One that wouldn't require raking raw emotions that still throbbed like old wounds. Just as she opened her mouth to do just that, she was granted an unexpected reprieve.

"Carpenter?" A short round man stopped at their table, then thumped Caleb on the back. "It is you. By damn...you came to Philly and didn't contact me? You aren't considering another supplier, are you?" Without waiting for an answer, the man narrowed his blue eyes and pulled up a chair. "You are, aren't you? By damn. Anyone who claims he can beat my prices, he's a no-good liar."

"Sean." Caleb's voice was carefully blank, immediately alerting Rachel's inner radar. "How have you been?"

"Can't complain. Of course if I find that you're dissatisfied with the merchandise, and you didn't bother to call me to work things out, I'll have plenty to complain about."

Caleb cut the man short with a raised hand. "I'm not in the city on business, Sean. Just a short trip with my fiancée."

The other man's expression of relief gave way to one of delight. "You don't say. Well, I'm doubly glad to run into you, then." He rose, and reached for Rachel's hand, bending over it with a courtly gesture that seemed oddly sincere. "Sean Conrad, miss, a business associate of your fiancé's."

As Caleb completed the introduction, Rachel studied the other man with interest. In a different season, she thought, Sean Conrad could get a job donning a red suit and taking Christmas orders from children. He was at least sixty-five, and bald but for a fringe of white hair. He wore wire-rimmed glasses over bright-blue eyes and possessed a girth to rival that of the jolly old elf's. The imagery was curiously warped, given his apparent association with The Brotherhood. An association Rachel was determined to explore.

"Would you care to join us for dinner?" Ignoring Caleb's closed expression, she smiled brightly at the other man. "We haven't ordered yet."

"Well, I don't mind if I do." He took the menu Rachel handed him and beamed a smile at them both. If he was aware of Caleb's lack of enthusiasm, he chose to ignore it. "Wouldn't think of horning in on the two of you, but I have a little business to discuss with your fiancé. Then I'll leave the two of you alone." He winked broadly. "Don't want to get in the way of romance."

So over steamed scallops and tender fillet, Rachel sat quietly at the isolated table at the back of the restaurant, more than content to listen to Caleb converse with the man who had joined them for dinner. And with each passing minute she grew more impatient. Each time Conrad would turn the conversation to whatever business he had with The Brotherhood, Caleb would smoothly steer it in another direction.

Nearing the end of their dinner, it was difficult to determine whether Rachel or Conrad was more frustrated.

In a deliberate effort to encourage a more open exchange, Rachel rose and excused herself. But she lingered only minutes in the rest room before starting back to the table, pausing before a small decorative fountain that was just within earshot.

"Three times the amount of the last shipment?" Conrad speared a piece of broiled swordfish and whistled. "That will cost you, son."

"With you it always does, you old reprobate. But can you supply it?"

She thought she detected real affection in Caleb's tone. It was obvious there was a history between the two men.

"Of course I can." Conrad sounded offended. "You couldn't get a better price anywhere on the market, and I know that for a fact. I was just making a general observation. I'll need a complete listing of your needs. I can make you a sweet deal on a shipment of armor-piercing rounds. I don't know that you included any on the last order?"

"Armor-piercing? I'll keep that in mind. I'm concerned about having enough ammunition for the AK-47s and SR-25s we'll have coming in."

"Got another order placed with Simon, do you? Don't worry, I can take care of your needs. It'll cost a pretty penny, too. You wouldn't believe the trouble I have to go to get my hands on ammunition for automatics these days." Conrad shook his head and sawed at his dinner, while Rachel strove to contain her sudden spike of excitement. The corroboration of her theory of Simon's involvement was given so offhandedly, it seemed almost anticlimactic. "Gun control legislation has really skewed the free enterprise system. Damn ex-mercs are swarming all over the business, trying to carve a piece of the pie for themselves."

Caleb's tone was unimpressed. "Quit trying to prime the

pump. I'm not going to sit still for a ten percent markup in your commission over the last shipment.''

Conrad looked hurt. ''Don't be so touchy. My commission hasn't risen that drastically. Why, I barely manage to cover my expenses these days. If it wasn't for my love of adventure…it's a mere three percent.''

''One.''

Slapping the table with one hand, the other man said, ''All right, for you I'll lower it to two. Don't let it get around. My reputation as a businessman would suffer.''

''One and a half.'' Caleb sipped imperturbably at his wine as Conrad sputtered protests. ''Take it or leave it. You're not the only one with contacts. You said yourself that I could go elsewhere…'' He smiled slowly. ''Despite my great affection for you, of course.''

''Thievery is what it is,'' sniffed the other man. His upset didn't seem to interfere at all with his appetite. He was devouring the swordfish enthusiastically. ''It's a sad day in this country when a businessman can't make an honest day's wage.''

''Yeah, I know. You'll probably be forced to buy your suits off the rack.''

The look of horror on the other man's face was comical.

Caleb took out his wallet and removed some bills, slipping them across the table. ''Here's a down payment. You'll get the rest on delivery.''

''Do you have a date in mind?''

''I'll call you.''

Rachel picked that moment to continue her way to the table, and noted that Conrad's disposition had visibly improved after he'd tucked the money out of sight into his pocket. He said jovially, ''Well, you drive a hard bargain, boy, but it's always a pleasure to do business with you.''

Caleb rose as Rachel appeared at the table, sitting only after she did. He picked up the wine and tipped more into

Rachel's glass, and then his own. "Believe me, Sean, the pleasure is all mine."

Once their dining companion had departed among effusive goodbyes, Rachel and Caleb headed to the lounge. There was a three-man blues band playing, and the plaintive wail of the sax seemed to wrap around them, vibrations throbbing in time to the flux of emotions coursing through her.

The conversation between the two men was uppermost on Rachel's mind. She toyed with the idea of contacting Jonah when they returned to the compound. Now that she could be certain of Simon's connection to The Brotherhood, a major portion of her investigation was satisfied. Almost immediately, she dismissed the thought. This case wouldn't be complete until she discovered the full extent of The Brotherhood's capabilities. And it would be far more valuable to SPEAR if she were to continue her search, and perhaps find something that could lead them straight to Simon himself. Far more rewarding if she could bring down The Brotherhood in the process.

As she toyed with the stem of her wineglass, she considered the fact that Caleb hadn't spoken of business to Conrad until Rachel's absence from the table. It was telling to discover that while she may have gained his trust on a personal level, she'd failed to do so on a business level. Not unlike some of the other militia heads she'd worked with, he was careful. And he was, as he'd warned her weeks ago, a very private man.

"This wasn't exactly the way I had planned for this evening to turn out."

Caleb's tone was faintly disgruntled, and she smiled at him across the candle flickering on the table between them. "Why? I enjoyed meeting your friend."

"He's not exactly a friend."

She sipped, replaced her glass on the table. "But you like him."

She caught the flicker of surprise on his face, before he inclined his head. "Unfortunately, you're right. Even knowing the old shyster feels loyalty only to the highest bidder, and then fleetingly. But I didn't bring you to Philadelphia to meet Sean Conrad, and damned if I'm going to spend the rest of the evening talking about him."

Because he would expect it, she forced herself to form the words. "I'm sorry the trip didn't turn out the way you'd hoped. I appreciated the opportunity to see my mother."

"What I had hoped was to ease your mind by arranging the visit. To maybe understand you a bit better." Resolutely, he reached for his glass, tipped it to his lips. He found himself in an unfamiliar position, wanting more from a woman than the physical, although God knew he ached to explore that aspect of their relationship as well. He was used to the strong craving that could only be physically satisfied, but was unaccustomed to the primitive demand for more. What he wanted, really wanted, was for Rachel to close the emotional distance between them of her own accord. To offer up bits of herself in an unspoken measure of trust that would be at odds with the remote caution that was so much a part of her, and that would satisfy him in ways he couldn't even explain.

He set the glass before him, his fingers toying with the stem. "We're alike, you and I." He smiled at the emotion that flickered in her eyes, interpreting it correctly. "We are. Perhaps you don't completely see it yet. But both of us move about the world shrouded in caution and privacy. It can make for a lonely existence."

The truth of his assessment chilled her. She was well-practiced in the art of keeping others at a distance, but thought she was a good enough actress that most didn't realize her efforts. That this man did so was daunting.

She searched for an explanation that he would accept, and

found one in the truth. "You're right, of course. I learned early on about the need to be careful. My parents couldn't afford a private school, and most of the children I knew grew up in very different environments, raised with different beliefs." Her voice was expressionless, as if the memory no longer had the power to wound. "My father was very verbal about his views. They often made him, and his family, unpopular."

She stopped then, but still he watched her, taking apart her words and reading what she had left unsaid. She could have been talking about a stranger, so calmly she spoke. But he could imagine the child she'd been, shunned by her peers because of who she was; who her father was. He felt a stir of pity, and knew instinctively how much she would detest the emotion directed toward her. He made certain it didn't sound in his voice. "You didn't have the companionship of others your age? Children of your father's followers?"

The shadows of the bar reflected those shading her thoughts. Unpleasant memories could still throb, their edge undulled by time. One of her earliest memories was going to a birthday party held for the child of her father's friend. The pinata had been an effigy of a black man with a noose around his neck. It always sent a dart of ice through her to think of how easily children accepted their parents' teachings; their attitudes, their beliefs. If it hadn't been for public school and the cultural diversity she'd come into contact with there, she may have grown up accepting her father's ideas without question.

"My father's organization wasn't on the scale of yours. Meetings were most often held in our living room. Children were rarely present, women only occasionally. But my mother and I were usually there." Yes, Rachel had often been there, through long nights of ranting and violent pledges. Watching silently from the fringes, wondering more and more often as she aged how people could let hatred control their lives. Shape their destinies.

Lead them to their deaths.

Aware of Caleb's close observation she forced herself to continue. ''After my father's death we found it impossible to continue living in Memphis, where I'd grown up.'' Impossible to contend with the media, the hate mail, the ostracization. Her mother had made the decision to move to a huge city, one that would swallow them up anonymously. And then had grown increasingly embittered about losing the only life that had held any meaning for her.

When the waiter returned to their table with more wine, Caleb waved him away with an absent gesture. The bar was dimly lit but she was able to discern the intensity in Caleb's eyes, was able to recognize the pounding pulse that started in her veins as a result.

She attributed the flux of emotions to her own uncustomary honesty. Sharing some carefully selected slices from her childhood might succeed in lowering Caleb's guard, but she was left to cope with the effect it had on her, as well. Rachel dealt better with the past when she could keep it neatly tucked away in a bruised corner of her mind. She usually considered her childhood as it related to her job as an agent. Only then did the bitterness and resentment she'd grown up with take on meaning.

But as quickly as the thought came, it was negated. Because she was reminded of her childhood, and all its bleak and desolate corners, each time she visited her mother; each time she saw the condemnation in her eyes.

As if reading her thoughts Caleb asked, ''I take it that your mother supported your father's cause.''

She nodded, fingers restless on the flute of her glass. ''She worshiped my father. I've never been sure if it was the strength of her own views or her belief in him that guided her, but she was his most ardent supporter. It was unusual in those days for women to have much power in the movement, but she was at my father's side consistently. I think he shared everything with her—each problem, each plan.''

"Is that the kind of partnership you look for in marriage, Rachel?" Caleb's voice slid through the dimness of the smoky lounge and glided sensuously down her spine. His tone, and the heat in his eyes, were curiously potent. She didn't know which of the two was responsible for her faltering response.

"I—I guess I haven't spent a lot of time thinking about it."

He picked up one of her hands and ran a finger over the smoothness of her skin. "I suggest you start thinking about it." His words were husky, laced with something she was afraid to identify. "I think we both should."

Even as she digested his words, he was reaching for her fingers, giving them a tug. "Dance with me."

Dismay made her awkward, desperate for an excuse to refuse. "I'm not...I don't dance."

His lips tilted. "I don't believe that." Slowly, inexorably, she was urged to her feet. And into his arms.

Pressed against Caleb on the tiny dance floor wasn't the way to avoid the intimacy she'd been skirting all night. Unwelcome memories had heightened her nerves, leaving them raw and exposed. It took more concentration than it should have to focus on the task at hand with her heart weary in her chest. The band played one tune after another, but it was the sax that echoed her emotions, one throbbing mournful note trailing to another.

"You lied."

The slight tensing in her muscles was as much due to the hand brushing the bare skin of her back as to his words.

"You dance as you do everything else. Superbly."

He spoke the low words in her ear, and a shiver chased down her spine. Wisdom was spiraling away. That was to be expected with emotion crowding in, clouding purpose. She desperately needed time away from the man, time to rebuild her shaky composure.

She shook her head, avoiding his eyes. "I'm not very

good company tonight, I'm afraid. Maybe I am a little tired after all."

He was quiet for a moment, and in the silence she was intimately aware of the closeness of their bodies; the firmness with which he guided her steps, the hand pressed against her lower back. The warmth that seemed so much a part of him transferred through their tangle of fingers, and warred with the chill that came from realizing the precariousness of her control.

"You're still upset. Seeing your mother affected you more than you admit. Did my presence today make it more difficult?"

Conversation, even about so personal a subject, was a welcome diversion from concentrating on the brush of their bodies. "Hardly. My mother had her first stroke midway through my sophomore year at college. She recovered, but she had several more right before I graduated." Shortly, she recalled, after she'd been approached by SPEAR, something she'd never dared reveal to her mother. "She would have preferred to stay in her home. I even checked into it but her needs are tremendous. Twenty-four-hour nursing, medications, speech therapy, physical rehabilitation, frequent doctor visits..." Her voice tapered off.

"You were faced with a complicated decision." His fingers tightened over hers. "I understand that. I've made a few difficult decisions myself along the way."

Slowly, she lifted her gaze to meet his. The light in his eyes was intent, sincere. Yes, she could believe that he'd made some tough choices. His relationship with his family had to have suffered because of them. But was he burdened with a conscience that flogged him for the hatred he preached? For the violence he planned? She didn't want to know. It was immaterial, at any rate. People were judged by their acts, not for the guilt that they suffered. She'd always believed that.

She directed her gaze over his shoulder. It was easier, far

easier than surveying him. "It seemed to be in her best interest to go to a home where there were health care workers,
equipment, suited to her specific needs. She would, of
course, be happier in an all-white center." Only she was
aware of the irony behind the words. *Happy* seemed an odd
word to describe her mother. Rachel could never remember
a time when her mother had seemed happy, or even content.
What loomed the most clearly was the vitriol of her beliefs,
the bitterness after her husband had died, the growing resentment as her daughter drew away from her. "I chose a
place that would be fairly close to me, so I could visit more
often. One with a good reputation…"

"Did you think I'd condemn your choice?" He gave in
to an urge to brush his fingers over her lovely nape, linger
there. "Given the liberal atmosphere of our country, I'm not
surprised that there's a shortage of the right kind of care
centers. Under arduous circumstances you did the best you
could. I understand that."

"Do you?" Her chin raised and she met his gaze. "I've
read The Brotherhood's doctrine, Caleb. I know what you
propose for people like my mother."

The hand at the back of her nape stilled. "That screed
was written with the greatest good of the country in mind,
Rachel."

"I know." The agreement clogged in her throat. "But
when reason wars with emotion, logic isn't always the win-
ner."

He moved closer to her, close enough that his lips brushed
her hair with his next words. "You have nothing to fear on
your mother's behalf."

"You can't guarantee that."

"I can. I do." He tipped her chin up until her gaze met
his and whispered the assurance again. "I promise. No harm
will come to your mother."

His gaze was strangely hypnotic. Incredibly, she believed
him. Even as she wondered at his certainty, she couldn't

question his sincerity. And that, perhaps, was the oddest thing of all. What was she expected to think? Was Carpenter merely a hypocrite, who would make allowances to his almighty dogma whenever and wherever it was convenient to him? Or was she to believe that it was out of some genuine feeling for her that he made the vow? If so, she should be elated. A good agent would use those feelings, wring them for every precious drop of information that could be had. Rachel had always considered herself a good agent, but ambition seemed to be failing her now. Duty was becoming increasingly burdensome. Never had her pretense weighed so heavily.

She was aware of his lips in her hair, at her temple. "Let's be selfish, shall we? Let's forget our obligations for a while and just concentrate on tonight."

He couldn't know what he was asking, Rachel thought wildly. Couldn't know how far removed from logic his request was. She couldn't afford to completely lower her defenses; had never known a time when she would have contemplated it. The stakes in this assignment were too high; the danger was growing too palpable. But the events of the day, aided by the climb and descent of the music, the deftness of his touch, conspired against her. Strength leeched from her limbs, a fraction at a time.

She would be expected to lean against him in just this way, wouldn't she? It would seem odd if she didn't shiver when his lips found the pulse at her throat, if she didn't arch against him when his fingers splayed over her bottom and urged her closer. Part of the job, she thought hazily, as he moved her in small circles on the dance floor. All of it was part of job.

Except, of course, for the pleasure.

And so they swayed together, endlessly, in time with the weeping of the sax and the low throb of the bass. The music tugged at sensitized emotions, seeped into their bodies and pulsed.

They didn't part until the band quit for the evening. The lounge had long since emptied. Pausing first at the table to collect her purse, they walked in silence to the elevator. Rachel was very conscious of Caleb's hand at the small of her back. He hadn't relinquished his touch since they'd begun dancing. She was acutely aware of him when his big body moved beside hers into the elevator; when he shifted closer to her to allow others to board the compartment.

The company of the others, a couple of men and a woman, should have shattered the air of intimacy that had enwrapped them while they were dancing. The chatter and accompanying laughter should have acted to banish the lingering memory of his body pressed closely to hers. But Caleb was too close, and his gaze was unwavering. Rachel dared to lift her eyes to his and swallowed hard at the sight. His eyes were heavy-lidded, intent on hers. His mouth was set, his jaw tense. And what she read on his face had the force to squeeze the breath from her lungs.

Desire. Naked, hot, unrelenting. She leaned a little against the wall of the elevator, needing the support. The corners of his mouth curled slightly, and he dipped his head toward hers just as a discreet bell sounded and the doors slid open.

"Getting out?"

It was humiliating that it was Caleb who recovered first, turning easily and guiding Rachel from the elevator. It was galling to admit that the hand digging for her door card was trembling, and that her breathing was slightly unsteady. Caleb was silent by her side, and when the green light refused to flash, he took the key card from her hand and had the door open with one quick swipe.

"Thanks." The word was difficult to form around the knot in her throat. Caleb pressed one hand flat against the door, ushering her inside. And then he followed her in, crowding her against the wall with a swiftness that had her senses reeling.

The naked passion she'd seen on his face was reflected in

his mouth—hard, hot and hungry. Dropping her purse, Rachel's hand went to his chest, as if to push him away. Instead her fingers stayed to knead.

Her pulse rocketed as his lips ravaged hers, drawing a response she couldn't control. Desire slammed into her, solid and painful. Submissiveness was foreign to her. Her arms twined around his neck and she raised on tiptoe to devour him. He tasted like primal, primitive male, aroused and wanting. She could feel the edge of his desperation, rearing beneath his ragged control. It made her heady with power. It made her long to make him lose that control, and free the full force of his desire.

His mouth shifted, went to her throat. Fast and greedy, it found all the sensitive places under her jaw, behind her ear. She wanted to touch him, and her fingers battled with buttons until she'd released enough to allow her hand to slip inside his shirt, skating over his chest possessively. Her purr of satisfaction was interrupted when he tugged the straps of her dress down her arms and buried his mouth between her breasts.

His tongue was painting the hollow of her cleavage with strokes of wicked fire, distracting her from the deft movements of his fingers. And then her bra was falling away. His hands went to her hips and hitched her off her feet. He bent his head and took her into his mouth.

A gasp strangled in her throat, and a kaleidoscope of colors fanned behind her eyelids. Somehow her legs became wrapped around his hips, her hands clasping his head, urging him closer. Her other breast was covered with his opposite hand, fingers teasing the nipple into aching hardness. The dual assault was shattering. A hot fist of need lodged in her belly, tightening steadily with each flick of his tongue, each tug of his fingers. She was writhing in his arms, trapped between the wall and solid, aroused male. The sensual onslaught was brutal, narrowing her world to one filled with exquisite sensation, burning urges.

His mouth left her breast and she cried out at the loss. With a quick savage turn, he carried her to the bed, followed her down on the mattress. They rolled across the bed, battling with clothing, wrestling for control. Neither of them would submit easily. Each was too strong for that.

So for each delicate nibble she took of his chest, his tongue trailed liquid flames across her collarbone. When her fingers danced along his rib cage, trailing teasingly to his loosened waistband until his breath hissed, his mouth tasted the crease beneath her breast leaving her body heaving for more. When she shoved him to his back and straddled him, lowering her torso to graze his chest with the tips of her breasts, it was his turn to groan. And then to reverse their positions, suckling strongly from her while one hand swept beneath her skirt, along one silk-clad thigh.

She paused a moment to savor the sensation then reached for him, molding his masculinity through his clothes, wanting desperately to feel him, hard and pulsing, in her palm. Her fingers went to his zipper, and were covered by his.

"Wait," he rasped, his breath sawing out of him. He kissed the frustration from her lips, but failed to soothe the desperation riding them both. Caleb opened his eyes, and lust punched through him. Rachel was sprawled beneath him, bared to the waist, her dress shoved up to her hips. And he could read the same passion on her face, the same impatience and longing. There was no distance evident now, neither physical nor emotional. He struggled to remember what had caused him to stop.

"We…I…" She moved beneath him, and his attention diverted to the sway of her breasts. "I can stop." The words were forced between clenched teeth, and he could feel the perspiration on his brow. That the words were uttered without conviction shouldn't outweigh the effort. "If you want." He groaned when one of her legs moved against his, and scrambled to regain his senses. "The Brotherhood…we respect a woman's chastity…outside of marriage." The sentiment was negated by the hand sliding up her thigh, pausing a fraction of an inch from where she was damp and aching.

His words were slow to penetrate the haze of desire. Rachel reached for him again, and then froze, one muscle at a time.

The Brotherhood. She squeezed her eyes shut. She'd almost slept with Caleb Carpenter. A man she couldn't trust; one she should despise. And God help her, she still wanted to.

"Do you want me to stop, Rachel?" His mouth was beneath her ear, his voice a sinful temptation, luring her to answer in the negative. She could still feel him, the heat of his body searing hers. Her eyes flew open, an effort to focus her other senses and what she saw wasn't guaranteed to ease her decision. The flush of desire was stamped on his face, nostrils flared, skin taut. His tie was loosened, his shirt undone, and his pants... Her eyes flicked away. In another moment she would have dispensed with those, as well.

A breath shuddered out of her, and then another. He read her answer in her silence. Slowly, painfully, he rose to sit beside her, not averting his gaze as she sat up as well and tugged at her dress to cover herself. Her image couldn't be erased from his mind, at any rate. He doubted anything could ever accomplish that.

Because he didn't trust himself to remain this close to her and not reach for her again, he moved off the bed and concentrated on buttoning his shirt.

"I think you deserve to know that the idea for me to take a wife grew out of a purely pragmatic decision." His words sounded raspy, so he cleared his throat. If ever there was time for honesty, it was now. If ever there was a person who deserved it, it was Rachel. "It was the future of The Brotherhood that we considered, rather than any personal sense of commitment on my part. In order for The Brotherhood to appear more welcoming to families, we decided it behooved me to have a family of my own."

His candor didn't make it any easier for her to speak. "I can understand that." She could feel the force of his gaze upon her, but didn't trust herself yet to meet it.

"Can you? Somehow it's gotten complicated. You've complicated things, Rachel."

In the silence that hummed and sparked between them, she forced herself to meet his gaze. "And how do you feel about complications?"

He reached for her hand, lifted it to his lips. "I've recently grown quite fond of them."

Chapter 10

If Rachel had been frivolous enough to believe in such things, she would have wished for a short stint of time travel, one that would whisk her back to the compound without having to spend uncomfortable hours with Caleb first. As long as she was at it she'd go back and change the past, as well. She'd erase the minutes she'd spent in his arms, devouring and being devoured. Her memory would be purged of his scent, musky and masculine, and her body would forget the dark, compelling flavor of his mouth, the certain possession of his hands.

Instead, she was forced to draw upon her tattered composure, her logic and training. An inherent survival instinct warned her to rebuild those invisible walls Caleb had scaled last night. The ones securing her fears, her vulnerabilities. It had nothing to do with concern over her cover, and everything to do with fear of allowing him emotionally closer than anyone had ever gotten.

Caleb was just as determined that her attempts would be met with failure.

Surely that was why he insisted, in his perfectly urbane manner, that she join him for a late breakfast the next morning. Why he delayed their departure, professing a longing to see an art exhibit at a well-known gallery in the city. The hour grew late, necessitating a languorous dinner before they could depart. When they finally reached the compound, it was nearing midnight, and Rachel's nerves were raw and jangling.

Her bedroom represented a haven, and when her luggage was deposited she said a quick good-night. Shutting the door, she leaned against it, her eyes sliding shut. She needed the next several hours alone, like a drowning woman needed a life preserver. And if the solitude held a curious void that hadn't been present before, well, that too, would be dealt with.

Pushing away from the door, she busied herself emptying her suitcase and readying for bed. With any luck she could arrange a full eighteen or nineteen hours before having to meet up with Caleb again. In an unfamiliar burst of cowardice, she welcomed the reprieve.

It was a measure of her preoccupation that realization dawned belatedly. It wasn't until after her shower that she reentered the bedroom and paused, aware for the first time of something that had escaped her before.

The trespasser had been back. Her gaze flicked about the room, shrewdly assessing. A better job had been done this time. The picture on her nightstand wasn't out of place so much as a fraction of an inch. The bureau drawers were in the right order, the clothes she'd hung on the back of a chair looked undisturbed. But there were traces of dirt on the light-colored carpeting, spaced evenly apart, as if from the sole of a shoe. There was no way that Anna, the fussy housekeeper, would have missed it. The intruder must have visited after Anna had finished here for the day.

Rachel followed the trail of dirt around the corner of the bed and tipped her head consideringly. The comforter, which the housekeeper regularly smoothed and fluffed to inviting perfection, hung just a bit crookedly. Closer investigation showed that the material was caught under the mattress in one spot.

Had she been aware of it, Rachel would have been relieved the way training took over, adrenaline spiking, proof that Caleb hadn't deadened her instincts, only dulled them a little. Carefully, she lifted the mattress until she could see what had been placed beneath it. She removed the brown manila envelope that had been concealed between the mattress and box spring and shook the contents out across the top of the bed.

Pictures. Frowning, she retrieved a pen from the bureau to separate them, surveying each closely. There were a half dozen Polaroid snapshots taken at various areas around the compound. There was one of the assembled troops, a few of Caleb and a photo of Sutherland. The one that her interest immediately honed in on, however, was the picture that had obviously been taken in the weapons storeroom. The one she hadn't yet discovered.

She peered closely at the picture, taking care not to touch it. Cases and shelves lined what looked like cement block walls, each row filled with assembled weapons. Handguns, scoped-lens rifles, machine guns, automatic weapons. There was enough artillery pictured to arm The Brotherhood members five times over. Enough to use that impressive store of ammo concealed in Caleb's hidden room.

The picture, while intriguing, wasn't her central focus. Rachel stared down at the array of photos and contemplated the possibilities. The more thought she gave, the more it appeared that there was only one likely scenario.

Someone was trying to frame her.

She hissed a breath out between her teeth and turned to pace. She couldn't help but remember the file on Sutherland's computer; the one detailing the candidates for Carpenter's wife, and the reasons for expelling the two who had come before her. Someone didn't want Caleb to get married, and that same someone was intent on making sure that he wouldn't be marrying Rachel. She had no doubt that some innocent discovery would be made, linking her to a nefarious spying scheme concocted by the perpetrator. The fact that the scenario shaved a bit too close to the truth for comfort was more than a bit awkward.

It occurred to her then to wonder how badly this unknown person wanted her off the compound. In light of this present discovery, her accident with the jeep was taking on a more sinister cast.

Shoving that grim thought aside for the moment, she began to search for the camera. She had no doubt that if the trespasser had hoped to pass her off as stupid enough to conceal photos where any brain dead person would look, she must also be careless enough to hide the instant camera in an equally obvious place. She found the camera in the largest of her empty suitcases, on the shelf in her closet.

Her lip curled. As frame jobs went, this one was offensively simplistic. That she was going to be exposed as someone so utterly lacking ingenuity and style was a personal affront. The sneer faded as she considered the fact that simplistic or not, the ploy could be shatteringly effective.

Intent on damage control, she spent the next hour considering options. Then taking a deep breath, she rose on shaky legs and went through her bathroom, donned her robe, and then rapped at Caleb's adjoining door.

As she raised her fist to knock again, the door opened before her, and Caleb filled the opening. Her breath strangled in her lungs. Almost every inch of him was bare, and he was overpowering in a way that had nothing to do with breadth and everything to do with sinewy strength padded beneath long-limbed muscle. Rachel allowed herself one quick sweeping glance that took in the form-fitting boxers then averted her gaze, swallowing hard.

"What's wrong?" He sounded alert. Either he hadn't

been sleeping, or he awakened as she did, senses immediately active.

She fixed her gaze on his face, and kept it there through sheer force of will. "I'd like you to come in here and look at something." When he moved toward her she added hurriedly, "You have time to put on a robe. I wouldn't want you to get a chill." It was far easier to face the slight smirk on his lips than his semi-nudity.

When he'd slipped into a robe and tied it loosely around his waist, she turned to lead him back into her bedroom. "What is it? A spider?" His tone was teasing. "Or...don't tell me. You're petrified of mice and you think you heard one under your bed."

"Not a mouse. But certainly evidence of some other type of vermin at work." She stopped before the bed and gestured, satisfied when the humor vanished from his face.

He studied the photos for long moments, then lifted his gaze to hers. She noted the careful blankness there, and knew she had to tread especially cautiously. "Who took these?"

"Presumably me. And the camera that I presumably used is hidden, rather unimaginatively, in one of my suitcases." She nodded at the pictures scattered on the bed. "I found them in the envelope under my mattress when I was getting ready for bed."

The warmth and charm she knew he was capable of was nowhere in sight. His expression was remote, his gaze chilly. "You're saying this is the first you knew of them?"

It was incredible, she thought, that his question had the power to wound. Amazing, since the truth was not far removed from the doubt expressed in his words. She inclined her head. "That's what I'm saying. Why don't you tell me what you know about them?"

He blinked at the reversal. "Me? Why the hell would I take pictures of my own property and hide them under your mattress?"

"I don't know. But I've had some time to think after I discovered these and it seems rather odd that I'd be the third candidate in a row to be proved undeserving of the almighty Caleb Carpenter." The nerves jittering in her stomach were ignored. "Just what kind of game are you playing here?"

She never saw him move. One moment he was beside the bed, the next he was crowding her against the footboard, one hand at her nape, the other capturing her chin. "Believe me, Rachel, I'm not interested in playing games with you. Not those kind."

His reaction was all that she'd hoped for, wasn't it? Then why was her heart thudding hard and heavy in response, the blood in her veins going slow and molten beneath the flame in his eyes? She managed to draw a shallow breath and struggled to follow strategy. "Not you, then. But someone in this compound is intent on discrediting me, trying to make me out to be a traitor, and it stands to reason that the same someone set up the two previous candidates, as well. Unless, of course, you're a great believer in coincidence."

It seemed an eternity before his brilliant-blue gaze left hers, before his hands dropped away, leaving a scorching brand of heat behind. He turned back to the photos, and she managed, barely, to suppress an urge to press one hand against her fluttering stomach.

"No. I'm not much for coincidences."

She turned away to stride to the window. The scene was playing well, better than she had hoped. She hadn't counted on Caleb touching her of course, hadn't counted on the rush of emotion his touch had elicited so quickly, but he was no longer considering her duplicity. She knew better than to underestimate him. She would lead him so far and let him draw his own conclusions. And perhaps she would solve a puzzle that had been troubling her since she arrived at the compound. "It isn't difficult to deduce that someone here doesn't want you married. You don't have any secret admirers ensconced on the compound, do you?"

"Actually, I have a legion of admirers, but none who make it a secret." He smiled, satisfied when his words hit their target and she jerked around to glare at him. "And none on this compound. What are you suggesting we do about this?"

She lifted a shoulder in feigned nonchalance. "I'm afraid this situation is a little beyond my realm of experience."

He merely arched a brow. "Don't be modest, it doesn't suit you. I'm beginning to understand a little just how your mind works. You've got an idea rolling around in there. Spit it out."

Uncertain whether to be flattered or offended at his words, she angled her chin. "All right. I suggest we do nothing."

"Nothing."

"That's right. Those," she inclined her head toward the photos, "are supposed to serve a purpose. Let's let them do so."

"And whoever brings them to our attention is the culprit, is that it?" He smiled, slow and devastating. "You have a quick and devious mind, Rachel. I admire those qualities in a woman."

"I have reason to believe that there are few qualities you haven't admired in women along the way." It suited her to imagine the pique in her tone was part of the pretense. Certainly Caleb seemed to believe otherwise.

"The past can't be undone, no matter how delightfully…"

Her gaze narrowed.

"…ah…varied, that past happens to be," he concluded. His smile faded as quickly as it had come. "It's the future we need to concern ourselves with."

Rachel shied away from the intimacy she heard in his tone, and concentrated on the photos. "Hopefully it won't be too far in the future before we solve the mystery of those pictures." And while she was at it, she wished that it wouldn't be much longer before she completely solved the mystery of Simon's connection with The Brotherhood. Hopefully she'd have some answers before she did something stupid and irrevocably irresponsible.

Like fall for the man she was supposed to be investigating.

The next day crawled by with maddening slowness, inching toward the one following it. Waiting for the "discovery" of the photos in her room had Rachel's nerves thrumming with tension. Waiting was never something she did patiently, and this time was no different. Perhaps she could blame that tension for the renewed sense of urgency she felt to wrap up this assignment. She'd discovered who supplied the ammunition for the weapons on the compound, and Conrad had confirmed her suspicion that it was Simon who supplied the guns. She had yet to find tangible proof of that, however. Nor had she learned the specifics of Caleb's plan for revolution. So that meant there was still a big hole in her investigation.

Strangely restless, she could only pick at the delicious fruit salad Eliza prepared for lunch. There had been no sign of Caleb. She would be surprised to see him before dinner. The certainty shouldn't have felt like a respite. Surely she wasn't that weak, that the thought of spending more time alone with the man should fill her with this sense of mingled dread and anticipation. But this assignment was teaching her new things about herself all the time, lessons she wouldn't have dreamed a month ago. Like how emotions could cloud reason, dull instincts. There was a danger here, one unrelated to the assignment or to Caleb himself. The danger lay with her, and her unfamiliar response to the man at the helm of The Brotherhood.

She sent her half-finished lunch back to the kitchen and wandered toward the library. She needed to formulate a new plan of action, one that would wrap this assignment up before she lost all judgment. This self-doubt, skewed perception…this wasn't her. One of her greatest strengths as an agent was her ability to weigh the odds, calculate the risks. And right now that same ability was telling her that time was running out, at least on a personal level. She had just enough objectivity left to tell her that she was close to losing hers. Why else would she be considering the inconsistencies in Caleb Carpenter, rather than focusing on the evil he preached? Why should it be his tenderness that lingered in her mind, instead of the violence he spewed?

Like a specter of that violence commanded by her thoughts, she rounded the corner and looked up into a familiar face.

"Tommy." The wariness in her voice was natural. She'd once thought she'd hate to meet this man in a dark alley. She now knew that even meeting him alone in the middle of the day in the house was enough to cause muscles to tighten, nerves to prickle. "Are you looking for Caleb?"

He didn't answer right away, just fixed her with that flat onyx stare. "You don't look any the worse for wear after your driving mishap."

"Caleb overreacted. I'm fine."

"Did he?" He gave her words more consideration than they deserved. "You should learn to be more careful. This is primitive country—anything could happen here."

Her heightened nerves may have been the cause for the warning she thought she heard in his words, but she didn't think so. This was yet another person who didn't seem completely comfortable with her being at The Brotherhood. She wondered how badly he'd like to see her go, and if it was bad enough to plant incriminating pictures in her room. Or tamper with the brakes of her jeep.

She was glad that she'd decided against mentioning a possible link between the planted pictures and the accident to Caleb. There was no telling how close he was to the person responsible for one, or both, incidents. She'd find the truth herself, in her own way, in her own time. But meanwhile, Tommy was right. She'd have to be more careful.

Aware that the silence between them had stretched, she said, "I believe Caleb is in the library if you'd like to talk to him."

"I know where to find General Carpenter."

She lifted a shoulder in feigned nonchalance and turned away. "Then I'll leave you to your business." She was aware of his piercing regard with every step she took. Entering the library, she didn't close the door, listening to the sounds of his retreating footsteps. What could be important enough to pull Tommy away from the shooting range?

But she spent little time on that question as another thought occurred to her. She couldn't imagine the store of weapons would be far from Mahoney's sight. Perhaps she'd been ignoring the most obvious place for the store of weapons.

While supervising the shooting range, maybe Mahoney was literally sitting on top of the rest of the cache.

"At least try it."

Rachel shook her head emphatically. "I have no intentions of eating Big Bird."

Caleb lowered the aromatic bite of meat atop his fork and contemplated her in the candlelight. "Big Bird isn't an ostrich."

"Whatever." She switched her attention to the rice pilaf on her plate. "There's something unappealing about dining on an animal that's noted for eating anything that's within its reach."

"Ostrich is considered a delicacy. Many of the finer restaurants are carrying it on their menus."

Rachel arched a brow. "Many carry seaweed on their menus, too, but I'm not dumb enough to order it."

Caleb shook his head. "Really, Rachel, I thought you'd be more adventurous than this."

"A pitiful attempt at manipulation, Caleb." Her voice reflected the cool amusement in her eyes. "But if it's adventurous you want, how about if we strike a little wager."

He leaned forward and reached for his water glass. "I'm all ears." A common enough expression, but not totally true in this case. Certainly he wouldn't want to suppress his sense of sight, wouldn't deny himself the chance to gorge himself on the vision she made clad in the deceptively simple dress, the color of the summer sky. She wore pastels often, he'd noted, and they suited her cool blond beauty. But the black dress he'd bought for her in Philadelphia suited the real Rachel even better, the woman she chose not to share freely with the world. The color of sin, the garment had wrapped lovingly around a body fashioned for the same. She was a woman suited for velvet and diamonds, a woman who would disdain both. It was a curiously sensual undertaking to discover just what it was that she did value. What she felt passionately about. For there was passion in Rachel Grunwald. That particular discovery of his had been responsible for more than a few sleepless hours recently.

"For someone who's supposedly all ears, you seem rather distracted."

He reacted to her rebuke with an easy smile. "I assure you, you have my complete attention." It was no more than the truth. Had been the truth for longer than he cared to recall. She was a dangerous diversion at a time when he could ill afford them. But he'd long since passed the point of trying to resist her allure.

"All right, then. I propose an even exchange. I'll try this…"

He didn't think her shudder was feigned.

"…novel cuisine. In turn, you'll try some rock climbing with me."

A gust of a laugh escaped him. "You call that an even exchange?"

"Isn't it? After all, I'm not afraid to try the ostrich, I'm actually ambivalent about it. Much as you feel about heights.''

His gaze narrowed, recognizing his own words being used against him. "You're on, sweetheart."

Her eyes widened at his easy capitulation. He didn't concern himself with his end of the pay off. The woman right here, right now, filled his thoughts.

He picked up his plate and moved to the seat beside hers. Selecting a particularly tasty morsel from his dish, he meticulously coated it with the sauce Eliza had prepared and offered it to Rachel.

A flicker of discomfit passed over her face. "I don't need to be fed."

"I insist." His teeth flashed. "As my part of the wager, I want to be sure you get the full impact of the taste." He watched, beneath lowered eyelids, as those shapely lips opened and took the sampling he offered. He observed the slight hesitation, as if the flavor surprised her, before it was chased away by a glimpse of enjoyment.

The sight was so reminiscent of the night she'd tasted *him,* that he could feel his muscles bunching in response. That brief pause, followed by a guarded response. And then later of course, the response hadn't been guarded at all but primitive, out of control. And for a man who'd valued control above all else for years, that response had been gut wrenchingly satisfying.

She was staring back at him now, wariness in her eyes, and something else, some reflection of his own thoughts. Yes, she would remember, too, how quickly control had spiraled away, and the memory wouldn't rest lightly. If he valued control, then Rachel demanded it. They were alike in that way. Her instinct would be to cloak herself in the shield she wore, gilded by her beauty, but a shield all the same.

He reached for her hand, brought the palm to his mouth. As defenses went, hers were damnably effective. A man used to patience, he wanted nothing more than to smash through them.

He tasted her skin, smooth and capable, and watched her eyes go to smoke. The sight tightened something inside him, something primal and viscerally male. It made a mockery of his much vaunted caution. Her single reaction made him want to clear the table with one sweep of his arm, lay her down on the polished surface and cover her body with his own. He wanted to reach down deep inside her and pull those responses from her again, even as he desperately needed her to offer them to him freely.

And he wanted to plunge inside her, to feel her nails biting into his shoulders and know that all the wanting, all the desperation wasn't just on his side.

His teeth nipped at the fleshy part of her palm and her hand began to tremble in his.

''Excuse me, General.''

The interruption was jarring. Caleb saw the exact moment when clarity returned to Rachel's eyes, and he wanted to curse.

Like the well-trained servant she was, Eliza kept her gaze trained on a discreetly distant spot. ''You're wanted in your office on an urgent matter.''

Rachel tugged lightly at her hand, and reached for her glass, the movement almost steady. Caleb pushed his chair back in a gesture of restrained savagery. He paused behind her on his way out of the room, his hands resting lightly on her shoulders. When he bent to whisper in her ear he could feel the shudder that worked through her, and was fiercely glad for her reaction.

''We'll continue our...discussion...later.''

Dinner had long since been cleared away. More than an hour passed before Rachel was summoned to the office. And she knew, the instant she opened the door, the instant she saw Caleb's carefully blank expression, what the urgent matter was. Colonel Sutherland was seated before Caleb's desk, his face set in serious lines.

"Sit down, Rachel."

She obeyed, slipping into a seat next to Sutherland's. She saw the envelope lying on Caleb's desk with the pictures spilling out of it and experienced a sense of déjà vu. She fought to recall senses that Caleb had half succeeded scrambling earlier that evening.

"The colonel has brought something troubling to my attention. Would you like to explain, Kevin?"

Rachel's gaze flicked to Caleb's. There was nothing there to hint at his thoughts, nothing to alert her to his reaction to the scene that had unfolded here before she joined them. How certain could she be that Caleb wouldn't have accepted Sutherland's description of her supposed duplicity? Nerves fluttered, were ruthlessly suppressed. In a movement designed to express poise, she crossed one leg over the other.

"Miss Grunwald, it has come to our attention that you have been taking an undue interest in some of The Brotherhood's more confidential matters." He rose, spread the pictures across Caleb's desk so each was visible. "Would you care to explain these pictures to us?"

She didn't spare a glance at the pictures, gazing steadily at Sutherland instead. "Would you care to explain how they came to your attention?"

Sutherland blinked, clearly taken aback at the question. "Anna, the housekeeper, found them when she was making your bed today. The envelope was half concealed beneath your mattress and some of the pictures spilled out."

"That was certainly careless of me," Rachel murmured.

"Quite. Anna rightly chose to bring them to my attention, and I, in turn, have alerted General Carpenter." At her silence, his voice went stern. "You have nothing to say about this, Miss Grunwald?"

"Oh, I have plenty to say." She raised a languid hand, began enumerating on her fingers. "One, I can say that you are quite correct. They were somewhat poorly concealed beneath my mattress. Two, you'll find the camera that took the pictures hidden in an equally obvious place. But I don't have to tell you that, do I Colonel? After all, you took the pictures yourself. You, or someone following your orders.''

His gaze widened, and he rose, taking one step toward her. Just one. He halted at the sound of Caleb's voice. "Kevin, return to your seat, please." Sutherland's hands clenched and released.

"Kevin."

The seconds dragged until the man did as he was bade, and he dropped into the chair beside Rachel's. "It's quite apparent what's going on here, General."

"I disagree," Caleb returned, sotto voce. "I admit to having a few questions about the whole thing."

"It might pain you to realize it, sir, but it's obvious that yet another candidate has failed to exhibit the high moral caliber that is imperative in your future mate."

"Because she's taken these pictures."

Caleb picked one up in his hand and Sutherland nodded. "Yes. I don't know for sure what she planned to do with them, but I will admit that I'm uncomfortable with her possible motives considering her previous relationship with Patrick Dixon."

Mention of the man's name sparked an unintended response. Caleb's jaw tightened a fraction, although his voice was deceptively mild. "And what do you make of that relationship?"

"Dixon is still being evasive about his intentions to unify with The Brotherhood. In light of this discovery," he gestured toward the pictures, "one might wonder if he's waiting for some very confidential information about our strength and our holdings. He stands to acquire a much higher standing in our new organization if he can approach us on an equal footing. Prior knowledge of our holdings and capabilities would give him an edge."

Caleb nodded slowly. "Plausible, I suppose." Rachel's attention jerked to him. Was he actually considering Sutherland's smarmy attempt to discredit her? It was impossible to say for sure.

"Could you tell me who found the evidence of the other candidates wrongdoings?" Rachel asked in a cool voice. "It didn't happen to be you, did it, Colonel?"

The naked venom in the man's eye was a little surprising. "As I said, Anna found these photos."

"And the other candidates? Just who was it that discovered one was a thief and the other promiscuous?"

"Your pathetic attempt to shift blame from yourself is ludicrous. My only goal is to be certain that General Carpenter's wife be of the epitome of purity, truly worthy of being his help mate."

"You wouldn't have a more suitable candidate for that position in mind, would you?" It was a shot in the dark, but Rachel knew the remark had hit its target by the stillness that came over the man's face. "Someone like your daughter, perhaps? Would Katherine be considered as worthy of marrying the general?"

"That's not a conversation I'm interested in having with you...."

"But it's one that interests me, Kevin," Caleb said quietly. "Especially in light of the fact that you and I have had that exact conversation before. More than once, in fact." When the colonel remained silent, Caleb went on. "And it would certainly explain this string of coincidences surrounding the unsuitable candidates, wouldn't it?"

Sutherland was rigid in his seat, his gaze focused on Caleb. "General, you can't possibly believe I contrived to deceive you in such a manner."

"What I believe is that you played me for a fool, Kevin." His smile resembled shark's, keen with purpose. "I tolerate that from no man."

There was indignance flitting across the other man's face,

anger, and then, finally, resignation. Slowly rising from his chair, Sutherland stood at attention, looking like a man readying to face a firing squad. ''Deception wasn't the motive here, General, nearly as much as pride. I hope that, whatever you decide, you will spare Katherine from your discipline. She knows nothing about my actions on her behalf. If I'm guilty of anything, it's of wanting too much for her.'' He turned and walked away then, his footsteps the only sound in the stillness of the room. Long after the door had closed behind him, Rachel allowed herself to breathe, feeling like she'd just fought a battle using only smoke and mirrors for weapons. She forced herself to meet Caleb's enigmatic gaze. It was harder than it should have been to ask, ''What will happen to him?''

''He'll be punished in a way I see fit.''

When he said nothing more she wondered if that punishment would include banishment from the compound. Jonah would be interested in that; Sutherland could prove a valuable source of information on The Brotherhood, if he could be made to turn on Carpenter.

''Come here, Rachel.''

The low, dulcet tones had the power to send an electrical current down her spine, flickering across her nerve endings. For her own peace of mind, she withstood the request. ''Will you send him away?''

A frown flickered across his brow, then was gone. ''No. He's too valuable to me for that.'' His eyes slitted then, and he regarded her from beneath his lids with lazy purpose. ''Am I going to have to come over there and get you?'' He reached out a hand, continued coaxing in that dark, seductive tone. ''We have a discussion to continue, remember?''

Transfixed by that low voice, the command in his eyes, it was too easy to convince herself to obey. To walk across the expanse of carpet. To take his hand. To let his fingers curl around her own. With one quick tug he had her on his lap, his arms around her, keeping her close.

She wet her lips in a show of nerves she would have denied. ''How—how will you know whether you can trust Sutherland again?''

His head paused just a moment in its descent toward hers, and the words he spoke were whispered against her lips.

''Because, Rachel, I make it a habit not to trust anyone.''

Chapter 11

It came to Rachel in the middle of the night, as ideas sometimes will when sleep refuses to be summoned. She'd spent the past hour trying to devise a way to search the area around the shooting range. It seemed the logical place to hide the weapons cache, given Tommy's proximity most of the time. Deciding how she was going to accomplish such a task was difficult. It was too far to walk, and, at any rate, if she attempted to do so she would surely be spotted. So she was going to have to confine her search to the daytime hours. However she hadn't yet hit on a successful strategy for doing so.

She shifted restlessly, the rustle of silk against cotton sounding a whisper in the night. Her strategy session might not be conducive to sleep, but keeping her mind busy kept thoughts of Caleb Carpenter at bay. He'd long since made a habit of seeping into her head. It was becoming a full-time job keeping him out of her heart, as well.

But, oh, it was difficult to keep her heart hardened to the man while his dark, mysterious taste still lingered on her tongue; when the feel of his heated touch still shimmered through her system; when her veins even now thudded in response to the memory.

Her reaction to him was totally unprecedented. Nothing in her experience had prepared her for the shattering moment when she began to doubt her own judgment. It was difficult to say when objectivity had eroded; when perceptions had skewed. Surely there could be no other explanation for the lance of ice that had pierced her when he'd whispered those words against her lips.

I make it a habit not to trust anyone.

It took only the memory of his statement to have regret swimming to the surface, battling with reason. Logically she knew his choices had been his own. A man who surrounded himself with assassins and troops on the lunatic fringe couldn't afford to let anyone close. The solitude he was steeped in as a result shouldn't tug at her emotions. It was symptomatic of her evaporating objectivity that it should affect her at all.

Rachel punched the pillow beneath her head, wishing she could banish thoughts of the man from her mind. Her assignment was to discover The Brotherhood's link to Simon. She needed to renew her focus on that connection. She was filled with a growing sense of urgency that had nothing to do with the investigation, and everything to do with her tumultuous feelings for Caleb.

...not to trust anyone...

An idea circled, began to gel. She sat up in bed, rapidly sifting through the possibilities. Did it make sense that Caleb would entrust the vast store of weapons to be hidden miles across the compound, even in the charge of a man he claimed some friendship with? A man who trusted no one—she ruthlessly ignored the pang to her heart—would most likely choose to stay close to the weapons cache. Extremely close.

Throwing the covers back, Rachel swung her legs over

the edge of the bed. Quickly, she exchanged her nightgown for a pair of dark leggings and a hooded sweatshirt. Slipping on a pair of tennis shoes, she found her hands unsteady. Emotion had dulled her instincts. Brutally, she forced herself to face the fact. A month ago the man's words wouldn't have distracted her from forming the conclusion she'd just reached. Her thoughts wouldn't have been clouded by feelings for him, by her own tangled feelings. So much could change in the span of a few short weeks. She refused to consider how long she'd be left to cope with that change after this case ended.

She paused long enough to collect the security detector, a pencil flashlight and her lock-picking tools. She wasn't certain where to look, but she was fairly certain of what she was looking for. There must be a basement under this house, one she'd failed to find in her earlier explorations. If it housed what she hoped to find, she could understand why the man would take such pains to keep it hidden. Silently, she opened her door and crept down the front stairs.

A single splinter of moonlight shone through the window in the front door. Rachel bypassed the hallway and kitchen. She guessed that Caleb would keep the stash close to where he spent most of his time. She headed toward his office.

The floorboard beneath her feet emitted a small sound and she stopped, not breathing. If she encountered anyone she was prepared to offer a story of insomnia, and a late-night walk. But she didn't want to put this off. Something other than logic told her she was on the right track.

When no sound followed the first, she eased into the office, finally allowing herself a breath when she found it empty. An architect faced with planning two concealed rooms, she decided, may well use a similar design for both of them. She spent the next hour and a half fruitlessly searching the wallboards for some clue to an opening.

Silently she moved to the library. Other than the break in the wall to frame the windows, the room was lined with bookshelves. Holding the slim flashlight in her teeth, she used both hands to tug on the individual shelves, and searched for a concealed switch that would release them.

It was on the last wall that she met success. And even expecting it as she did there was still a sense of disbelief when the set of shelves swung soundlessly toward her. With only the thin beam of the penlight to illuminate the paneled wall before her, it took a few minutes to find the almost invisible crack defining the opening of the concealed entrance.

Rachel fumbled for the security detector, moved it along the crack in the wall. Eyes trained on the tool, she paused when its telltale light began winking. Using both hands to steady it, she remained motionless until the light flickered out. Whatever security measures were held within, cameras, alarms, or both, they were deactivated for the moment.

Dropping to her knees, she used the flashlight's beam to focus on the lower left corner of the door, where she'd found the concealed switch on its mate upstairs. In the near darkness it took her long minutes to find. But then she felt the give of a depression beneath her fingers, and the door slid open.

There was no second door behind this panel, only a yawning pit of darkness. The beam of the tiny flashlight was almost ridiculously inadequate against the well of blackness. Picking up the remote, Rachel slipped it into her sweatshirt again and started for the steps.

A draft of cooler air washed over her face. She needed the flashlight to find the steps. Focused as it was at her feet, she had the sensation of being swallowed by the inky darkness as she cautiously made her way. She descended with care, trailing one hand over the wall at her side for balance. It was cold to the touch; concrete walls, just as the picture found in the envelope in her room had depicted.

When she reached the bottom of the steps she swept the area with her beam. The sheer amount and variety of weapons were staggering. Playing her light over the locked glassed-in cupboards lining the wall, she found them stocked with every imaginable kind of firearm. There were a few handguns, high-powered rifles, and shotguns. But the majority were lethal automatic firearms banned in this nation. Guns created with one purpose in mind—mass murder in the time it took to pull a trigger.

The chill tracing down her spine had nothing to do with the cooler air in the basement. Surrounded as she was by the tools of violence, The Brotherhood's stated intention for revolution was sounding less fanatic rhetoric and more like a very real possibility.

Forcing herself to move, Rachel crept down the rows fashioned by stacks upon stacks of unopened crates. She wondered how many more firearms had yet to be unpacked. Surely there was already enough stockpiled here for serious warfare. Yet she'd overheard Caleb speak to Conrad about ordering three times as much ammunition as he had previously to match the new weapons order he planned. Simon must wield a great deal more influence than she'd ever considered, to be able to deliver such huge shipments.

She stopped for a moment and played her light over one of the crates, squinting at the writing on it. Large black letters were stamped across the top. She couldn't make out what the words said, and she leaned forward for closer examination. The writing wasn't illegible, as she'd first thought. These words weren't in English. And although she couldn't read the writing, she could identify the language with some degree of certainty.

Arabic.

Rachel stared at the crate, digesting this new information. The guns were probably Russian or Chinese made, she imagined, easy enough to procure in the Mideast. And with the unrest in that area of the world, she knew for a fact that the arms trade there was lucrative, indeed. So Simon had

contacts in the Mideast. But what did arming The Brotherhood have to do with betraying SPEAR?

Lost in contemplation of that question, Rachel grew belatedly aware of how much time had passed. Quickly she
examined the rest of the area, then ascended the stairs again.
Once the door was closed behind her, she climbed on the
chair still sitting nearby and ran the sensor detector along
the top of the basement entrance. With the security reacti-
vated, she could hope that no one would ever know the place
had been infiltrated. She nimbly jumped down and replaced
the shelves and chair. She flicked the light around the room,
and then, satisfied that she'd left nothing out of place, tucked
the flashlight and remote back into her sweatshirt.

Returning silently to her room, Rachel felt a renewed
sense of purpose. There was no doubt in her mind that she
was nearing the end of her investigation. All that remained
was to find some shred of evidence that would lead them to
Simon.

And for purely personal reasons, the conclusion of this
case couldn't come soon enough.

"Where's that famous sense of adventure?"

"Since when does an astronomy lesson at midnight con-
stitute adventure? I've seen stars before." She'd been gen-
uinely dismayed when Caleb had made the suggestion at
dinner that evening. Cowardly, she'd prefer to spend as little
time in his company as possible. Things were so much
clearer when they were apart. Her sense of clarity had a way
of dimming in his presence. It was becoming increasingly
difficult to separate that easy charm, that quick wit, from the
man committed to revolution. Increasingly confusing to consider the dual facets of his personality.

It was instinct rather than logic that had had her trying to
find reasons to avoid him for the past two days, but her
efforts had been thwarted at every turn. Her plea of exhaustion last night had been met with a plan for a quiet evening

in the library listening to their favorite composers. And this evening…well, she had more to fear from Caleb Carpenter in the moonlight than simple astronomy.

"No, you haven't." Those words, coming so quickly on the heels of her thoughts, had her attention jerking back to him. "At least," he continued, "you haven't seen stars like these. I couldn't believe it myself when I first came out here. Stargazing in a wide-open space like we have here is a novel experience for those of us used to dwelling in huge cities."

"I'll take your word for it." Doubt laced her words, layering the trepidation coursing through her. A moonlit night, a handsome companion, with whom she'd already shared some disturbing moments of intimacy, coupled with her own warring emotions, could be no less than a recipe for disaster. Mentally, she readied her guard. She wouldn't let him tap into that doubt she was increasingly having to silence, the one that insisted, *needed,* to see some good in the man. Instead she focused on what she knew of Caleb's intentions. That should be enough to keep those inner walls raised high.

He pulled to a stop and switched off the jeep's ignition. "Here we are."

Rachel looked at him. In the vehicle's darkness he was no more than a shadowy profile. "This exact spot on the entire compound is the one area suitable to look at the stars? You're certain?"

His teeth gleamed in the dim interior. "I've given this very careful consideration, Rachel. Trust me."

He opened the door, then reached into the back to remove a blanket. She got out of the jeep more slowly. Trust him? The idea was completely foreign to her nature, to her mission. But there was no denying that a part of her yearned to be able to do that very thing. And that same part of her, left unchecked, would certainly lead to her undoing.

She started after him. Only a sliver of moon was visible, making her path more difficult. He waited for her to reach his side, and slipped an arm around her waist to guide her steps as they moved away from the vehicle.

"Where did you get your expertise in astronomy, Caleb?"

"Years of research. My interest caused me to pursue the subject with some diligence." Although she thought she detected a tinge of humor in his words, he said nothing more for a few minutes as they walked. Then he proclaimed, "Here we are. This is the perfect spot to observe the constellations." He laid the blanket on the ground, then sat. Reaching out a hand, he urged her to sit beside him.

Rachel wrapped her arms around her raised knees and tipped her head back, ignoring the senses that sparked and hummed in response to his proximity. The wide expanse of sky was unlike the scanty patches evident between skyscrapers in the city. That was one reason she'd sought a home in the country. The renovated barn was perfect for her. Isolated and peaceful, it was an island of tranquility in her otherwise challenging life.

A quick sense of nostalgia wafted through her, and for an instant she thought of home. She could use a little peace right now, away from the constant battle between reason and emotion. But she realized that the inner war would travel with her. Distance wouldn't lessen the confusion. She wasn't quite sure what would.

"Can you find the North Star?" Rachel couldn't prevent herself from stiffening beneath the casual arm around her shoulders, nor could she prevent the accompanying sensation from skating over her skin. Her gaze trained upward, she nodded, trying to gather scattered nerves.

"No, that's Venus," he replied when she pointed. "Beautiful, isn't it? Over here. See it? Now look to its side, opposite the Big Dipper. That's Cassiopeia. If you look closely you can see an irregular letter *W* formed by five of its brightest stars."

To her surprise, Rachel could see the pattern he described. "What are those stars to the south of it?"

"Andromeda."

"Daughter of Cassiopeia?"

He turned to her, smiled in the darkness. "You know your Greek mythology."

"I remember a smattering of it. What about that one over there?"

"That's Vega, one of the brightest stars, and my favorite. I could see it from my bedroom window when I was a kid. Over there is Saturn. You really need a telescope to appreciate its rings. And there," he reached for her hand, drew out her index finger and guided it, "is Mars, Jupiter, Mercury and Saturn." He shifted her hand as he mentioned each planet, and to her delight, she could see them easily. "You can pick out the planets because of their brightness, and the fact that they shine rather than twinkle like the stars seem to do."

More impressed than she cared to admit, she asked, "Care to share just where this interest in astronomy came from?"

He stretched out beside her, resting on his elbows. "I believe my fascination with heavenly bodies occurred when I was about thirteen."

She managed, barely, to avoid rolling her eyes. "Puberty. Who would have guessed? Did you find teenage girls pretty susceptible to starlight and glib patter?"

"You have a very suspicious nature, Rachel." The feigned hurt in his voice made her want to smile. "I simply enjoyed sharing my appreciation for astronomy with—"

"...other heavenly bodies," she finished with him. "You were obviously a depraved adolescent. No wonder they locked you up."

"I wasn't locked up," he corrected mildly, tucking his arms beneath his head. Although in truth, he thought, it had often felt like it. "I just went to a rather strict academy."

"Uh-huh." Her words were completely devoid of sympathy. "And I'm sure the mothers of teenage daughters in San Francisco slept easier because of it."

"We've already discussed your complete misunderstanding of pubescent boys."

"Oh, I understand all right. I still remember Johnny Franklin walking me home from the library, eager to share his endless fascination with astronomy. After the shortest of lessons, *anatomy* seemed to become his area of expertise."

"What happened?"

She stretched out her legs, crossed them at the ankles. "The shiner he was sporting for the next week caused far more interest than any stars he could have named."

He chuckled, feeling a fleeting sense of sympathy for the unknown young man. "You were a formidable opponent even then, hmm?"

The memory still had the power to ache just slightly. "The incident did bump my reputation up from outcast to surly outcast, so it wasn't without its advantages." She'd seemed like fair game, she imagined, to boys brave enough to dare talk to her. With a father often in the news spouting his bigoted beliefs, she'd been lucky to avoid worse.

He rolled to his side, his head propped on one hand. "Were you lonely?"

"I was alone. There's a difference." Her nonchalant tone hung in the air, sounding like a lie to both of them. Perhaps it was the shrouding darkness that made the truth come easier. "Yes, I was lonely." Even in her own family, *especially* in her own family, she'd felt set apart, foreign. She hadn't understood what had driven her father, or what drew her mother to follow him blindly. Her lack of comprehension had seemed yet another failure at a time in her life when she'd begun questioning everything about herself. Her work for SPEAR had laid many of those old regrets to rest, and soothed the others. Her job as an agent had been the only thing in her life to give her painful childhood some sense of meaning.

Caleb watched her silently. The urge to touch her was strong; the reasons not too even stronger. Physically, of course, he'd been ready soon after they'd met; soon after he'd begun to discover the fascinating appeal of Rachel Grunwald. But emotionally…his mind skittered away from the thought. Rachel would demand all of a man…heart, body, soul. That depth of commitment hadn't been his intention in seeking a bride. He'd been looking for a woman who could help his cause, and with Rachel's background she suited him perfectly. It was all the other areas in which she suited him that made her so alluring. And so damn dangerous.

"I got a phone call after dinner this evening." The change of topic was abrupt, and not the way he'd meant to broach the subject. When it came to Rachel, very little seemed to go according to plan.

"I remember."

"It concerns you. At least, your mother." His words had an immediate reaction. She jerked around to face him, causing him to regret his careless wording. "She's all right. I made a few calls on her behalf, that's all. I've gotten a promise from Francis Thorpe to see her, and oversee her physical therapy program. He has national expertise in the area. I thought he could be helpful to her recovery."

Rachel stared at him in the darkness, speechless. "You made arrangements for her…without telling me?"

Feeling at a disadvantage, Caleb rose to sit. "I wasn't trying to usurp your authority. I just knew how concerned you were about her progress in recovery and I wanted to help." As each moment ticked by in the ensuing silence, he felt increasingly uncomfortable, like a small boy excruciatingly aware of the clumsily wrapped package he offered to the girl he cared about. "Thorpe is white, of course, and his credentials are impeccable. I can go over them with you if you like. He's currently affiliated with the Mayo Clinic in Rochester. I didn't want to mention it to you until I had a firm commitment from him."

She registered his words on some distant level even while

she struggled to comprehend the reasons behind them. "I—I didn't realize... I can't believe you did that. I have been troubled by her lack of progress. But the Good Shepherd has a wonderful staff—they just haven't been able to motivate her to participate in her own recovery."

Feeling on steadier ground, he said, "I kept that in mind when I was researching the experts in the field. Thorpe has published some of his work with patients like your mother. In our conversation I described the difficulty she was having, and he thought he could help her."

Her thoughts still refused to focus, insisting on swirling and colliding within her. But there was no denying the surge of warmth that his effort on her mother's behalf caused. "Thank you." It was all she could manage at the moment. Would she ever understand this man? "Is that what you brought me out here for in the middle of the night?"

Her easy acceptance of his meddling had his lungs easing. "I had many reasons for bringing you out here, but none of them concern your mother." Because he sensed the questions on her lips, he went on. "Stargazing is best done on a clear, moonless night. This one was almost perfect. And—" his smile sounded in his voice "—there's enough of the thirteen-year-old boy inside me to be certain that you'd be exquisite dusted with starlight."

"Ah, ulterior motives again. The man didn't stray so far from the boy, after all."

"Perhaps." His thoughts turned reflective. "I've always found a sense of perspective sprawled on my back contemplating the planets and thinking about my place in the galaxy."

"And were you in need of perspective just now?"

He gazed at her in the darkness, glad she didn't know how close to the target her words were. Because she was absolutely right. Regarding her, he was desperately in need of perspective.

* * *

Tommy stared somberly at Caleb from across the desk. "Have you ordered the next shipment yet?"

"I'm working on it." Caleb, turned the yellow legal pad before him around and pushed it toward the other man. "I think I have everything on here that we discussed."

Picking up the pad, Tommy meticulously perused the lengthy list. "That's everything," he finally concluded, setting the pad down again. "How soon before delivery can be made?"

Caleb shrugged. "Hard to say. Simon is proving elusive. Obviously his other business interests keep him occupied. But when I do speak with him I'll emphasize the urgency of our need."

"We may have to wait for an order that size."

Caleb shook his head. "I have a time line in mind. A lengthy wait is not acceptable. I'll make that clear to him."

But Tommy didn't appear mollified. Over the years Caleb had found the man to be a stickler for details. "How sure are you that he can even deliver a shipment of that size?"

"Believe me, this guy is one of the few who *can* deliver. He's a dependable source—we can count on him."

The other man nodded. "If you say so. There's something else I wanted to talk to you about. Maybe it's nothing, but it's been bothering me. I'm wondering if we should purchase a new security system for the weapons storeroom. Especially with this extra shipment we have coming in."

"Why?" Surprise sounding in his voice, Caleb leaned back in his chair. "You picked that security setup yourself."

The reminder brought a frown to the man's face. "I know. But I found a glitch in the security camera. It may be shorting out. The tape I removed yesterday had a problem. It looked like the camera may have shut off, and then started again."

"I don't claim to be the expert in that area, but I can't imagine a glitch would cause that."

Tommy shook his head. "I don't know either, but there's clearly a spot on the tape where there's a moment of static, before its starts taping again. And when I replace tapes every day, there's usually ten minutes left to run on them. This one had more than forty minutes left."

Mulling the information over, Caleb asked, "Could the tape have been defective?"

Tommy responded, "Maybe. I didn't notice a problem on the one I changed today."

"What about the alarm set on the weapons? Any indication that the alarm system had turned off, then back on?"

Understanding where Caleb was heading, Tommy said, "Not a chance. Something like a power outage would have automatically put the alarm system on backup, and I would be alerted to that when I checked it."

The desk chair squeaked as Caleb leaned back in it. "What are the possibilities that security was breached?"

"Sutherland, you and me are the only ones with the code to activate and deactivate the security system, and you alone have the master code to supersede even that. Unless you've shared it with anyone?"

Shaking his head, Caleb said, "It was my understanding that the code was impossible to be surpassed from the outside."

The other man rolled a shoulder. "I thought about that. I don't like it, but it's probably just a glitch, like I said."

"Give it a couple more days, review the tapes and see if you notice the problem again. If you have even the slightest concern, come back and we'll see about replacing the system. I don't want to take any chances now, especially with the extra shipment we'll be expecting."

Tommy accepted his advice with an incline of his head, but made no move to leave. Instead he gazed at Caleb with his flat stare for long enough to have Caleb raising his brows.

"Something else?"

"Maybe. Might not be my place, but I'm wondering about the woman."

The men exchanged an even look. "The *woman* has a name."

"Rachel Grunwald, then. What are your plans for her?"

Caleb crossed one leg over the opposite knee, meticulously smoothing the crease from his trouser. "I think I've been quite clear with all the troops about my purpose for selecting a bride."

"I remember your purpose perfectly. I was just wondering if it had changed."

Tension filled the room, an almost palpable sense of strain. Caleb's voice was mild, revealing none of the temper trapped inside. "Why don't you get to the point, Tommy? It's obvious that you have one."

"All right." The man inclined his head, his gaze never wavering from Caleb's. "The Brotherhood is in the midst of some very delicate negotiations. But you seem somewhat distracted from the matters at hand."

"Care to expound on that?"

"C'mon, you know what I mean. Trips away from the compound together, moonlit walks…I've seen the way you look at her. Can you really tell me that you're giving your complete attention to the mission laid out before us?"

"Don't let our long-standing relationship cause you to forget who and what you're questioning here." Layered beneath the softness of Caleb's words, was an explosion waiting to detonate. "I'm the man at the helm of The Brotherhood. I haven't lost my focus or my commitment. But you're causing me to believe that perhaps the same can't be said for you."

Mahoney's jaw tightened. "I'm just reminding you that we can't afford to mess things up right now. If you claim things are under control, I'll believe you."

"How generous of you."

Rising, Tommy looked at Caleb one last time. "I'm just

as dedicated to this cause as you are, Caleb. We're too close to everything we've worked for to let it slip through our fingers because of one woman. She's a tool, nothing more.''

"I'm perfectly aware of Rachel's reason for being here. I suggest you attend to your duties and trust me to do the same."

The two men exchanged a long look before Tommy nodded and strode from the room. It took a conscious decision for Caleb to relax the fingers that had curled into a fist. He didn't need anyone reminding him of his obligations. He'd given his life to achieving his objectives. Despite his family's continuing inability to understand the compulsion that drove him, he'd spent years working to just this point. He'd never put all he'd fought for at risk. Not even for Rachel Grunwald.

But there had been a thread of truth in the man's words that resonated with Caleb, and he couldn't refute them even if he wanted to. Rachel *was* a distraction. He'd long admitted that. She was an enigma he was desperate to solve, a woman he was equally desperate to possess. He could damn Tommy for questioning Caleb's focus, but he couldn't deny that his relationship with Rachel went far beyond what was The Brotherhood's original intent. The time had long passed when she could be considered merely a tool. He'd struggled with that knowledge for some time now.

But despite Mahoney's doubts, Caleb's commitment to his goals hadn't faltered. The distraction Rachel posed wouldn't interfere with his plans. Her future was entwined, irrevocably, with his. He was willing to go to great lengths to prove that to her. He was, in fact, looking forward to it.

Chapter 12

The soft lips against the back of her neck were instantly recognizable, but it was instinct that had Rachel twisting around in her seat with her fork raised threateningly.

Caleb backed away, his hands raised in mock surrender. "Don't hurt me."

Feeling slightly foolish, she lay down her puny weapon. "You should know better than to sneak up on people like that. You're lucky I heard you coming."

Eyes gleaming, he dropped down in the chair beside her and snitched a strip of bacon from her plate. "Liar. You were completely lost in your thoughts. Daydreaming about me?"

"Hardly." She managed the wry tone despite the kernel of truth in his guess. *Daydreaming* would hardly be an applicable description. *Agonizing* would be closer.

"You're a tough woman. What does a guy have to do to impress you?"

It was, she thought, a peculiarly apt question. Several weeks ago she wouldn't have been able to think of a single example. But now they crept into her mind, stealthy as thieves—a trip to Philadelphia, when he could ill afford to leave the compound; fussing over Rachel after the jeep accident; and most confounding, arranging for an expert to tend to her mother. She was still struggling with the ramifications of that one.

Aware that he awaited an answer, she replied, "There was a man who impressed me once." She waited for his gaze to narrow before adding blandly, "He managed to scale the Sears Tower with little more than a harness and grip boots."

"Spider Man?"

She swallowed a chuckle. "No."

"Whoever he was, when he came down again I'm certain they were waiting for him with a straitjacket."

The smile broke free. "I believe he was evaluated, yes."

"Which only goes to show—" he reached over for a piece of her toast "—that climbers are crazy. I've known it for years. You'd do well to temper your passion for heights. No good will come of it."

"There goes my plan to invite you climbing down the canyon wall."

He managed, barely, to resist a shudder. "Thank God."

She was just quick enough to save the last piece of bacon from his encroaching fingers. "Did someone forget to feed you this morning?"

"Strangely enough, I find my appetite heightened around you."

With effort, she succeeded in swallowing around the boulder-size knot in her throat. She knew him well enough to know the innuendo was planned and not quite playful. The knowledge had her system, already weakened by that one light kiss, jittery with nerves. It took all her considerable poise to look directly into his gaze and suggest, "If you're feeling uptight I'd be glad to work out with you at the gym again. Some men find it relaxing to have their butts whipped on the mats."

His smile settled in his eyes. "While the thought of wrestling with you again, sweaty and half-naked, does hold a certain appeal, I have business to attend to."

"What sort of business?"

He reached out, amused when she moved to protect the last piece of toast on her plate, and settled for taking her hand instead. "I need to make a perimeter observation. I usually try to do one every couple of weeks. I thought you could come with me." He must have read the reluctance on her face. "If you have plans today, I can postpone the task until tomorrow."

Since he appeared determined that she join him, she shrugged. "I don't have any other plans today."

"Good." He brought her hand to his lips, nipped at her knuckles. "Shorts are fine, but bring a sweatshirt in case it cools off. I'll have Eliza pack a picnic lunch."

It was hard to say which had her senses swirling, the warm heat of his mouth, or his words. "Picnic? Is... I mean..." she corrected lamely, when he looked at her quizzically, "...are we going to be gone that long?"

"Several hours, I expect. Long enough to get hungry." He took advantage of the nerveless grasp she had on the toast to reach for it, take a bite, and hand it back. With a wink, he started from the room. "I believe in being prepared, at any rate. Be ready to leave in an hour."

Rachel told herself that this outing with Caleb could prove fruitful. If nothing else, it would give her a chance to observe the security of areas on the compound that had been difficult for her to do on her own. That benefit, of course, was offset by having to spend several hours in close proximity with him.

There was nothing she could do about the nerves jumping in her stomach, except to be sure her anxiety didn't show. After last night, and the offer he'd made her, she didn't know what to make of the man. Why would he go out of his way to help a woman who was, by The Brotherhood's standards, part of the unworthy they were committed to eliminating? It made no sense to her. Either his views were flexible, swaying to convenience, or he was willing to put his feelings for Rachel ahead of his own beliefs.

It was the last possibility that was the most seductive, and it was a measure of her lack of objectivity that she would even consider it. She tried, and failed, to remember one time in her life when another person had set her feelings above their own.

This pattern of thought was insidious, creeping into her subconscious, capable of softening her toward a man with views diametrically opposed to her own. In some ways he was very much like her father, with his attitudes about white supremacy and the lengths he'd go to accomplish his goals. But it was Caleb's other traits that muddied the waters and made her dubious about her own perception. It was much easier to retain dispassion about a subject when that target had few redeeming characteristics, and certainly no tender ones. It was tougher to separate the acts from the man when his enticing qualities were as apparent as those she found so abhorrent.

"You're quiet. Did I keep you out too late last night?"

She shook her head. "I slept in this morning."

"I noticed." His voice was wry. "I'd already completed a dozen phone calls and some correspondence before I heard you at breakfast."

Unwilling to let an opportunity slip by she prompted, "I hope the phone calls netted good news."

"Actually, among others, I heard from Dixon." He made no effort to keep the satisfaction from his voice. "I have his commitment to join our unity effort, with a few details to be ironed out at a later date."

Rachel could well imagine what details he was referring to. Unless Patrick Dixon had changed a great deal since she knew him, he'd be finagling for a position of power in the unified group.

She reached out a hand to lower the temperature on the air conditioner. "What about the others?"

"Word of Dixon's alignment with us spread quickly. We've achieved one hundred percent membership pledged from the western militias we've contacted."

A wave of nausea twisted viciously in her stomach. "Your achievement is remarkable." And it truly was. As individually as most of the supremacy groups operated, it was nothing short of astonishing that all major organizations in the western states were willing to join with The Brotherhood to create a new entity. Surely it was a mark of Caleb's standing among the branches; with his finances and plans as the foundation, the unity effort seemed much more like a frightening reality.

It took more effort than it should have for Rachel to chat normally with Caleb, to ignore the questions and confusion that continued to plague her. When he stopped, she got out of the jeep and stayed close to his side as he checked the supervision logs and talked to the guard on duty, Private Eppley.

Flipping through the pages in the log, Caleb was silent for several minutes while the guard stood at attention. Then he looked up, handed the log back to the guard and nodded. "Everything looks to be in order, Eppley. Anything to report?"

"No, sir. Haven't seen no sign of trespassers, other than a coyote we chased off last night."

"Excellent." Caleb turned, prepared to leave. "Just don't let the duty get to be routine. That's when mistakes can be made."

"Won't be no spics sneaking by on my watch, sir."

"Good man. If anything out of the ordinary turns up on your watch, I want to be notified immediately."

The soldier's answer drifted after them as they made their

way back to the jeep. It was lost, at any rate, amidst the earlier slur he'd made so matter-of-factly. The one Caleb accepted so nonchalantly.

This was what she'd needed to observe, Rachel told herself. Something to remind her of the reason for her presence here. She'd never discovered the fate that had befallen the trespassing Hispanics the first day she'd come to the compound. But it was a measure of how much she'd changed in that she'd been prepared to believe Caleb capable of murder at that time; now, despite the scene she'd just witnessed, she was unable to imagine it.

Had she come to understand him so well, or were her growing feelings for the man shrouding her judgment? She already knew the answer to that question. It wasn't one guaranteed to put her at ease.

Over the course of their journey, she was able to observe that the posts were located approximately twenty miles apart, with fewer guards stationed along the canyon's ridge, and double the number on the two sides edged by the Sawtooth Mountains. After several stops, Rachel concluded that the guard rotation took place every eight hours, and continued around the clock. Their schedule appeared similar to that of the guards posted closer to the house. Caleb made no effort to check with those charged with the security gate in front, and when she questioned him about it he said that he checked their logs daily. No other information was needed, at any rate. She'd gotten close enough on a couple of occasions, and aided by the nightscope, had never observed fewer than a dozen sentries posted across the front of the property.

When it came to security measures on The Brotherhood of Blood compound, Rachel was well aware of the efforts taken. Today's outing answered whatever questions she had left. For some reason, the extent of her knowledge failed to satisfy.

Caleb steered the jeep toward the southern border of the

property. "Can you wait a while longer to eat, or are you ready to start gnawing on the picnic basket?"

She edged away from the hand he would have placed on her knee, feigning an interest in the scenery. "I'm really not very hungry yet." It was no more than the truth. The thought of food did nothing for the nerves clutching and grinding in the pit of her stomach.

"Good." He drove with speed and control, and with the expertise that was so much a part of him. "I want to take you to one of my favorite spots on the property."

"I thought we visited that spot last night."

"That was the best spot to watch the stars," he corrected her. "We're going to the best spot to picnic and laze away what's left of the afternoon."

"I hope this appreciation of nature, unlike your interest in astronomy, doesn't stem from your adolescent fantasies."

"Brat." The rebuke was mild and laced with amusement. "Wait until you see the spot. I guarantee it'll impress even you. I was going to show it to you one other time, but we got sidetracked by your discovery of the shooting range." They drove in silence for a time until they were at the foothills of the mountains. Then Caleb brought the jeep to a halt. Rachel watched him retrieve the picnic lunch Eliza had packed, and a blanket. "We have to hike from here," he said in response to her questioning look. "It's a spot near the pass, totally secluded. It's a ways, but I promise it will be worth it."

Rachel was much slower to get out of the jeep, his words causing needles of unease to dart through her chest. *Secluded.* It shouldn't matter. She tried to shake off the feeling of trepidation. Caleb had already shown himself, on more than one occasion, to be respectful of her wishes. Physically at least, she knew she could trust him. She just wished she was as certain that she could trust herself.

The path they followed was strenuous enough to make conversation nonexistent. It was a good twenty minutes before the underbrush they waded through gave way to a clear area, surrounded on two sides by steep mountains.

"Over here." Caleb pointed, then plunged ahead. Rachel stopped, cocking her head. She thought she heard water running. Curiously, she followed Caleb into a clearing sheltered by some large rock formations, then stopped again, amazed.

Water trickled off the side of the rocks and formed a small brook, which twisted through the clearing, disappearing into a large crevice at the base of the mountain. The pastoral scene was so unlike the rest of the compound, she blinked in astonishment. "It's beautiful."

While she stared, Caleb laid out the blanket and opened the picnic lunch Eliza had prepared. "I told you," he said, with only a hint of smugness. "How about it? Impressive?"

"Very." She joined him on the blanket, took the sandwich he handed her. "Are there any other spots like this on the compound?"

Caleb bit into a sandwich with huge enjoyment, and shook his head. "Not that I know of. That's part of its magic— it's totally unexpected in this location." He watched her as she paid far greater attention to the scenery than to her food, and he thought the same words could be applied to Rachel. Certainly she wasn't what he'd bargained for when he'd advertised for a wife. There was no doubt that she could fill the position as specified, but there was more, much more to be found with her than that. He'd never contemplated emotions getting in the way of his goals, but that was before he'd met her; before he'd gotten close to her.

"How did you happen to find this place?"

It took a moment for him to gather his thoughts, another for him to answer. "Actually I found it by accident. What are you doing?" He made a grab for the bag in her hand, missing as she held it out of his reach. "You can't break open the cookies before you've eaten your sandwich."

"Wanna bet?" Sitting cross-legged on the blanket she

ripped open the bag of fresh cookies Eliza had baked and waved one in front of him. "Tempted?"

He was. Almost overwhelmingly so. "I distinctly remember my grandmother informing my mother that eating courses out of order made for poor manners, and worse digestion."

Contemplating that, Rachel took a bite of the cookie and chewed with something approaching ecstasy. "And did your mother believe her?"

"She believed everything my grandmother said. Still does. It was like having a well-oiled army come after me when the two of them confronted me about some misdeed."

And those misdeeds, she had to remind herself, were legion, with even more in the works. Her sudden burst of appetite vanished. She couldn't allow herself to be blinded by his charm, unexpected kindnesses and easy personality, not when she'd witnessed repeated episodes of his bigotry; had listened to him proclaim his intent to start a racial war. Never in all her years as an agent had she been swayed from her purpose by dwelling on a target's better qualities. Never had she found it so difficult to reconcile two opposites of the whole, and focus only on the part that mattered to her investigation.

A small wad of paper whizzed by her cheek. Glancing up she saw Caleb, legs outstretched, his hand in the bag of cookies, watching her. "You were a million miles away. Worried about your mother?"

"No," she murmured. Her attempt to regain her objectivity wavered yet again. "I'm sure she's going to be in good hands."

He cocked his head. "You didn't eat much."

"I guess all this fresh air has made me more sleepy than hungry."

"Come here."

Her eyes flew wide open at the low command, senses immediately alert. "Not on your life."

"Rachel, I'm hurt." His tone certainly didn't reflect his claim. On the contrary, the words were full of laughter. "You really are going to have to curb your suspicious nature. I was merely going to offer a back rub. Maybe you can doze off."

It was that suspicious nature that he was decrying that provided the only type of defense she could muster with him these days, and even then it was proving woefully inadequate. Common sense may be in short supply recently, but feminine instinct shrieked a warning she had every intention of heeding. Defenses dangerously shaky wouldn't be sturdied inviting Caleb's touch.

"I'm fine over here."

"You do look fine." The admiration in his words distracted her from his easy agreement. Too easy. A moment later he moved, a blur of motion, grasped her ankle and tugged her closer. When she would have rolled away, he reversed his position and landed above her.

His face was close; too close. Teeth flashing, male smugness stamped on his face, he was asking for an upset. She drew in a quick breath, found her lungs strangled, her limbs strangely weak. "I really don't find wrestling conducive to a good nap."

"You're right. It can be oddly…stimulating." The smile left his eyes as he pushed a strand of hair away from her face with one finger. "It's hard to decide if you're more exquisite under the stars or in full sunlight. It's a question I could commit myself to researching—" his face lowered to hers "—much more closely."

She, was, she told herself, braced for his touch. His lips pressed against hers, and the accompanying onslaught of sensation called her a liar. Her fingers speared into his hair, dragging him closer, and she lost herself to pleasure.

His mouth was lazy at first, coaxing, with just a hint of demand that tasted like an intoxicating dare. She met that dare with one of her own, gliding her tongue along his.

Teeth clashed, lips melded, and dark flavors rose. The semblance of ease was shattered. Fires too long banked took little to flame and immediately Rachel realized her mistake. There was no readying herself for this, no thought, no concern for defenses. There was only speed, desire hurtling to the surface, surpassing logic and reason. She shuddered when he deepened the kiss, and dived recklessly into the passion they created together.

Reckless falls, a dim alarm reminded her, had only heartbreak waiting at the bottom.

She tore her mouth away from his, and relentlessly his lips pursued. Her breath coming in gasps, she raised a shaky hand to his chest, but failed to find the strength to exert pressure. His lips cruised her jaw, her throat, until infinitesimally he became aware of her hesitation.

She could feel the power raging through him as he fought with control and desperation. The same battle waged within her, so much so that her body was trembling against his. There was one brief moment when he pressed against her, as if absorbing those shudders with taut, tense muscles quivering with restraint. And then, in a move as sudden as the one that had begun this, he moved away.

Rachel pressed her lips together to still their trembling. Neither spoke. The air was strained, throbbing with unfulfilled need, turbulent emotions. Ragged fists of frustration twisted in her belly, and a quick glance at Caleb was almost her undoing. There was a sheen of perspiration on his face, and his eyes... Lord help her, his eyes had darkened to midnight. All that frothing crashing energy was visible in his gaze.

Without constant volition, her hand went to his arm, where the muscles clenched and jumped at her touch. "Caleb—"

"Don't." Because the word reflected the savagery that he was still working to bank, he took a deep breath. "I told you before I'd respect your wishes." The words tasted like a lie while mixing with the flavor of her that still lingered on his tongue. "There's nothing more to be said."

Her hand dropped away and she lay back, uncertain. It was painful to watch the need chase over his expression, particularly when she knew the emotion was reflected on her own face.

Her eyes closed to block out the sight, but pictures of him fragmented beneath her eyelids. She was acutely aware of his ragged breathing, hearing attuned to the conscious effort he made to slow it. It didn't help that his struggle for control so closely mirrored her own, or that regret shimmered, dark and persistent, churning with emotions she'd rather not feel, and couldn't quite control.

Minutes ticked by, one melding into the other. The brook murmured nearby, the birds called to one another in the distance. The sounds were easier to focus on, and far more calming. As devastating as those few desperate moments had been, it was even more shattering to acknowledge how little restraint she'd possessed. In only a few more moments there would have been no turning back...for either of them. And while Caleb would have no trouble dealing with the aftermath of their lovemaking, she was certain that she'd be left destroyed.

The sunlight caressed her skin, and the small sounds of nature acted as a lullaby. She dozed, that curious stage between wake and sleep, and was unable to find peace from Caleb even there. He'd lodged deep into her subconscious. Somewhere in the dim recesses of her mind she knew that she'd never be completely free of him.

Distantly, she was aware when he rose. Still he said nothing to disrupt her, and Rachel could feel herself sliding down the steep path of slumber, until something alerted her, and niggled at her consciousness. He was moving away.

It took more effort than it should have to force her eyes open, and then to make them focus. Turning her head, she spotted him making his way toward the pass. But he wasn't striding openly. His movements were stealthy.

All drowsiness vanished. Even when Caleb was far enough away to not have to worry about awakening her, his movements remained furtive. Senses sharpened, Rachel rose to follow him. If there was something he didn't want her to see, she was doubly certain she wanted to witness it.

Using the large boulders scattered nearby for cover, Rachel followed Caleb to the base of the mountain, and beyond. Something rustled in the brush beneath her feet and she ducked for cover, hoping he was too far away to have wondered at the noise. When Rachel finally dared to start after him again, she rounded the rock she'd used for concealment and then halted abruptly in her tracks.

Some distance away, Caleb had stopped as well, and was conversing with someone. Rachel's fingers crept to the small of her back, unconsciously reaching for a weapon that wouldn't be there. Because the person Caleb was talking to was a woman. And she was Hispanic.

Disconnected thoughts and fears veered across her mind, and rational thought had to dodge emotions. The scene that took place in Caleb's office the first day of her arrival rose in her memory, and with it came the doubts she'd long entertained about the conclusion of that meeting.

Caleb stepped toward the woman and Rachel tensed, everything in her surging upward in vehement denial. She wouldn't, *couldn't,* believe that he would hurt an unarmed woman, regardless of his racial views. Even as she poised to act, she refused to contemplate that her worst fears were being realized.

In the next moment he reached into his pocket and withdrew a slip of paper, which he handed to the woman. Rachel watched, thunderstruck, as he put his hand on the unknown woman's shoulder and spoke to her, his gaze intent and serious on her face. The woman nodded and smiled, and made a reply. And through spiked adrenaline and heightened senses, came a realization that pounded home its truth.

The meeting was amicable.

Torn between hope and disbelief, Rachel stared as the woman began to back away, still smiling and talking. Belatedly, she became aware that Caleb would be making his return soon, and she slipped away, returning to the blanket covertly.

She reached the site of their picnic, and dropped weakly to the blanket, resuming her earlier position, and feigned sleep. When Caleb returned he would see nothing out of place, nothing changed. But a change had not only occurred, it had rocketed through Rachel's system, to be joined with a deeply feminine rejoicing she didn't completely understand.

She felt…validated. Her instincts hadn't gone completely faulty, derailed by the man's culture, wit and charm. There *was* something decent in Caleb Carpenter, perhaps even something he would refuse to admit to. The scene she'd just witnessed was yet one more piece of a puzzle that still made no sense. But it was impossible to continue rejecting that genuine goodness existed in the man. She'd seen evidence of it time and again. She just hadn't trusted in it.

She sensed his presence a few moments before she felt his lips on hers, brushing lightly. When he would have moved away, her lips parted beneath his, inviting him to linger. It was an invitation he didn't resist. The warning alarm still buzzed somewhere in the recesses of her mind, but it was muted now, by equal amounts of confusion and wonder. There was satisfaction in knowing that her judgment hadn't been completely impaired. He was a man of enigma, and she was a woman with her own secrets. But whatever the future held, she'd never again doubt that slice of decency in him was real, not imagined.

Caleb gathered her closer, and deepened the kiss. It would have taken the strength of a plaster of paris saint to resist the temptation of Rachel's lips, and he'd never pretended to be a martyr. He cupped her jaw, her throat, and felt the delicate pulse beat against his palm. Every pulse point inside him throbbed in response.

This woman called to him, in a way as primal and ancient as the land surrounding them. The urge to mate was keen and pure, a savage churning of desire that was wrenching and intensely personal. It wasn't any woman who could satisfy him now; it was only Rachel. She was responsible for the ache low in his belly. She was the cause of the tight fist of need clenching his lungs.

He indulged himself by nipping lightly at her mouth, fingers moving nimbly up her blouse, releasing the front catch of her bra. And then smooth satiny skin was bared to the crisp air and his hands were free to touch. To explore.

The perfect breasts he cupped were surely made for his hands, his possession. Her narrow waist curved in a natural indentation he ached to claim. Desire, edgy and fierce, sharpened talons in his gut, and control was forgotten as lips and fingers went on a sensual journey.

Rachel found it difficult to summon reason with Caleb's heated mouth at her breast, pleasuring her with each hot pull of his lips. He was the same man she'd feared becoming involved with, and yet he was more. The doubts she'd long harbored hadn't dissipated. But they were joined now by certainty of an equally compelling, if contrasting, goodness in him. Head battled heart; instinct warred with logic. But it was the memory of those unexplained decent qualities of his that tempered the doubts and had her responding to his touch in an untempered response.

His mouth ate at hers with a pent-up hunger that was all the more thrilling for its fierceness. Rachel reveled in his ferocity. Some women would want tenderness this first time, some would want wooing. All Rachel wanted was raw emotion, honest and undisguised. It was, perhaps, the only honesty they could offer each other.

The razored edge of his desire honed her own and her mouth twisted under his, just as hot, just as searching. Speed and desperation were a heady mix. Rachel and Caleb rose to their knees, arms entwined around each other, lips urgent. Her fast, impatient hands tugged at his shirt, desperate for the feel of his skin. Caleb made short work of the task by pulling his shirt off and tossing it aside. Rachel leaned into him, their groans mingling at the first touch of heated flesh to heated flesh.

Caleb pressed her back until she lay on the blanket and made a place for himself between her thighs. This was no gentle seduction; Rachel's need was as strong and demanding as everything else about her. She matched him, stroke for stroke, longing for longing. Every reckless craving he had was indulged, returned. There would be no submission, from either of them. It would be a race until every vicious need, long controlled, was quieted.

He lowered his head and smoothed his lips over the scar that curved across the top of one breast. Then he took the nipple between his lips. Her low moan stoked a savage need he had to please her, and himself. He smoothed his other hand inside the leg of her shorts, along a length of silky thigh, dipped his fingers beneath the elastic of her panties and cupped her moist heat.

The shock of the intimate touch had her back arching off the blanket, her hips twisting toward him. It was a moment before she could focus beyond the knot forming low in her belly, the sudden clawing hunger. But her pleasure would be measured by how much she gave as well as received. Her hands went in search of his waistband, loosened it, then found him to circle, mold, possess.

His world went abruptly gray. He pulled away to divest them of the rest of their clothes and the battle took on an increased urgency for them both. Hot mouth to fevered skin, the scrape of teeth, pulses whipping in unison. He filled both hands with her, molding her with his touch. She found him with teasing fingers, gliding, smoothing, stroking.

He obeyed her urging and lay on his back, the breath searing through his lungs when she straddled him. In a sensual explosion, she dominated his every sense. Her scent was in the air, her breath coming in short heady pants. The sunlight dappled her body, and he knew he would never remember this place again without the vision of her swamping his senses.

He retained just enough sanity to reach for his discarded jeans, remove the shiny foil packet. Rachel sheathed him, then lowered herself to him, one torturous inch at a time, until he was sheathed again, within her tight moist heat. He could feel her inner muscles clench and release, tiny, infinitesimal adjustments to their position, and his last remaining semblance of control shattered. His fingers curled on her hips and he gave a violent surge upward that she met, matched. And then the race began in earnest, with each of them warring to bring the greatest pleasure to the other before the sharp spear of release destroyed them both. Clinging to his own dwindling control he lunged upward into her, over and over. She braced her palms on his shoulders and stayed with him, movement for movement, as their bodies bucked and strained together.

The wildness of their passion vibrated within them, reckless energy that pulled and pounded and punished. She was greedy in the pleasure she took from him, relentless in the pleasure she returned.

He felt her movements quicken, her body tighten. He reached out for her and found her slick dampness, and stroked her to a shuddering violent release. The pulsations of her climax worked his own. He was helpless to stop himself from tumbling over the edge with her.

Awareness returned one gossamer layer at a time. Caleb's lips brushed Rachel's hair, his hand slid possessively over her hip, returned to stroke. It was amazing, he thought, that hunger, so recently assuaged, could stir again so quickly. Stunning to realize that even now he doubted his ability to let her go. The decision he made then came from no conscious level, but from a deeper more primal part of him that he hadn't been aware existed.

"I think," he said, stroking her delicate spine lightly, "that it's time to end this engagement."

Comprehension lagged for several moments. When his words finally registered, Rachel lifted her head, met his gaze with her own.

"Tonight," he drew one finger down the curve of her jaw, satisfaction filling his words, "we get married."

Chapter 13

The house seemed to vibrate with activity. The servants bustled about, following unknown orders, one dodging the other as preparations were made. A steady stream of people paraded through the house—Sutherland, whom she hadn't seen except from a distance since he'd confessed to trying to discredit her—Mahoney, others who were strangers to her, and a man Eliza identified as the Chaplain of the Faith.

It was the sight of the chaplain disappearing into Caleb's office that had Rachel heading for her room. The surreal situation was beginning to take on a measure of all too frightening reality.

She was marrying Caleb Carpenter.

Her room seemed an oasis of calm after the commotion downstairs. She paced across the floor and back, driven by a need to move. How had this situation moved so rapidly out of control? Although she'd known the pretenses under which she'd ostensibly come to the compound, she'd had no intention of going through with the ceremony. A month had been plenty of time to wind up the investigation, or so she'd

thought. But Caleb had rushed things a bit with his procla-
mation that afternoon. And she'd let him.

Putting a hand to her grinding stomach, she forced herself
to take a breath. She caught a look at her reflection in the
mirror then, eyes wide and dazed. Dammit, she *wasn't* that
woman, never had been, refused to be. She was in control
of every situation in a case, or else she found a way to turn
it to her advantage. She wasn't some love-struck adolescent
waiting for her prince to sweep her off her feet.

Love-struck. Oh, God. Oxygen seemed in short supply
and her lungs felt strangled. Comprehension punched
through her like a sneaky left jab.

She was in love with Caleb Carpenter.

How had this happened to her, of all people? With her
background she'd been the perfect agent to take this case.
What did it say about her that she hadn't been able to forgive
her parents their flaws, yet fell for Caleb, who shared the
worst of them?

But even as the question sounded in her mind, she rejected
it. She wasn't sure what Caleb was. Not completely. But
she'd come to realize that there was far more to the man
than she'd previously believed, more even than Jonah knew.
There was an inherent decency in Caleb that contrasted with
his venomous views, an uncompromising honesty that was
evident even when he had secrets in his eyes, on his lips.
She'd worried that her professional judgment had completely deteriorated. Perhaps, instead, it was time to take a
step back and readjust her focus on the man and his role
here.

The plan eased her lungs, and she began to pace again.
There was renewed purpose in her movements, in her
thoughts. She still needed to prove Simon's link as The
Brotherhood's arms supplier, but her objective had become
two-fold. While she looked for such a connection, she'd also
unravel the truth about Caleb.

Checking her watch she discovered that it was six-thirty.

The ceremony was scheduled for nine o'clock, before the assembled troops. From the looks of things downstairs, Caleb would be kept busy with details for some time yet. And with the adrenaline pounding through her veins, staying here doing nothing was not an option.

She went to retrieve the pencil flashlight and small packet of lock-picking tools, and tucked them inside her waistband, under her shirt. Somewhere on this compound existed the evidence she needed to prove Simon's involvement and explain the mystery surrounding Caleb. She wasn't going to put off the opportunity to search for either.

Unlocking the adjoining bathroom door between her and Caleb's room, she peeked her head in. It was empty, as she'd assumed. Losing no time, Rachel crossed to the secret panel and within a couple of minutes had both the doors opened. Practice, as they said, did indeed make perfect.

Carefully closing both doors behind her, Rachel shone the flashlight around the concealed room. She had to believe that Caleb kept more detailed records than what she'd found so far. It made sense that those records, in whatever form they were, might be kept in one of the most highly secure places on the compound.

She prowled up and down the aisles constructed by the stacked crates of munitions. It quickly became apparent that there was nothing inside the room besides the boxes, but one discovery gave Rachel hope.

There was an electrical outlet on each of the walls.

Standard blueprints called for outlets in each living space in a house, but she wasn't sure this area qualified as such. She was hoping the outlets meant something else. Tapping the flashlight against her palm, she considered the possibilities. The most likely one was that Caleb kept another computer, one with much more sensitive files. The type of files that just might contain the answers to all of her questions.

The crates would have to be searched. Rachel stifled a sigh. There wasn't a lot of room to move around, and trying to move these heavy crates silently, if she could move them at all, was going to be a chore.

Never one to back down from a challenge, she chose the crates lined closest to the outlet for her starting point. But she'd no sooner laid hands on the top one than she froze, one muscle group at a time.

There were sounds right outside the doors.

She snapped off the flashlight, barely daring to breathe, and crept closer to the entry to the room, straining her ears. The noises came again, and they were unmistakable. Someone was about to enter the room.

Caleb. She slipped through the darkness of the cramped enclosure, picking the farthest corner in which to conceal herself. She would have thought he'd be occupied for the next couple of hours, easily. He'd shooed her from the office while he took care of all the details for the evening. It had seemed a perfect opportunity to take care of a little detail of her own, but she'd allowed her eagerness to overcome caution.

A minute ticked by. Two. Three.

She let at least ten minutes crawl by, then moved silently to the entrance again and listened. The sounds were still present; someone was obviously trying to get in.

But it wasn't Caleb.

Anyone who was supposed to have access to the room would surely know how to open the panel; would certainly have a key to the second door. Whoever was attempting to gain entry was trying it the old-fashioned way, just as she had—by breaking in.

Brows skimming upward, she contemplated her conclusion in the darkness. The more she thought about it, the less likely it seemed that someone would try breaking in for the ammo. So that meant she wasn't the only one looking for much more.

It took long moments for her consideration to be interrupted by a realization of even greater ramifications.

She was trapped.

And as long as someone was outside this room trying to get in, she wouldn't be going anywhere.

Caleb stood on the porch and took stock of the progress that had been made in the front yard. As ordered, men had erected the dais, and the finishing touches were being put on the decorations. Flowers from the garden adorned every imaginable corner of the area. Sets of tiny twinkling lights had been strung, a vague reminder of the stars he and Rachel had sat beneath just nights before. Sweeping the area with an assessing gaze, he was satisfied that his directions had been carried out to the letter.

The troops began filing into place before the stage. He resisted the urge to look at his watch. He'd finished changing and returned downstairs some twenty minutes ago, but Rachel hadn't yet made an entrance. As a matter of fact, he hadn't seen her since they returned to the house earlier that afternoon. He refused to let that fact shake him. Given only a few hours warning in which to prepare for her wedding, she was entitled to every minute.

Wedding. He sipped from the glass of wine he'd carried outside with him and concentrated on its smooth taste. Everything was in place now. Every plan, years in the making, was unfolding without a hitch. This ceremony, joining him to a woman with impeccable background, gave his organization a broader, additional appeal. The strategy had been meticulously crafted for the good of The Brotherhood, designed without a specific woman in mind. He was finding it a completely different matter entirely to contemplate the ceremony with Rachel as his bride.

His fingers tightened on the stem of the wineglass, the only outward sign of the nerveless energy singing through him. With Rachel involved, the marriage was far more than a mere convenience, another rung achieved en route to an objective. She complicated matters in a way he hadn't previously considered possible. He hadn't planned for the eventuality of emotion entering into his design. Emotions were messy, dangerous things that fogged reason and made fools of lesser men. He'd never been particularly susceptible to them. But if he wasn't mistaken, they were exerting a firm grip on him now.

Chaplain of the Faith Steven Davis approached him, his tall thin frame slightly stooped as he walked up the steps. Caleb watched him impassively. The man owed his title to the office The Brotherhood had bestowed on him, and he took it seriously.

"General." The chaplain's voice was respectful. "It's just about time to begin."

Caleb did check his watch then, and saw the man was correct. It was two minutes to nine. "The bride needs a little more time."

The chaplain took off his glasses and wiped them fussily with his handkerchief. "I would have preferred to have been able to meet with her beforehand, as I did with you. She wasn't in her room when I went to do so."

Caleb frowned. He'd gone in her room himself before he'd gone to change, to surprise her with flowers for her bouquet. She'd been absent then, too.

"This is a very big step and I really would prefer to go over the vows with her before I—"

"Rachel understands her vows." Caleb cut the other man off. That was, after all, what had brought her here, wasn't it? To become the wife of the powerful General Carpenter, to provide heirs for the future of the white race? He couldn't yet make the claim that he understood all there was to know about Rachel Grunwald, but he knew enough to be certain that nothing would shake her commitment, once made. And she'd come to The Brotherhood voluntarily to become committed to him.

It wasn't, he discovered, nearly enough. Downing the wine under Davis's disapproving eye, Caleb decided that the commitment he needed from Rachel entailed far more than he'd originally planned. Visions of that afternoon were indelibly stamped on his mind. Visions of Rachel under him, astride him. The accompanying surge of possessiveness was unfamiliar, and impossible to suppress. He needed to believe that she'd offered herself to Caleb that afternoon, not General Carpenter. He wanted to think that her desire had been for the man, not the office, and had sprung from something far deeper than the shared beliefs which had brought her here. He refused to accept less from her.

"General." The glasses planted firmly on the bridge of his thin nose, the chaplain tucked the handkerchief back into his pockets. "Perhaps someone should go and fetch Miss Grunwald. I'd be glad to do so. It wouldn't be uncommon in her situation for her to be in need of some spiritual support."

"No need to send in the troops." The quiet voice soothed the ragged nerves that Caleb refused to admit to. "I'm not that late, am I?"

Turning, he set the glass down on the porch floor. "There were some ready to report you missing in action, but your arrival is timely enough."

He watched her approach, her loveliness striking him hard in the chest. As she came closer he could see that her cheeks were flushed, and there was a hint of anxiety in her eyes, but her hand, when she placed it in his outstretched one, was steady. She wore the pale-yellow dress he'd seen her in before, and her hair was pulled up in an ornate knot, adorned with some of the flowers he'd left for her bouquet.

The troops grew quiet as she took his arm and accompanied him across the lawn. "Your pulse is racing," he murmured, as he guided her up the steps of the makeshift stage. "Nervous?"

She denied it with a shake of her head, the quaking in her veins calling her a liar. The events of today had all but shredded her control. Making love with Caleb, discovering her love for him had been shattering enough. Being locked for hours in his secret room, while somebody on the outside of it had tried, in vain, to enter, had been nerve-racking. Faced with the very real possibilities of discovery, or of missing the wedding, had given her more than a few bad moments.

Upon the stage she looked out over the gathered crowd. The little lights that had been strung for the occasion cast a flickering illumination on the assembly. Which of them, she wondered, as the chaplain began his address, had been the one on the other side of the door?

"The sanctity of this marriage will strive to duplicate the very holiness of a pure white race, one blessed by The Brotherhood and the God above."

Familiar faces stood out among the crowd of strangers: Eliza, Tommy, Sutherland and Kathy. Others she recognized by sight. It was impossible to know what one of them had hoped to find in the secret room.

Her hand was encased in warmth, and her gaze rose to meet Caleb's. She'd narrowly avoided discovery by him, as well. It had been his approach upstairs, she imagined, which had frightened the intruder away. After the noises had stopped for a while, she'd raced to make her escape, but once she'd opened the inside door she could hear Caleb moving about in his room. She'd spent another half hour in an agonizing wait.

"Their union is a sign of the bond forged among the brethren of our faith, a promise to the future."

Caleb had an enemy within the compound, someone desperate enough to assault what should be a secure hiding place. Her gaze went to the troops again. What had that person been searching for? And how was it going to be used against Caleb?

"Repeat after me, I swear beneath the almighty God of the Aryan race…"

Rachel's attention jerked back to the ceremony. She dutifully repeated each of the lines he announced, unable to meet Caleb's intent gaze.

"...and to bear his sons, for the propagation of our Lord's holy war..."

Hesitating only slightly over the words, Rachel forced herself to echo them.

"...and to commit myself to the service of my husband and the goals of this Brotherhood."

Her hand was raised to Caleb's lips, and a soft kiss brushed her knuckles. Surely that would explain the slight tremble in her voice, should anyone notice it. A shiver worked through her as she parroted the words, and then she was unable to look away, while Caleb took his turn.

"...I do solemnly swear..."

The fire in his blue gaze was intense, bathing her in heat. She felt scorched by it, branded in a way she couldn't explain.

"...that this union is but part of my dedication to our sacred cause..."

Rachel couldn't help imagining, just for an instant, what it would be like to be sharing vows with Caleb in a church. With love between them instead of The Brotherhood. With no secrets left, no puzzles left unanswered. The forlorn fantasy sent needles of pain stabbing deep in her heart.

"...and to protect her, and honor her, for as long as we are both bound by The Brotherhood..."

She stiffened knees that wanted to waver and angled her chin, as if she could banish the vulnerability through sheer force of will. She was exchanging vows in a ceremony that wasn't legal, with a man she loved, but didn't really know, before a crowd concealing someone planning to betray him.

Weakness was the last thing she could afford right now.

They shared a light supper of fruit and cheese following the ceremony. The meal had immediately taken on an air of intimacy. Rachel was keenly aware that the house was empty save the two of them. The troops had dispersed, the help had gone back to their quarters. She felt alone with Caleb in a way she had never felt before, because never before had she acknowledged her feelings for him.

The churning emotions made her appetite uncertain. Caleb noticed and commented on it.

"You must be hungry. You barely ate this afternoon, either."

Their gazes met, and both knew the other was thinking of appetites that afternoon that had run unchecked. Rachel was the first to swallow and look away. That particular memory wasn't designed to calm the nerves clawing through her. "No, really, I've had enough."

"Well, I haven't." His eyes were trained on her, bathing her with warmth. "I haven't had nearly enough yet." He picked up her hand, send a thumb skimming across her knuckles. The emotions chasing across her face were an endless fascination, at odds with her usual poise. The evidence of her discomfort left him with an unfamiliar desire to soothe. "I'm not used to having to wait for you. If you hadn't shown up on the porch when you did, the chaplain might have been called upon to administer The Brotherhood's last rites." He laid his hand over his heart.

The jittering in her pulse steadied slightly. "Weak heart. You? I've never known anyone less likely to have difficulty with that particular organ."

"You'd be surprised," he murmured, sliding a finger over the soft skin covering the back of her hand. "It's been a bit unreliable recently."

"Too much red meat?"

"Too much of you. And yet not enough." He refused to release his grip on her fingers, despite her discreet tug. He wasn't letting go of her. Not in any way. "This is more than I prepared for. More than I imagined wanting."

Helpless under his gaze, she understood his meaning. The candidates…the marriage…all were part of a well-thought-out strategy. She'd known that going into this. Having him reaffirm it shouldn't have the power to wound.

"I understand that."

"I don't think so," he disputed, a slight frown forming. "How could you? I barely understand it myself. All I know is…" He hesitated, seemed to choose his words carefully. "I'm not sorry about the way this turned out. I don't want you to be, either."

His words softened something inside her, something she wouldn't have been able to identify. "Did I seem sorry to you this afternoon?"

To her delight, he took a deep shuddering breath. "Ah…no. No, you didn't. You seemed…" He rose, tugging at her fingers, so she stood as well, stepping into the circle of his arms. Cupping her face in both hands, he murmured against her lips, "You seemed perfect. And more, far more, than I deserve." His lips moved against hers softly at first, and then with a possessiveness that was oddly thrilling. She blamed the disorientation she felt on the dizzying taste of him. It was a moment before she realized she was in his arms, moving up the staircase. He never released her mouth. She sighed a little, linked her arms around his neck and leaned into the kiss.

Flickers of candlelight weaved and danced in the darkness of his room. Her eyes didn't flutter open until he lowered her to the bed, and lay down beside her. Candles and flowers filled the room, their scent stinging the air. Something in her chest squeezed hard at the sight.

"You went to a lot of trouble."

"A lady's entitled to a little romance on her wedding night."

She stared into his sober gaze, so close to her own, so full of secrets. So full of more than she'd ever imagined finding. Romance had been an element oddly lacking in her life, one she'd never missed. So his effort, his desire to please her, meant more than it should have. Much more.

He leaned over her, found the pins in her hair and began removing them, one by one. He was meticulous in his task, and when her hair tumbled down, he dropped the pins on the floor and speared both hands into the free strands, cupped her scalp and kneaded. She managed, barely, to resist a purr.

"Glorious," he muttered, combing his fingers through it. "I wanted to do this the first time I saw you."

Her voice was very nearly breathless. "What else did you want to do?"

"Wicked acts." He took her earlobe in his teeth and scored it lightly with his teeth. "Sinful deeds." His mouth was on her neck, cruising to her chin. "Shameless pleasures."

Her skin quivered in response to his lips, her veins throbbed in response to his words. There was a surreal feel to the moment, to the setting. A kind of magic that shimmered between them, around them, encasing them in a sort of wonder that couldn't be duplicated. Could never be repeated.

She slid her hands along his jaw, brought his mouth to hers. "Show me."

And he did.

The night misted dreams. She was awash in the sensual images, aroused by the erotic sensations. Skin to skin they pressed, stroked and explored. His body was an endless fascination to her. She found the places where she could touch and elicit a hiss of breath, where she could linger and stroke, bringing a groan to his lips. And she discovered how one could balance, poised, on the keen blade of desire, its edge pleasurable and painful at once as the magic spun out. Sharp and sweet. Stoked and soothed. An endless ritual of passion.

His hands mapped her body, marked her for his own. There was exquisite softness to be found in the curve of her breast, a whisper of intriguing strength beneath the silky skin of her thigh. There wasn't an inch of her that he didn't want to taste, to possess. Before the night was through he was determined he would succeed.

Her spine was delicate beneath his dancing fingers. He followed it with his lips, dipping his tongue into the twin dimples at the base of her back. His mouth skimmed lower, over smooth rounded curves. He grazed one satiny globe with his teeth, and was rewarded with a gasp. He soothed the spot with his tongue and reveled in her sigh.

She learned the sinew and angles of his shoulders, his arms, his chest. He was power leashed in long lean muscles, strength that flexed and pulsed beneath her touch. She drew her leg along his, thrilling in the contrast of smoothness against hair-roughened skin. Her hands shaped the narrow masculine hips, fingertips deliberately skirting the area where he was hot and straining.

His mouth could spread flame, summon nerve endings to the surface so that they hummed beneath her skin, helplessly quivering in anticipation of release. And then he'd use his lips to soothe, almost, just enough to dull the slashing need a fraction, and leave her trembling helplessly as his attentions shifted. His technique was deliberate, knowing and mind-numbingly shattering.

Her hands smoothed up his sides, her nails scraped across his nipples. He made a noise deep in his throat, so she repeated the action. She tested the strong cord in his throat with her teeth, nipped beneath his jaw line. This wasn't the flash and fire of this afternoon. That had been simpler somehow. This was slow and languorous, and infinitely devastating.

He stroked her breasts, trailing a delicious path of heat in his wake. Her nipples were so taut that the first touch made her whimper and press closer. He obeyed her unspoken wish and took a nipple in his mouth, batted it with his tongue. Her fingers speared into his hair, one long leg drew up to clench over his hip and he drew strongly from her. Her cry summoned something primitive inside him, some unfamiliar response that usually lay dormant beneath a veneer of civility. But polite social trappings were gone, replaced with a man at his most primal level. He wanted to trap that cry with his mouth, let it echo into his system. He wanted to feel her bones melting beneath that sleek, tight flesh, and feel the music of her response flow over him, through him, filling a void he would have denied he had.

He wanted, quite desperately, to possess her. In a way that could never be denied, nor forgotten. In a way that would brand them both in an indelible searing heat that reached clear to the soul.

Her fingers found him, circling him in a sweet tight grip that played havoc with his senses and his determination. He caught her hands, and manacled her wrists on either side of her hips. Sliding down her body, he pressed openmouthed kisses against the skin of her belly, using his tongue to trace the muscles that jumped and quivered beneath her skin. Sensing his intention she stiffened beneath him, but his lips were lazy, patient. The warmth of his breath caressed the slick bundle of nerves between her legs a moment before he pressed his mouth against her and steeped himself in her taste.

Sensation after sensation crashed through her. Each sharp lance of pleasure threatened to be the one that toppled her over the keen edge of release, a free fall into mindlessness. She fought the promise of sweet climax until she could have him inside her. Deep. Pounding. Until their systems overloaded and the storm broke over them. Together.

''Caleb.'' His name was a sob, a demand. He couldn't resist the sound of his name on her lips, the plea that echoed his own desire. He moved up her body and entered her with a long, slow stroke. Muscles quivering, he remained motionless above her an instant, letting the heat streak over them like lightning.

Her hips slammed up to his, and he cupped her bottom, forcing her to the rhythm he would set. Her legs went around his hips and he groaned, scrambled for the last ounce of control. Sweat beaded on his forehead as he moved in her with long slow strokes. This time it wasn't a race, it was a prayer. Something offered, something received. Pleasure spun in luxurious waves, the glorious friction building to a gradual release. The flickers of candlelight waved and danced around them, illuminating their bodies as they moved on the bed.

"Look at me," he murmured. Her eyes opened, dazed and unfocused. The sight of her lost to pleasure chipped away at his last ounce of restraint. He reached for her hands, stretched them over her head, linking their fingers. His breath gusted out of him in huge ragged pants, the cost of his control. He moved harder, deeper, and watched her shatter, her body twisting mindlessly under his own. And when he followed her into explosive ecstasy, he thought of nothing but her.

Chapter 14

Rachel awoke alone, disoriented. She sat up in bed, pushing her tangled hair off her face and searched for some sign of him. The room was empty. The candles had been extinguished. She remembered them gutting, one by one, through the long hours of the night, until by dawn there had been only a handful of flames weaving in the darkness.

Her gaze fell to the pillow beside her, the one that still bore a slight indentation where Caleb had laid his head. One perfect white rose lay in the depression, each of its satiny petals edged in the palest pink. She reached for it, brought it closer to inhale its sweet scent and allowed herself a smile.

The clock on the bedside table pointed to after noon. She was unsurprised. There had been very little sleep last night as the time had spun golden around them. They'd been steeped in each other, and the experience had been exquisitely sensual. But the solitude she was left to now was welcome. She wouldn't care to have to deal with these emotions in front of Caleb.

She was, for the first time in her life, utterly terrified.

She'd faced down a sword at her heart with more equanimity than she was capable of now. Making love with Caleb all night had drained her to all but mind-numbing sensation, exquisite pleasure. But thought was crowding in now, and with it, panic.

Last night had stripped her bare. She was so vulnerable it was almost painful. Love left her exposed, in a way she hadn't before contemplated. She needed time to examine her options, to shore her defenses.

Because it was difficult to separate the woman from the agent while she sat in her lover's bed, nude but for his scent, she made a strategic decision and headed for the shower. The needles of spray would shake the dreams out of her mind, chase away the lethargy that still pervaded her limbs. Time, which had ceased to exist last night, was now a precious commodity. Whoever had used the uproar of the sudden nuptials as a cover under which to break into Caleb's secret room would be back. Rachel was determined to deny the intruder a second opportunity.

Worry speared through her, one too ingrained to be denied. Resolutely she pushed it aside. She wasn't losing sight of the investigation, she was merely widening her focus. Within the framework of proving Simon's involvement with the arms shipment, she'd unravel the truth about her new husband. Both goals were equally vital. One to her career, the other to her heart.

Rachel didn't leave the upstairs until she heard Anna making her way down the hallway. She'd be occupied in the upper story for hours, her presence, hopefully, a deterrent to anyone bent on snooping. Leaving the door to Caleb's bedroom open, she went downstairs to where she knew she'd find him.

Once inside the office door, her steps faltered. Caleb was deep in conversation with Colonel Sutherland. They broke off at her entrance, and Caleb's eyes gleamed as he immediately rose to meet her.

"You look rested." The murmur was audible to her ears only, but that didn't stop an unfamiliar flush from heating her cheeks.

"I am." Her gaze went over his shoulder in Sutherland's direction, and Caleb turned her, walked her to the hallway and closed the door behind them. Then he took her face in his hands and kissed her thoroughly.

When she could manage a breath, she stepped back…away from temptation. "I was surprised to see Colonel Sutherland here this morning."

"Were you?" His palm cupped her jaw, marveling in the softness of her skin. He'd touched every inch of her last night but it hadn't been enough. It had only whetted a thirst that he was beginning to doubt could ever be quenched. That doubt made it doubly difficult not to reach for her again. He dropped his hand and jammed both fists into his pockets. It was a deplorable habit, and utterly ruined the line of a fine pair of trousers. It did, however, keep him from dragging her closer.

She wasn't completely unmoved, although that remarkable composure of hers was mostly intact. He smiled slightly. The return of her customary poise made it all the more intoxicating to remember her stripped of it, when both of them had been lost to everything but the primal need for each other.

The look in his eyes did dangerous things to her pulse. Rachel forced herself to swallow around the knot that had formed in her throat and reach for her scattered logic. "Do you have a busy day planned?"

Her words had the intensity fading from his expression, to be replaced with resignation. "I do. We have quite a few arrangements to make."

"And Colonel Sutherland is helping you make them?"

She saw the moment when comprehension registered. "I need his help with this, yes. We're married, Rachel. His attempts to separate us failed."

An image of the jeep heading straight for the cliff flitted across her mind. There would probably be no way of ever knowing if that had been simple bad luck or something more. And if Kevin Sutherland had had anything to do with it. "You forgive easily."

"No, as a matter of fact, I don't." Although his voice was even, it held an underlying thread of menace. In his next words it was absent, and she was left to wonder if she'd imagined it. "I've got a mountain of arrangements to work through for a party I'm hosting, one to celebrate our marriage. The guest list is substantial. It's a lot to pull together in two days."

"Two days?"

"It'll be held tomorrow night. We didn't have time to invite anyone outside of the compound to our wedding. I'm afraid all the guests will be business associates of mine. If you have someone special you'd like to invite, perhaps it can wait for a more intimate gathering."

"No," she murmured, watching him closely. "There's no one."

He didn't make mention of his family, and she was unsurprised. He'd said once the only contact he had with them was when he visited them at their home. She wondered how he would explain his marriage to them, or if he planned to do so.

It wouldn't matter, she thought grimly, if she didn't find something, quickly, that would answer the many questions she still had about Caleb. Without those answers, his family would have far more to deal with than his unexpected marriage. And so, for that matter, would she.

"All right then." Nonchalance gloved her response. "If you're going to be busy I can certainly entertain myself. I'll see you at dinner?"

"It's a date." He swooped in for a kiss, catching her off guard, and lingered for another when he found her lips softly parted. He paused to lean his forehead against hers for a moment. "Later." With resolution on his face he turned around and headed back to the office. Only when he reached the door did he dare take his hands out of his pockets.

It took longer than it should have for her mind to work properly again. But when the office door closed behind Caleb, Rachel gave herself a mental shake and turned to go back upstairs. With Caleb occupied for the next several hours she had a chance to work on both of her goals: discovering The Brotherhood's link to Simon as well as information that would clear up the enigma of the man she married.

She waited until Anna had finished in Caleb's room before she entered the concealed room again. This time, she was determined, she would find what she was looking for. She was doubly certain that she was on the right track. Someone else apparently agreed that there was more contained in here than the ammunition.

The crates were the most likely places to conceal something, but Rachel soon learned that despite her top physical shape, she was ill equipped to move any of them by herself. Nor was she tall enough to check the lids of the top ones to see if they were secured. So she climbed each of the stacks, balancing precariously at the top to test them. None had been loosened.

Next she inspected the sides of each stacked crate, searching for an edge that would lift up or slide away completely. She found what she was looking for in the fourth box she investigated. The wooden side didn't fit as securely as the others she'd checked, so she pulled harder on it. It came off completely, revealing a computer case inside.

Her excitement mounting, Rachel lifted the case out, squatted on the floor and unzipped it. Inside was a laptop computer. She pushed the case over to the outlet in the wall, plugged it in and turned it on.

She switched the pencil flashlight off. The computer screen provided all the light she would need to work by.

Impatiently, she waited for the screen to clear. When it did, the anticipation in her veins did a slow freeze.

The computer was protected by a security system, a different type than the one that was used on the computers in the office. Her excitement dissipated, to be replaced with grim determination. She'd cracked the code on the ones downstairs. She could do it again on this one.

A distant voice in her head reminded her that it had taken her two very long nights to do so. It would be so much easier, she thought wistfully, if she could manage to discover his password. She'd wasted valuable time trying just that when she'd investigated the office computers, without success. Nevertheless, she racked her brain for a word that might have some meaning for him, but obscure enough to escape detection.

Cassiopeia. She typed in the word with bated breath, remembering their night under the stars. Incorrect. Quickly she tried some more. Andromeda. Saturn. Venus. She scowled as the balloon popped up over and over, alerting her to the incorrect password. She stopped for a moment, ready to give up on the fruitless task. There had been another star he'd mentioned. Rachel scrunched up her brow, trying to recall it. One that had been his favorite, yet she'd never heard of it before. It had started with a *V*...

V-E-G-A, she typed. And then her stomach did a slow roll as the password was accepted and the hard drive became accessible. Her mouth went abruptly dry when she realized that she might be moments away from having all her questions about this case answered.

There were several encrypted files kept on the drive, she discovered. She clicked on one, and when it opened, one of the concerns that had been plaguing her was clarified.

A full database of guns ordered and received was logged with dates of contacts and deliveries. At the bottom of the list were the letters, SIMONDAMSYR, followed by twelve numbers.

Rachel stared at the information, barely able to believe what she'd found. The lettering on the crates used to ship the guns had signified a tie with the Middle East. Rachel stared at the letters after Simon's name. Damascus, Syria was in the Middle East. And unless she missed her guess, the series of numbers following would be a contact number for him there. She was certain that Jonah would be extremely interested.

She repeated the numbers to herself until she had them memorized, then closed out of the file. She opened another, and as she skimmed the long document she could feel the blood in her veins slowly go glacial. In intricate detail, Caleb had charted out his future plans for revolution. The western unionization was plotted, as were targeted hits in New York and Baltimore. The details were horrifyingly thorough.

Her stomach did a slow nauseating roll. Forcing herself to skim several more pages, she found references to the national union Caleb had talked about in his address to the troops.

She also found further reference to Simon. Apparently his ties to the Middle East made him useful in more ways than one. Caleb's written intentions spelled out the other man's role clearly. Simon, it appeared, had agreed to supply terrorists to help The Brotherhood's national union with the revolution. When The Brotherhood succeeded in their rout, the terrorists would be destroyed in turn.

Her vision blurred. She rubbed at her eyes, which had grown tired and strained from staring at the small screen. Had she found this information any sooner in the investigation, it would have only underscored her earlier belief that Caleb was the worst kind of monster, capable of the most heinous deeds.

The horrible doubt was back, crowding at emotion, making her question decisions made, allegiances given. There was, she discovered bleakly, no turning back. And there was a fierce burning conviction inside her that wouldn't have allowed her to do so, at any rate.

The information she'd chanced upon just gave further particulars of the strategy Caleb had spoken of time after time to the troops. It didn't change anything, and it certainly didn't help her detect something that would prove what she knew in her heart. There was more to Caleb than his connection to The Brotherhood would suggest.

She found an item that supported her belief a half hour later in yet another file. She scrolled down the listed names and dates uncomprehendingly. Consuela Ortega. Manny Rodriguez. Arturo Perez. Jeff Kirby.

It was the last name that first snared her attention. Jeff Kirby, son of an ex-SPEAR agent, who had been found buried alive, on The Brotherhood's compound. Suspicion of Simon's involvement in the incident had precipitated her own investigation into The Brotherhood. What did Caleb know about the kidnapping?

Checking the date by Jeff's name, she thought it must be approximate to the time he'd been rescued. The other names had dates, also, she discovered, one by each of the men, and a full half dozen by Consuela's. She suspected the file had been meant to document contacts with civilians, or nonmembers of The Brotherhood. One of the dates matched the day of Rachel's arrival at the compound. The day Caleb had received word about the trespassing Hispanics, and had left the house armed.

It took conscious effort to breathe. Rachel had no doubt that Consuela was the Hispanic woman that she'd seen him talking to yesterday. There was nothing in the document to suggest what their conversation had involved, but she'd seen for herself that it had been friendly. It occurred to her that the names of the three Hispanics might prove to be valuable, if they could be traced and then shed some favorable light on Caleb. It was little to go on, but it was a start.

She double checked the dates after Consuela's name, but

failed to find yesterday's date. If her guess was correct, Caleb hadn't yet had opportunity update his files.

Thoughts of him doing so had her glancing at her watch, and cursing mentally. There were a full half-dozen files that she hadn't opened yet, but clearly, there would be no time to continue now. She would need to hurry to get everything put back in order here and get ready to meet Caleb for dinner.

As she returned the computer to its case, then back to its place of concealment, she made a mental vow to return tomorrow to look at the rest of the computer files. Surely there was more information within there that would unravel the rest of the truth about her husband.

Making her exit from the concealed room was always the trickiest part of the situation, especially the moment when she stepped out of the paneled wall and moved to lock both doors behind her. She didn't breathe deeply until she'd done both, then headed directly toward the bathroom. She was sure she bore the visible effects of spending hours in the airless dusty area. Replacing the lock-picking tools and flashlight in her room, she stripped and showered, feeling as if she washed a little of the stress of the last two days away as well as the grime. But there was grim satisfaction inside her, as well. She was close now, very close. She knew Simon's involvement, and she could pass that information along to Jonah. If the traitor was going to deliver the guns Caleb had ordered, it would be a perfect chance for SPEAR to catch him.

And while she was waiting to do so, she'd unlock the dangerous puzzle that was Caleb Carpenter.

When Caleb entered her room she was sitting on her bed clad in nothing but a robe, devoting painstaking attention to the task of painting her toenails. He stopped in the doorway, drinking in the sight. Her position made his bones ache just contemplating it and almost drew his attention away from the blade of disappointment that had stabbed deep when he hadn't found her in his room.

It was ridiculous to feel this possessive after one night. It was especially ridiculous given the circumstances that surrounded their marriage. But logic, he was finding, was a poor defense against primal urges that owed little to reason. He shut the door and leaned his shoulders against it.

"Hi." Concentrating on her task gave her a reason to avoid his gaze, so after her greeting she redipped the brush and meticulously drew it across the next toenail.

"Looks fun. Need any help?"

"I don't think so. This is kind of a one-man...make that a one-woman...operation."

He cocked his head. "That doesn't seem quite fair."

A smile lurked at the corners of her mouth. "I have another bottle if you want to do your own."

He pushed off from the door and ambled in her direction. "I'd rather assist you."

"Caleb!" Rachel rescued the bottle which had started to slide as he sat down next to her on the bed. He picked up one of her feet and brought it to his mouth, blowing lightly on the damp polish.

That warm breath skating across what was proving to be an incredibly sensitive area had the air backing up in her lungs. "I...ah...really, that isn't necessary."

He looked up at her with a grin that held pure wickedness. "I know, but it sure is fun."

"You know what would be even more fun?" She reached for one of his feet and stripped off the sock. "If we shared...everything."

"Not a chance." He made a lunge for the polish just as she reached for it again, and they rolled across the bed, giggling and wrestling like children.

"You're going to spill it," she gasped, helpless with laughter, as she strained to keep the polish out of his reach.

"Anna will blame you if I do. Aha!" He pried her fingers

off the bottle and sat upright again, triumphant. "I'll finish the job for you. Hey, come on," he complained, when she shielded her foot from his ministrations. "I'll have you know I'm incredibly artistic."

"For every nail of mine you paint, I get to paint one of yours."

"I'll take the suggestion under consideration," he hedged. When he had the narrow feminine foot across his lap he bent over it with the utmost care and began to draw the tiny brush across one of her nails. "Hold still. The artist is not responsible for an unsteady foot."

"Shouldn't we be getting ready for dinner?"

He attentively reapplied paint to the brush. "I think we should have dinner delivered upstairs. From the looks of this job it may take several hours." He looked up then, and the light dancing in his eyes did odd things to her stomach. "In fact, this may take well into the night."

For the second day in a row, Rachel awoke confused. She frowned, rubbed her eyes. Comprehension came sluggishly. When the bed in her room had become a jumble of bedcovers, they'd moved to Caleb's. He was responsible for the furnacelike heat at her back. His arm was a heavy weight across her waist, keeping her at his side. She had no desire to be anywhere else.

She felt him stir. It was infinitely preferable, she decided, to wake with him than to do so alone. It couldn't be more than an hour past dawn. It was tempting to snuggle back into bed, into the arms of the man beside her and spend the next several hours making memories. But an increasing sense of urgency was riding her since her discovery yesterday. She desperately wanted a thorough look at the rest of those files on Caleb's second computer as soon as she could manage it.

The arm at her waist tightened, and a stubbled jaw nuzzled her ear. "Morning."

"Hi." Rachel arched her neck to allow his lips better access to her throat, enjoying the faintly prickly rasp of beard against her skin.

"Did we get anything to eat last night?"

"Eliza delivered supper on a tray before she left for the evening." His mouth cruised over her shoulders.

"Oh, right." He nipped at her delicate skin. "Do you think we could convince her to deliver our breakfast?"

She gave a breathless laugh, and he transferred his attention to the nape of her neck.

A knock sounded at the door. Caleb lifted his head. "Boy, she's fast."

Rachel turned to watch him roll from the bed, and walk, gloriously nude, across the room to don his robe. He looked, she thought, delight curling her toes, disheveled, sexy and totally male. The only bit of incongruence to the picture, she decided as he pulled open the door, were the two pink toenails he sported, one on each foot.

"Kevin." He stepped into the hallway, pulling the door half shut behind him. "I'll be in the office shortly."

"A fax just came in for you, General. I thought you'd want to know. Your guest from Damascus has responded. He plans to be here tonight."

The rest of the conversation was lost on Rachel. For a moment, it felt as if every organ in her body failed. Lungs strangled, veins clogged.

Simon would be at the compound tonight.

Breathing became a conscious effort. One hand went to her heart, as if to ensure it continued to beat. She was half-shocked to find that it did.

With the information she'd discovered linking Simon to the arms, and knowledge of the man's presence here tonight, she'd have to contact headquarters. They couldn't pass up this opportunity to capture the man who was out to destroy SPEAR. There would be no further opportunity in which to discover the truth about Caleb.

Time, that most precious of commodities, had abruptly run out.

"Rachel, there you are."

It took more effort than it should have to arrange her face into a smile before turning and greeting Caleb. His hand went to her back, left bare by the strapless dress she wore. Nerve endings shimmied beneath his touch.

"When you volunteered to check the ice supply, I didn't know you were going to disappear for so long." There was concern beneath the smile, and had she been less jittery herself she would have wondered at it. He'd barely let her out of his sight all day, and the constant proximity, in light of the events she'd arranged, were bittersweet. There had been an accompanying awareness that those moments might well be the last she'd have with him.

She showed him the small purse in her hand. "I had a lipstick emergency and had to freshen up."

He considered her lips, as if contemplating arranging another emergency, then looked past her to the house. "The ice delivery made it without incident?"

"Yes." His hand went to her elbow, guiding her away from the shadows outside the house and back toward the crowd. People had begun arriving in the late afternoon, and Caleb had kept her busy supervising the arrangements. She'd had to consult with Eliza on the food, and with the soldiers acting as bartenders on the drinks. For some reason it had been imperative that she be at his side while he gave tours of the compound to the suitably impressed visitors.

The only time she had had alone today, she recalled bleakly, was when Caleb had left her to shower that morning. While the spray had beat down in the empty tub, she'd carefully assembled the small transmitter she'd smuggled in parts for. And with that transmitter she'd arranged for an assault on the compound.

"I don't believe we've danced together this evening."

Troops had been busy all day assembling the wooden decking on the lawn. Trucks had arrived every hour, with tables, outdoor lighting, fine food. No expense had been spared for the celebration Caleb had arranged. She wondered dully if anyone would get an ounce of enjoyment out of it before the revelry was shattered.

The noise of the crowd enveloped them as they drew near. Rachel had recognized a few of the militia leaders from around the country who had come tonight. For many others, she'd recognized their names. She nodded again as she caught Sean Conrad's eye. He gave her a broad wink. He'd been one of their earlier arrivals.

"Keeping your lovely bride to yourself, Caleb? I can't say that I blame you."

She recognized the smarmy voice even before she turned around. "Patrick." Because she couldn't avoid it, she offered her hand. He seemed loath to release it.

"Dixon." Lukewarm welcome was in Caleb's voice, and murder was in his eye. Tension seemed to come off him in waves. "Glad you could make it."

"Well, it's an important day, Carpenter." Dixon let loose Rachel's hand and raised his glass to the crowd. "And it appears you have many important friends who have come to wish you well. I may have underestimated your influence."

"Underestimating Caleb is always a mistake," Rachel said evenly. "Would you excuse us? We were just on our way to dance." Before they'd gone a half a dozen steps, they were joined by a newly arrived couple.

Caleb introduced the man and his wife, but Craig Forester needed no further introduction to Rachel beyond his name. He was the leader of The White Empire in California, and his sect was one of the more violent in the nation.

"Damn glad to be here, Carpenter, and even gladder to be part of your plans. This country has been ruined for too long by these spineless liberals. I just wanted to give you some suggestions you might keep in mind. Worked well in my state, and I can't see why they wouldn't work even better in a regional organization...."

"Why don't I find a waiter to take your drink orders?" Rachel slipped away from the group, disregarding Caleb's faint frown. She wended her way through the crowd, pointed a waiter in the couple's direction, and then continued strolling, until the crowd and the voices were in the distance.

She ducked into the shadows near the house and took a deep trembling breath. She never remembered having nerves this raw, this exposed, before the break of a case. Of course, a case had never before involved Caleb Carpenter. With an effort, she tried to summon that icy calm that usually served her so well in an investigation.

But the calm seemed beyond her. She could feel the weight of the derringer in her purse, the kiss of cold steel where she'd strapped the slim stiletto to her thigh. Tools of her trade. Objects she'd feel naked without.

It was difficult to maintain her usual equanimity on the job knowing that when the assault began, Caleb would be swept into custody along with everybody else. It would be another successful case for the agent they called Angel. Nobody would know just how horribly she'd failed the man she loved.

The hushed voices around the corner of the house were an annoyance. Rachel wanted, more than anything right now, to have a few moments of solitude. But as the voices became more audible, her annoyance turned into interest.

"No, I won't leave it to you. I'm through leaving it to you. You've made a mess of things from the beginning."

"You dare to speak to me like that? To me?"

She could barely make out the words. Silently, she crept closer to the arguing couple.

"Face it. You've lost your nerve. My way was best, and now we've missed our opportunity."

"Your way." The second voice snorted. "I told you not

to be so impatient. It's because of you that Carpenter caught on to what we were up to in the first place. Taking chances isn't the answer, I told you. Searching her room was a stupid risk. Cutting her brake lines was worse.''

"And your way was better? You were supposed to arrange it so you and I would share in the power of the new Brotherhood.'' The sneer in the voice didn't make it any harder to recognize. The voice belonged to Kathy Sutherland. "You'd get rid of all the candidates, you said. I'd be Carpenter's mate with access to his money, and both you and I would be in a position of control.''

"He didn't prove to be as malleable as I had hoped. We're left with no choice.'' Kevin Sutherland's voice was eerily matter-of-fact. "Carpenter will have to be eliminated. I'm the natural one to succeed him in The Brotherhood. My position of power in the new union will assure your own.''

"But what about his money? Without his finances we don't have the kind of influence in the new organization as we would have with him.''

"He just placed another order for weapons. More than enough to see us through the reorganization and to set the stage for revolution. I'm certain I can find the strategy he's hidden detailing the steps he's planning. It's enough. We don't need him anymore.''

"You'll take care of it tonight?''

"I'll arrange an accident.''

Kathy considered that for a moment before asking, "What about Grunwald?''

"She'll have to die, too, of course. She's of no use to us.''

Rachel had heard enough. She slipped from the shadows and crossed the lawn, stumbling a bit in her haste. She had to find Caleb and warn him. She had to protect him.

Halfway across the lawn she looked over her shoulder to see the Sutherlands trailing behind her. She spotted Caleb up ahead, in the middle of a group of people. He raised his head and met her gaze.

The mob of people made it difficult to get to him. From the corner of her eye she saw Tommy nearby, observing her closely. She gauged the distance again between the Sutherlands and Caleb. Tommy followed her gaze and then reached behind his back, beneath his jacket. She knew instinctively that he was reaching for a gun.

She picked up her pace, elbowing her way through the crowd, surreptitiously opening her purse and palming the derringer. Caleb's gaze narrowed, and he made his way toward her, calling her name. "Rachel?"

And then chaos struck the compound.

Blinding spotlights flooded the area from overhead. A voice blared from a loudspeaker. "This is the FBI. Remain where you are. Put down your weapons." A woman began to scream. Shouts filled the air. The crowd seemed to explode, people pushing in all directions.

The first helicopter was joined by three others. Ladders dropped from each and men began descending from the air.

There was a rush of running feet and black-garbed agents burst into the area holding high-powered rifles ready. "Stop! Hands in the air." They swarmed over the crowd, and confusion reigned. Rachel looked wildly around for Caleb, but couldn't find him. Tommy, too, had disappeared. She saw an agent cuffing Sutherland, and then she was jostled, pulled around by the shoulder. She was divested of her purse and gun just as she caught a glimpse of Caleb, shouting at a man with FBI emblazoned across the back of his jacket.

The last thing she saw before her hands were manacled and she was pulled aside, was the sight of Caleb being slugged by an agent. He crumpled, and two others dragged him away.

Chapter 15

The punches came fast, hard, and found their mark. Over and over Rachel pummeled the body bag, expending the frustration that was so thick and tangible, she'd spent the last two weeks choking on it. She stopped for a moment, breath coming in huge ragged pants, bent at the waist and rested her hands on her knees.

The relief from the restless energy that plagued her would be momentary, she knew, but even short-lived it was welcomed. There would be no relief in sight for the heaviness in her heart. That could come from only one man. And Caleb was lost to her; lost deep inside the judicial system.

She had no idea where they'd taken him after the assault on the compound. She'd gone through booking herself, a necessity to keep her cover intact. The biggest catches made at the party had been taken elsewhere. Discreet inquiries had been met with closed doors.

She'd failed him. She could almost face that now without flinching. She'd spent enough long nights alone going over every bit of her guilt. If she'd put aside a lifetime of suspicion just a little sooner, she may have found the one thing that would have spared Caleb arrest. She may have discovered the piece of the puzzle that would have reflected every facet of the man that she'd tried, unsuccessfully, to piece together.

The cell phone rang, the line only Jonah would ring. The call would be totally secure, thanks to the SPEAR technology that rendered Jonah's call untraceable.

"I have good news, Angel," the voice on the line began without preamble.

She sank to the floor, resting her back against the wall. "You have a new case for me?" Another assignment would be welcome. It would take her mind off the endless regrets that haunted her nights, and her days. It would give her something to focus on besides the organ in her chest that seemed to be cracked beyond repair.

"Seventy-six of the guests caught up in our little net a couple of weeks ago are facing federal charges. Another dozen will be taken care of at the state level."

Because he seemed to expect a response, she said, "That's quite a haul."

A low chuckle sounded in his ear. "It is, indeed. I believe five or six of the militia leaders captured had been underground for years, to avoid outstanding warrants for their arrests. The FBI should be kept busy with the paperwork for quite some time."

It was customary, if arrests were made in the course of their investigation, to have another agency be visible, while the SPEAR agents faded back into the shadows. Shadows were where she was most comfortable, she assured herself. But there was a poignant memory of lovemaking in the full light of day that called her a liar.

"I still regret that we missed Simon." That was one more fact that ate at her. "I don't know how he could have slipped by us."

"It's more likely that he got word somehow of the

planned assault, and didn't come at all.'' Jonah's tone was grim. If that scenario was true, Simon still had reliable informants deep within law enforcement. ''Don't worry yourself. The information you were able to give us about his link with The Brotherhood is a valuable lead. We've already shut down the pipeline of guns he was smuggling. That should put a crimp in his cash flow. You did another fine job.''

''Thanks. Now tell me that you have another one lined up for me. I'm going crazy.''

That low chuckle sounded again. ''So impatient. I should have something arranged for you in a month or so.''

''A month!'' She straightened, horrified. ''I can't keep myself sane for another month!''

''Any agent who brings down an organization like the one Caleb Carpenter spearheaded deserves some time off.''

''Jonah.'' Rachel took a deep breath then plunged ahead. ''About Caleb…''

''Enjoy yourself for the next four weeks, Angel.'' And then the line went dead.

She flipped the phone off and sent it skittering across the mat. Jonah wouldn't have answered any questions she put to him about Caleb, regardless. He could have; she had no doubt that he knew every detail of the aftermath of the assault. But details were something he was very stingy with.

Springing to her feet, she readied for another round. She was going to have to piece together her life again. Her foot shot out and caught the body bag high on the side. She had her career.

Spin, twist, kick.

Her mother was making slow but encouraging progress.

Spin, feint, kick, dodge.

The thought of her mother brought other thoughts shoving in, thoughts of the man who'd made the progress possible, so she pushed herself harder. If her life was hollowed out by the absence of something she'd never known she was lacking, well she would find something else to fill it. Somehow.

Flying kick, twist.

"That's a lot of energy to waste on an inanimate object."

She reacted to a presence behind her before thinking. She spun, her foot shooting out. Caleb ducked, narrowly missing the connection to his jaw.

"Is that any way to greet your husband?" The amusement in his voice overrode the feigned hurt.

Rachel went completely still, gaping at him. "What are you doing here? Are they looking for you?"

"I sincerely hope not. At least, not for a while." He watched her carefully, gauged his chances for coming closer. "I've earned some time off after dedicating the last two years of my life to the job."

"To the job?" Parroting his words, she sounded like a nitwit, but didn't care. She was too busy gorging herself on the sight of him.

"Yes, to the job." He pulled a leather case from the pocket inside his jacket, and flipped it open to display the gold shield. "FBI." When her jaw dropped, he added dryly, "I assume you've heard of it."

An FBI agent. Questions, answers, whizzed across her mind, clicked into place. "I knew it!"

"You did not." He sounded affronted. "You never had a clue, I made sure of that. Believe me, it was the only thing that saved my pride, once I found out I'd been lusting after a secret agent for weeks."

"There's no way you could have known," she said by way of explanation, still struggling to make sense of it all. "I'm good."

His mouth quirked. "Aside from your overwhelming modesty, I'd agree."

She dragged her gaze from him with effort and turned to pace. "I *knew* something wasn't right. You weren't adding up. There was more to you than a venom-spewing racist, but I couldn't quite make all the pieces fit.''

''I passed as a venom-spewing racist for two years,'' he reminded her.

''But you arranged for a specialist to see my mother, who supposedly was one of the unworthy you professed to hate.''

He lifted a shoulder. ''I could have just been crazy about you.''

She went on as if she hadn't heard him. ''And then there was your obvious friendliness with Consuela Ortega.''

His brows skimmed upward. ''You saw us?''

At her nod, he explained, ''One of the biggest headaches in an operation that size is making damn sure no civilians get hurt. But there was a group of Hispanics who routinely spent the summer in the mountains, on the other side of the pass, waiting for the potato season to hire on at local operations. I don't think I ever did impress upon any of them how dangerous their trespassing was. When I could, I'd slip them a phone number of someone who could help with money and food.''

''Yes, I found references to Consuela and the other civilians in your secret computer files.''

His expression abruptly altered. ''You were in my files? In the concealed room?''

''I told you I was good.''

He grimaced, still grappling with what she'd just revealed. She'd been in the hidden room. She'd broken into his computer. He sent her an aggrieved look, which she didn't seem to notice. It was a kick to the ego to realize that all the caution he'd expended, all the planning that had gone into the operation, could have been compromised by one slip of a woman with a will of iron and nerves of steel. Not for the first time, he considered the possibility of putting her into safekeeping for good. The risks she'd taken in this assignment, believing what she had about him, were enough to chill the blood.

"What about Sutherland? He must have been a danger to you from the start." Briefly, she related the conversation she'd overheard right before the assault.

"Teaming up with him was a calculated risk, but unavoidable. Aligning myself with a well-known militia leader was a critical first step into the supremacy circle. He needed my money, I needed his connections. He was the one who put me in touch with Simon. I knew all along that I'd have to watch my back with both of the Sutherlands. I'm beginning to believe that Kathy was even more lethal than her father."

Caustically she said, "Hmm, yes, I suppose it's a bit disconcerting to realize that had circumstances been different, you could have wedded her. And likely been murdered in your bed."

He grinned at her words. That edge in her tone could have been caused by ire or jealousy. He preferred to believe it was the latter.

"As enticing a prospect as Kathy was..." He waited for her gaze to heat and narrow before going on. "I couldn't afford to let the Sutherlands get that close to me. So I told the Colonel we needed to broaden our base of support by searching for a candidate from another region. It made too much sense for him to refute it. Tommy was kept busy tracking them after-hours. We knew they wouldn't settle for their lesser positions in The Brotherhood."

But she'd stopped listening after mention of the familiar name caught her attention. "Tommy? He's FBI, too?"

"He is. At this moment I believe he's on a beach in Maui taking a well-deserved vacation."

Picturing the menacing Mahoney on a beach required more of a stretch of imagination than she was capable of. Of course, she was a bit distracted. Her gaze returned again and again to Caleb, roaming over his form bemusedly. She'd never been one to believe in fairy tales and happily-everafters, but the sight of Caleb, here, in her home, was too gratifying to be denied.

Abruptly, reality sliced neatly across her sense of wonder. If she'd been on the job at the compound, well, so had he. And Caleb had had reasons to find a bride, reasons to marry one, that had nothing to do with her.

Driven to move, she began to circle him, scowling. He'd summoned two other women to The Brotherhood with every intention of marrying them, hadn't he? It was only due to Sutherland's interference that Rachel had been the one he'd wedded. In a ceremony that was as bogus as the reasons behind it.

He turned to keep her in sight. Sensing her abrupt change of mood, it paid to stay cautious.

Snappishly she observed, "The FBI must have a curious code of ethics to expect an agent to marry as part of the job."

He grinned, slow and wide and knowing. "Well, it wasn't a real ceremony, you know."

"I know that!" She gave a regal toss of her head, a gesture at odds with her casual dress. "Do you think I would have taken part in it if it had been real?"

He stroked his chin, pretending to give it some thought. "Yes," he concluded finally, "I do."

Her chin angled and she stopped prowling, as if readying to pounce. "What's that supposed to mean?" If he was smiling at her expense, he was going to land facedown on the mat, no question about it.

The smile had faded from his face to be replaced with that familiar intensity. "You married me because you loved me." When she didn't, *couldn't* answer, he corrected himself. "Well, you many have married me for the job, but you made love to me because you loved me. Isn't that right, Rachel?"

Her mouth went abruptly dry. She'd rather feel the cold

prick of a blade against her skin than to take the risk she was about to take. "I suppose so."

He refused to identify the easing in his lungs as relief. "Please, stop. Your fawning is getting embarrassing."

Feeling exposed made her irritable. "Well, why did you…" She blinked, strangely reluctant to put voice to the words. "Why did you make love to me?"

With more care than the act called for, he slipped his hands into his trouser pockets. "I suppose I love you, too."

Hope spiraled, fueling a giddy sense of amusement. "Is that the best you can do, Carpenter? With your experience I'd expect something a little more articulate."

She should have been warned by the glint in his eye. One moment he was standing several feet away, the next moment he had her wrapped securely in his arms. "I don't need to be articulate when I've got a sure thing here. You're going to marry me again, Rachel. Legally this time." He ignored her sappy grin and cocked his head, surveying the room. "I like this place. We could use it to whip each other's butts on the mats. You know, like foreplay."

"You have disgracefully low standards, Carpenter." She linked her arms around his neck and nipped at his bottom lip. "I've always admired that in a man."

Sobering now, his gaze sought hers, held. "Jonah said he thought he might have some openings for husband-wife field teams. How do you feel about joining up with me for good?"

She gave a leap and wrapped her legs tightly around his hips. The joy bursting her heart bubbled out in her voice. "You've got a deal. If there's one thing I learned on this assignment, it's that you and I do our best work together, *undercover*."

* * * * *

Next month, look for
NIGHT OF NO RETURN
by Eileen Wilks
as Intimate Moments' exciting
A YEAR OF LIVING DANGEROUSLY
continuity series continues.
Turn the page for a sneak preview...

Chapter 1

He didn't want to die.

It was a disconcerting thing for a man like Alex Bok to learn at the age of thirty-four. He sat at one of the wrought-iron tables on the western terrace, dripping with sweat as he watched the southern California sky turn gaudy with sunset over a darkening ocean. If the air could have held one dram more of that eye-burning orange, he thought, he'd be able to pluck it like a guitar string.

Color. Life. He drank them both in, relishing the way the muscles in his thighs jumped and the burn in his calves. His heartbeat pleased him. It was almost back to normal, though he'd just finished a five-mile run in the scrubby mountains surrounding the resort. If he wasn't at quite the peak of conditioning yet, he was well enough. His body had done everything he'd asked of it. He was fit again, ready for assignment.

He was the only guest on the terrace at this hour. The heat kept most people inside, or in the pool. A waiter had brought him a glass and a pitcher of ice water when he first reached the terrace. The staff here at Condor Mountain knew him; he'd stayed here before, though never for as long as he'd been here this time.

Too damned long, he thought. He needed to get back into action.

The air was dry, smelling of dust and creosote...yet he could have sworn he smelled lilacs.

"Brooding again, Alex?"

The voice belonged to another woman—not the one he associated with lilacs. Alex looked over his shoulder. "Hey, I don't brood. I'm enjoying the sunset."

"You do look like you're having a good time melting. You actually like this heat, don't you?"

"Heat is good. Come sit down and we'll talk about it. There's body heat, for example..."

Alicia Kirby pulled out the chair across from him. She was twenty-four, brilliant, and looked, he thought, like a forward on a high school basketball team, with her long, elegant bones and that boyish cape of auburn hair.

Pretty, yes, but it wasn't a long, rippling fall of hair as black as the desert sky, and smelling like lilacs.... Dammit. He had to stop thinking about a woman he'd never see again.

"Life must be painfully dull," Alicia said, "if you have to flirt with me to add a hint of danger to your humdrum existence. No more than a hint, of course. East doesn't take you any more seriously than I do."

As if on cue, a tall man with shaggy brown hair stood in the doorway, one eyebrow raised, "Trying to make time with my wife again, Alex?"

"I do my best," he said cheerfully.

East Kirby walked over and pulled out a chair. "I just talked to Jonah. You're to call him."

Alex was on his feet instantly. "I'll let you take over with the flirting, then."

"Come back down after you've talked with him," East

said. "I'm supposed to brief you on some of the background."

"Will do." Alex was already at the door.

He went past the regular elevator in the expensively rustic lobby to one that the other guests at the resort couldn't use, taking out the key required to operate it. His blood was up, his heart pumping with excitement.

A call from Jonah could mean only one thing—an assignment. He was ready for it physically, and if he still had a ways to go emotionally...well, he'd shake down just fine once he got into action again.

A man never felt more alive than when he was challenging his limits. He'd teetered on the slipperiest edge more than once while on assignment, but until a month ago he'd never gone over. But when he'd been left for dead in the Negev Desert, he'd skidded well down that dark slope...until she found him. His lady of the lilacs.

As soon as Alex entered his suite and closed the door behind him, he picked up his cell phone. This phone had special properties. The signal was digitized and encoded, so that even if someone did manage to intercept part of the transmission it wouldn't do them any good. It wasn't dependent on normal cells, either, but used a system established by orbiting satellites. He could talk to anyone from anywhere on the planet.

He punched in a number he knew well, hung up and waited. A few minutes later the phone rang, then a cool, dry voice said, "Are you ready to go back to work, Alex?"

Ten minutes later he disconnected. No surprise that he was going back to the Mideast. That was where his expertise lay. Among other skills, Alex spoke Arabic and Greek fluently and could make himself understood in Hebrew; he knew smugglers in five countries and scientists in three. He'd be going in as an archeologist—a cover he'd used often, since it dovetailed so neatly with reality. Nor was his assignment a surprise; the people who had left him for dead a month ago had ties to the terrorist organization whose base he would be hunting.

No, none of that was unexpected. But the dig he'd be participating in as part of his cover, and the person in charge of that dig—oh, yes. That had surprised him.

The scent of lilacs drifted across his memory again, and Alex smiled slowly. Never say never, he thought, his spirits rising. Not only was he going to have a chance to exorcise the fear that clung to him like a bad smell, he would get to work another distracting memory out of his system.

A memory named Nora...

INTIMATE MOMENTS®
Silhouette®

presents a riveting 12-book continuity series:

A Year of loving dangerously

Where passion rules and nothing is what it seems...

When dishonor threatens a top-secret agency,
the brave men and women of SPEAR are prepared to
risk it all as they put their lives—and their hearts—
on the line.

Available September 2000:

NIGHT OF NO RETURN
by Eileen Wilks

Hard-edged Alex Bok fought valiantly to keep his emotions
in check when a dangerous undercover assignment reunited
him with the virginal beauty he found irresistible. Could he
accomplish his mission...*and* surrender his heart to love?

*Available only from Silhouette Intimate Moments
at your favorite retail outlet.*

Silhouette®
Where love comes alive™

**Don't miss
an exciting opportunity
to save on the purchase of
Harlequin and Silhouette books!**

Buy any two Harlequin or
Silhouette books and save
$10.00 off future Harlequin
and Silhouette purchases

OR

buy any three
Harlequin or Silhouette books
and save **$20.00 off** future
Harlequin and Silhouette purchases.

*Watch for details
coming in October 2000!*

PHQ400

Coming Soon
Silhouette Books presents

Weddings in White

(on sale September 2000)

A 3-in-1 keepsake collection
by international bestselling author

DIANA PALMER

Three heart-stoppingly handsome bachelors are paired
up with three innocent beauties who long to marry the
men of their dreams. This dazzling collection showcases
the enchanting characters and searing passion that
has made Diana Palmer a legendary talent
in the romance industry.

Unlikely Lover:
Can a feisty secretary and a gruff oilman fight
the true course of love?

The Princess Bride:
For better, for worse, starry-eyed Tiffany Blair captivated
Kingman Marshall's iron-clad heart....

Callaghan's Bride:
Callaghan Hart swore marriage was for fools—until
Tess Brady branded him with her sweetly seductive kisses!

Available at your favorite retail outlet.

Silhouette®
Where love comes alive™

Celebrate
Silhouette's 20th Anniversary

with *New York Times* bestselling author

LINDA HOWARD

and the long-awaited story of
CHANCE MACKENZIE

in

A GAME OF CHANCE

IM #1021
On sale in August 2000

Hot on the trail of a suspected terrorist, covert intelligence officer Chance Mackenzie found, seduced and subtly convinced the man's daughter, Sunny Miller, to lead her father out of hiding. The plan worked, but then Sunny discovered the truth behind Chance's so-called affections. Now the agent who *always* got his man had to figure out a way to get his woman!

Available at your favorite retail outlet.

Silhouette®

Where love comes alive™

COMING NEXT MONTH

#1027 NIGHT SHIELD—Nora Roberts

Night Tales

Even though he'd agreed to protect her cover…even though her own dad
vouched for him, Detective Allison Fletcher refused to trust a shady
character like Jonah Blackhawk…even though her pulse raced at his touch.

#1028 NIGHT OF NO RETURN—Eileen Wilks

A Year of Loving Dangerously

When a near fatal incident put Alex Bok at death's door, virginal
archaeologist Sarah Lowe gently nursed him back to health. Now, for the
first time, the love 'em and leave 'em SPEAR agent was contemplating
happily-ever-after with the one woman worth fighting for. But could he
complete his deadly mission before fate intervened and spoiled their
chances at forever?

#1029 CINDERELLA FOR A NIGHT—Susan Mallery

36 Hours

Business tycoon Jonathan Steele never dreamt that a masquerade ball would
land him the woman of his dreams—and a little boy *he* was responsible for.
And not only was Cynthia Morgan beautiful, but she had a soft spot for
children. Could Jonathan convince Cynthia to go from live-in nanny to full-
time mother…and wife?

#1030 I'LL BE SEEING YOU—Beverly Bird

Kate Mulhern's perfect evening was ruined! First the guest of honor at an
event *she'd* catered wound up facedown in his salad, and now her life was
being threatened by the mob. Her only chance at survival came in the
disconcertingly virile form of detective Raphael Montiel. Without his help,
Kate didn't stand a chance…and neither did her heart.

#1031 BLUER THAN VELVET—Mary McBride

The moment sexy, velvet-clad Laura McNeal walked through his door,
private investigator Sam Zachary knew he'd have a difficult time keeping
the relationship professional. But Sam had to remember why Laura was
there *and* that her life was in danger. When an unexpected twist kept them
in close quarters, Sam saw that a future with Laura was the only solution—
and the greatest danger of all.

#1032 THE TEMPTATION OF SEAN MacNEILL—Virginia Kantra

Struggling single mom Rachel Fuller was none too pleased to find sexy
carpenter Sean MacNeill living in her girlhood home. Although, truth be
told, Sean's presence had made the threats on her life a little easier to
handle. Too bad things weren't so simple when it came to her feelings….